THE EVOLUTION OF A WARRIOR

▼

A Book of Personal Transformation

Christopher J. Regan

Writers Club Press

San Jose New York Lincoln Shanghai

The Evolution of a Warrior
A Book of Personal Transformation

Writers Club Press
an imprint of iUniverse.com, Inc.

For information address:
iUniverse.com, Inc.
5220 S 16th, Ste. 200
Lincoln, NE 68512
www.iuniverse.com

This book is a fictitious work. Any similarity of the characters in this novel to any person alive, dead, or somewhere in between, is purely coincidental.

ISBN: 0-595-19211-4

Printed in the United States of America

The Evolution of a Warrior

To Barbara and the Beagle

CONTENTS

Preface ix

Acknowledgements xi

Chapter 1 The End 1

Chapter 2 The Art of Hunting 23

Chapter 3 Crushing Enemies 55

Chapter 4 Increasing Power 77

Chapter 5 Riches 99

Chapter 6 Discovering the Heart 118

Chapter 7 Harmony 138

Chapter 8 Setbacks 164

Chapter 9 Healing 191

Chapter 10 Searching 216

Chapter 11 Directions 239

About the Author 271

PREFACE

Before us lie many paths. Some paths lead to happiness. Some paths lead to destruction. It is simple to know what path you are on now even without having come to the final destination. Choose your path well for that is how your life shall be. Choose your path purposely or others will choose for you.

ACKNOWLEDGEMENTS

I wish to thank Brother Leo Richard for his guidance during troubled times. Even in death, he is a beacon that has given my life direction.

My late but heart-felt thank you to Frank Paul Beslity. Fate took him far to early from this earth.

A special thanks to Colleen Alford for her assistance with the manuscript.

CHAPTER 1

▼

THE END

"When a man loses everything and succumbs
to despair he awaits death. When a man loses
everything and realizes he has nothing left to
lose, he becomes
powerful and fearless."
from 'How I Got Lucky and Bumped into God', the author

A thick blanket of gray clouds ominously darkened the morning sky. Droplets from a cold blustery mist filled wind collected on my face and ran down my cheeks like tears from my eyes. I did not carry an umbrella to shield me from the elements, nor did I care to have one. The weather matched my gloomy disposition and I desired to experience it fully.

With the rain and wind as my companions, I began my routine four-block walk from my Queens apartment to the subway going into New York City. The underground stop I ventured to each workday was the first on that line, or the last depending on your direction. Along with other members of the working class herd, I waited for the train to pull in to start my early morning commute to Wall Street.

I stood among one of the many small dense circles of people positioned precisely on the platform where the doors of the train would eventually open. I glanced at an older man with graying hair immediately to my left. He was holding a plastic cup of coffee in one hand and a skillfully folded newspaper in the other. The pale, dry, flaking skin of his face suggested ill health. I shifted my eyes to a middle-aged woman on my right. Heavy makeup layered her face in an obvious attempt to maintain a youthful appearance. She looked straight ahead without deviation as if staring transfixed into a void. My eyes wandered downward at the tracks. No amount of effort could ever completely cleanse the grime and dirt that soiled them. I felt that my soul shared the same fate. After years of turmoil, I doubted that it would ever regain its once peaceful state.

An empty train pulled into the station. It became time for the subway version of musical chairs. The doors opened allowing a flood of humans to enter and compete for whom had the privilege of sitting. The event was particularly mastered by later middle-age women who moved with surprising speed and agility when threatened with the prospect of not getting a seat.

When I was a commuting novice, I almost sat on a woman's lap by accident after she somehow managed to dart into the seat I intended to occupy between the moment I turned around to sit to the moment I began lowing myself into the seat. Finding myself the victim of this seat pirating on numerous occasions, I became agitated. I decided to make my presence felt the next time it happened by remaining seated on the woman's lap and pretending to not notice her for a while. I foolishly reasoned this tactic would discourage future seat stealing. Unfortunately for my rear end and me, the first time I tried it, the woman immediately produced a sharp pin to encourage my eradication from her lap. I never attempted the tactic again and resigned myself to accepting I would just have to stand.

As I became a veteran of the commuting hoards, I developed a number of habits in an effort to insure survivability and ease of passage. For example, at this particular station on the line, there was the choice of taking the local train, which stops at every station, or taking the express train, which stops between every station. The express train was my first choice though I was fully aware that the term express was used loosely at best.

I always carried a hard-shelled briefcase with me, even if empty, for self-defense. It was infinitely useful for blocking off other commuters as I forced my way into or out of trains. I also rationalized it would come in handy as a shield if I was ever attacked by a knife wielding assailant. Inside the briefcase, I carried my personal panic button - a military grade tear gas canister courtesy of a friend in the army reserves. One pull of the pin was more than enough to clear out any subway car. My front shirt pocket hosted another weapon - an innocent looking black pen that concealed a thin two-inch blade sharp enough to remove an appendix. Thankfully, I never had occasion to use the pen for anything more than opening envelopes. The tear gas was another story but I digress.

After I gave up the idea of ever sitting in a subway seat again, I would casually enter the subway car and simply stand. This was something of an advantage in that I could easily view the entire car and all the people in it. The scene I witnessed was not a pleasant one. Tired and unhappy faces lined the seats. I was also tired and unhappy. The only difference I could discern between us is that they seemed numb to the pain while I felt acutely aware of it.

The train pulled out of the station with a lurch and the human herd began its trip. On its way to the city, the subway car periodically stopped or started abruptly jerking us back and forth. Invariably, announcements each morning over a statically sounding speaker alerted us to delays. On those occasions, I would observe the faces in the subway car and marvel at the state of indifference. The emotionally anesthetized responses seemed strangely symbolic of the way most people resign themselves to accept suffering as their fate. I always fancied myself, perhaps whimsically, as a rebel grimily determined to never become a numb robot like the others. The trouble is I did not know who the enemy was.

We arrived like we usually did each morning except when there were blackouts, track fires, or the all encompassing switching problems, to our particular stop. The mindless herd moved from train, to elevator, to another train for those of us heading downtown. In this train as well I was forced to stand. However, random fortune bestowed upon me an enjoyable diversion. A few feet away from me, in clear line of sight, stood a very attractive young woman with long blond hair. I gazed at her unnoticed appreciating the disparity of her splendor to the foul underground. I was close enough to pick up a scent of perfume that pleasantly masked the underground's heavy dead air. Her presence was like finding a lone colorful flower in the middle of a desert. The contrast of her beauty against the surrounding ugliness gave me a fleeting sense of hope. Though I stared at her overtly for some time, she never noticed. In the crowded humanity of a human sardine can called a subway car, everyone did his or her best to completely ignore each other.

My final stop arrived. The other people and I who shared this destination trudged up the station stairs to a dull gray morning light inside the canyons of Wall Street. The early autumn air was damp and chilly. I wanted to stop a moment to look up and see if the sky was clearing. However, the steady push of the human herd at my back propelled me forward preventing any sustained gaze. One has to always move with the crowd here or risk being trampled. New York is the home of the champion fast walkers. The rat race is highly competitive and the rats are quick.

I worked in one of the better known brokerage houses. After exiting an elevator, I entered the office area on the 33rd floor and made my way down a corridor of desks, side offices, file cabinets, and the occasional water cooler.

It was my habit in the morning to scan the office area and observe how the more attractive women were dressed that day. Tammy was one of my personal favorites. I often made minor detours around the office to pass by her desk. She was a pretty, dark haired, 26-year-old, Chinese woman who managed part of the trading floor. I had considered an attempt to get to know her in a more intimate sense. However, I found out in conversation that she had a live in boyfriend. Tammy mentioned she periodically shaved her boyfriend's back so I assumed this meant they had a close relationship. I sometimes daydreamed about what she allowed her boyfriend to shave on her. In my active imagination, Tammy was frequently a lead cast member of various erotic fantasies. In the real life, she was a nice person and we got along well.

My desk was immediately adjacent to Rob who served as my unofficial mentor since I started at the firm two months ago. I was training to be an account representative, which is a fancy term for stockbroker. The job was certainly not the type of career I was interested in. However, it was the only work I could find at the time after searching for six months. Previously, I had been employed as a programmer at a defense contractor. Unfortunately for me, my programming experience consisted of arcane computer languages used only by the military. This left me with little transferable skills for the private sector when laid off from the contractor after five years of service.

"Good morning Rob."

"Hey Tony."

Rob had the peculiar habit of rarely making eye contact even during face to face communication. His ability to alter perceptions of financial reality for his personal profit contributed to his success in the industry. In his late twenties, he suffered from an ever-expanding waistline and a generally ill-tempered disposition. Despite our collective personality shortcomings, we got along well. Our amiable relationship developed from the ability to be brutally direct with each other without taking offense.

"You're running out of notches on your belt you fat bastard."

"F—you too."

"Maybe you should cut out those deli cheeseburgers for breakfast."

"Mind your own business. Here's the latest sucker list," he said handing me a long sheet of names and numbers.

The so-called sucker list contained a directory of prospective customers. We also had a second sheet listing stock recommendations for clients. My job as a new broker was to cold call people from the list and persuade them to open an account and purchase suggested securities.

Naively, I asked Rob what the firm's recommendations were based on. That is, why did the firm believe certain stocks were going up in price as opposed to others? He looked at me with an air of disbelief.

"You're kidding me, right?"

After hesitating for a moment to consider if I asked a foolish question I replied, "No. I'm serious. What do the analysts base their recommendations on?"

"Tony, Tony, Tony…" he began with his head shaking. "We just recommend the stocks that are already popular. All we are looking for are accounts and commissions. That's why we have so many stocks on the Buy list and we don't even have a Sell list."

He gave me an expression with face and shoulders as if to ask, "Get it?"

Rob then continued educating me. "The only specific stocks we really push are the ones we have in inventory and we are trying to get rid of. The firm dumps those stocks on the clients first and only sells them on the open market if they cannot find enough buyers among their customers. Now, get on the phone and get with the program." His head was still shaking in disapproval at how I could ask such a stupid question.

I started down the list calling perfect strangers and attempted within a five-minute phone call to get them to trust me with their money. My success was limited at best but enough to keep me professionally afloat.

Countless calls later, the day wore on slower than the revolving electronic ticker tape around the office. At that time in my life, the green and red scrolling electronic numbers held little interest for me. My attention was focused on more primitive needs mainly the potential of exploring the intimate pleasures of the opposite sex. After the break up of my marriage six months ago, such urges went unsatisfied.

My ex-wife, who I married three years after graduating college, had initiated the divorce. Years of feeling neglected and alone in the relationship took their emotional toll on her until she finally left me.

Since the breakup, my sex life had the excitement of a dried out tortoise shell. Fortunately, a potential light at the end of the tunnel presented itself. I had an ally, a self-appointed matchmaker, to help me rise from the ashes of unintended sexual abstinence.

Susan, a divorced woman in her late forties, worked as a secretary in the office. Over the months we became friendly and frequently conversed about personal matters. Based on our conversations, I concluded that both her life and personality bordered on the bizarre. She seemed to be a cross of a mature sixties hippie and a modern New Age person. Since my life style was conservative by her standards, I often wondered why she valued me so much as a friend.

Susan did not intend to intervene directly to end my social drought but rather sought to match me with potential candidates. Susan mentioned that she had a girlfriend who had a daughter who apparently was anxious for, shall we say, male companionship. Naturally, this piqued my interest.

"What does she look like?"

"Well, she's pretty, a bit on the short side, and blond. She's well groomed too."

"What?" I asked puzzled. "What do you mean by well groomed?"

Susan, who was seated at her desk, leaned over to me and said in a low voice, "When she shaves her legs she doesn't stop at the top."

She winked at me. My eyes opened widely and my interest in the woman increased proportionately.

"Okay," I said deliberately, "What is her personal baggage report?"

This question was my polite way to ask if she had any significant emotional issues that I should be aware of.

"Let's see," Susan started, her eyes shifting upward and to her left, "She's never been married; just a few boyfriends here and there. The last one was eight months ago. She never had a lesbian experience unless you count that time in the kitchen with her cousin when she was twelve."

"In the kitchen with her cousin?"

"You know. Girls like to experiment." Susan said matter-of-factly.

"No, I don't know," I replied inquisitively, "Is there a video I could get?"

"Oh, you!" she said with a wave of her hand, "Girls experiment. For example, I learned how to french kiss during sleepovers with my girlfriend Arleen when we were thirteen."

"I don't know if I should be listening to this."

My stated reluctance to hear such a personal revelation failed to discourage Susan from expounding on the subject.

"Of course, we both grew up to experiment together using our tongues in different ways."

"Susan, really…"

"Before my first sexual experience with a man," she interrupted, "I practiced to make sure I could accommodate a male if you know what I mean."

"Practiced? How?"

"You know, with carrots, cucumbers, and have you ever noticed the neck on certain shampoo bottles?"

I decided not to encourage any further elaboration despite a natural curiosity.

Susan moved real close to me, her breath tickling the inside of my ear, and said in a pleasant singing voice, "This girl hasn't been with anyone in a long time."

Wink.

"When is she free?" I asked.

Susan laughed and delighted in her role as a matchmaker, a function that provided her with far more excitement than her secretarial job. The following day happened to be a Friday so she made a few calls. The next thing I knew we had plans to meet a twenty-something year old woman named Grace for Happy Hour.

"Everything is set." Susan said with a devilish smile.

I smiled too. It had been a long time since I had something to look forward to. I meandered back to my desk to continue the dull task of calling prospective customers. No sooner had I sat down than Rob grabbed me by my shoulders and shook me vigorously.

"Look!" he said excitedly as he pointed my body in the direction of a quote screen. "That stock is taking off just like I knew it would. Everyone is getting in!"

He mentioned this stock to me before. It was one of those high tech companies popular at the time.

"I told you! I told you!" Rob shouted quite pleased with himself. "You should get in now before it's too late," he suggested.

"Who else is in?"

"Practically everyone on the floor!"

By everyone, Rob meant the traders.

I had about forty thousand dollars saved up. My ex-wife, Diane, an inherently kind person not given to bitterness, did not go after my money when we divorced. I did not have to pay alimony and we had no children. Therefore, I was able to put away a nice sum from my once high paying programmer's job.

"Open an account with the firm." Rob suggested. "This stock has already doubled. It could go up ten times from here!"

Rob's optimistic projection caught my attention.

"Wow," I thought to myself. Ten times forty grand is four hundred thousand dollars. With that kind of money, I would be well on my way of getting out of this miserable rat race. Maybe this was my ticket! Maybe my luck was finally turning for the better. Still, despite growing feelings of greed and hope, I hesitated.

"Are you going to be a wimp, or are you going to go for it?" Rob asked with a tone of a high school football coach.

Questioning my manhood cinched the decision for me.

That same afternoon I opened an account and bought forty thousand dollars worth of the stock. I reasoned that Rob seemed to know the business and his money was in it too. Later in life, when I was better educated on such matters, I learned that people engaged in questionable acts will often attempt to recruit others to their way of thinking to psychologically reinforce their beliefs. Unfortunately, at the time, my mental discipline was not yet evolved enough to avoid falling into this trap. I foolishly followed the crowd.

On the commute back home that day, I became increasingly hopeful for my near term financial and social prospects. I felt on the verge of revitalizing my love life and making big money in the stock market. What more could I ask for?

*   *   *

The next day, Friday, I went about my work in a cheerier mood than usual. The tickertape revealed that the stock the other brokers and I purchased for an anticipated windfall leveled off in price. However, the decline was small so it did not alarm us. In fact, Rob said the dip in price was like a springboard that would help propel the stock to new heights. We all anxiously waited for it to explode upward.

I went through my normal routine of calling potential customers and trying to get them interested in whatever stock of the day was on the menu. My success in getting new clients was minimal. I suppose this was because my heart was not really in it. I simply went through the motions for the sake of collecting a paycheck every other week.

My mind wistfully wandered during the day wondering what degree of pleasurable success might be obtained that night with the blind date Susan arranged. I prepared for the evening by dressing in my best suit, wearing cologne, and having a readily available form of contraception just in case.

The Boy Scouts taught me to be prepared. Each passing hour increased my sense of anticipation until finally the end of the workday came.

Susan and I left the office together and headed to one of the many bar restaurants within a comfortable walking distance. We pushed ourselves into a crowded Irish tavern and looked around for Grace who turned out to be already seated at a small table. She waved at us to get our attention. Susan noticed her and we walked over. I involuntarily took a deep breath.

Grace smiled at Susan and stood up to greet us. She checked me out in a not so subtle way by scanning the entire length of my body with her eyes. I sensed she was pleased by what she saw judging by her reaction. Both her eyes and smile were wide and she wet her lips. I would like to say her response is because I am a devastatingly handsome guy, but I think it was really more of a case that I was just better than she expected. Regular trips to the gym honed my body well above the average late twenties male. My blind date seemed to notice this despite the fact that I had a business suit on.

Returning the favor, I visually studied Grace. Her face was only average looking though okay. The body seemed somewhat chubby though it looked like most of the fat resided in the right places. A generously sized chest and natural blond hair added a few points to her overall score. She wore tight jeans that hugged her curvy hips and round buttocks. Overall, she was acceptable for a blind date I thought.

"Hi Susan!" Grace enthusiastically greeted. They hugged each other tightly.

"Hi Grace! How are you? Grace, this is Tony."

Grace extended her hand and I gave it a polite single shake. Her hand was noticeably warm and moist.

"Hi Grace, nice to meet you."

"Nice to meet you!"

She dragged out the "you" in her sentence indicating immediately that she liked me. I began to sense the distinct possibility of a physical encounter later that night.

With the pleasantries completed, we all sat down, ordered drinks, and started to chat. The conversation was an assorted mix of typical subjects like how we all came to know each other, our jobs, and New York City in general.

As prearranged, a half an hour after arriving there, Susan bid us goodnight. This left Grace and I alone to get to know each other without the presence of a third party.

I don't recall exactly what Grace and I talked about the next two hours. The exact subject matter is irrelevant. What I do remember is lots of flirting, laughter, humorous innuendoes, light touching, and six drinks consumed each. To be honest, I did not find myself particularly attracted to her. Nonetheless, the lack of initial attraction was nothing alcohol couldn't cure. Besides, this was the most fun I had had in a long time.

"Where do you live?" I asked.

"Right here in Manhattan. I have a small apartment in SoHo."

"Really? Did you ever go to one of those underground clubs where people dress in leather and do bizarre things to each other?"

I asked this question just as a joke - mistake number one for the evening.

"Well, I used to have a boyfriend into those kind of things so I do know of a place," she said with a sly smile and twinkle in her eye.

"Really?" I repeated. "You know, I have heard of clubs like that but I have never been to one."

"Would you like to go?" she asked with a big grin.

"Well, uh, I don't know."

She grabbed my hand and yanked me off the chair. "Come on! I'll take you!"

I quickly downed my seventh drink and she dragged me out of the place with her arm wrapped tightly around mine.

Though I have my own set of unique sexual preferences, bondage and leather is not one of them. This is just my own personal taste and I do not disparage those who like it. Some of my best friends are intensely interested in bondage and the paradoxical experience of simultaneous pain and pleasure.

I, for one, do not like to be tied up. Of course, if a woman requested that I restrain her with handcuffs or some other device, I would happily accommodate. For me though, there is no extra thrill associated with a helplessly bound female. I prefer more active participation.

A short subway ride and a walk of a few city blocks brought Grace and I to our destination.

Down a few steps just off the sidewalk, there stood a huge unmarked black door like a sentinel guarding a forbidden domain within. Grace knocked on it assertively. A black painted window slid open. She stood on her toes to reach the window with her head and said something but I could not hear what. Perhaps it was the secret password.

A doorman garbed in leather and chains from head to toe watched over the entrance just inside the passage. From the wrist to the shoulder, his arms brandished tattoos reminiscent of sexual fantasies and bad dreams. He gave me a dirty look as if disapproving of my business like attire.

Grace and I descended into a dark smoky abyss filled with intermingling humans in various forms of dress and undress. The gender of some people was questionable at best. Odors of leather and sweat permeated the air.

On a small, elevated stage, a floorshow progressed for the benefit of the patrons. The entertainment at the moment consisted of a leather-clad woman whose specially designed outfit did not cover any of her rear end. While her backside was very much exposed, her face was covered with a leather mask including a metal zipper over the mouth. I assume the mask is designed that way so participants in this kind of behavior can indulge without disturbing their neighbors.

The woman on the stage stood bent over, her wrists handcuffed to a pole. Another female, looking very much like a dominatrix, repeatedly smacked the meaty buttocks of the shackled female with a paddle. Curiously, the crowd seemed unimpressed and bored. I assumed the display was tame by their standards.

,

The next act on stage involved multiple men and women alternately inflicting erotic pain on each other. Clothespins dangled from nipples both male and female. Men enjoyed the tweaking of appendages I cringed at while witnessing. Audience participation was actively encouraged and the crowd's collective interest perked up. Two women ended up completely in the nude. My eyes fixated upon numerous tattoos painted on their flesh. Body piercings were evident in very private places.

I looked over at Grace and observed her evilly grinning at the display of bondage and affliction.

We did not speak much inside the club, as it was very loud. She hooked herself onto my arm and kept me close.

Next to us, two couples decided to get friendly and experiment with each other's partner. They started to engage in voracious tongue exploration and roaming hands. The two women of the group alternated between the newfound boyfriend of the night and each other.

The next stage act involved three men testing the limits of their male member's elasticity with the assistance of a scantily clad female and a few heavy objects attached to straps.

During the last three stage acts, drinks eight, nine, and ten were consumed. Surprisingly, Grace drank as much as I did. It always makes me a little nervous when a woman can drink as much as I can.

The sight of unnaturally elongated male private parts from the last act must have aroused Grace. She started to run her hand over my backside. She seemed quite skilled with exploring its contours.

The alcohol and bizarre atmosphere began to take its toll on me. My conscious awareness began to fade in and out. The rest of the time spent in the club was a blur. I hazily recall Grace biting and running her tongue along my neck while forcibly pulling my head back by the hair. She grabbed my crotch and rhythmically squeezed it. I believe another couple made an offer of group sex but I could be mistaken.

Though feeling dizzy and unsteady on my feet, Grace got me out of the club safely. My head cleared a little when we were outside.

"You feel okay?" Grace asked.

"Uh, yeah. I've just had a little too much to drink."

"Why don't you sleep over at my apartment? Its pretty close by."

Her voice sounded sincerely concerned for my well being. However, I thought I detected a suppressed grin. The trap was closing fast.

"Uh, if you don't mind. Okay."

Bait hooked.

"Great! Let's go!"

The fish, that's me, was being reeled in.

Grace guided me by holding my arm as we walked. My head was spinning counter clockwise. I toyed with the idea of trying to get it to spin the other way but had no success. I barely remember how we got to her place. She lived in one of those skinny railroad apartments.

"Do you want a drink?"

That's number eleven if you are counting.

She lit some candles and joined me on the couch I had collapsed into. The lights were off. Smelling blood, she went in for the kill. Leaning toward me, she inserted her tongue into my mouth and began to tango inside. The combination of an alcohol induced daze and the long period of sexual inactivity weakened my resistance. What the heck? I'll go along for the ride.

In her ravage passion, Grace nearly sucked my tongue out of my head. In fact, the next morning, it hurt. Next, she made road tracks on my neck with her teeth while running her hand over my chest.

With her breathing getting noticeably harder, she tore off my shirt and began sucking on my nipples. Hey, I thought I was supposed to do that. She then went to her knees, freed me from the rest of my clothes, and began to toot the tuba. Her mouth engulfed me like a high powered out of control vacuum. After a few minutes of applying enough action to siphon a gas tank, she stood up, stepped back, and undressed urgently.

The dim candlelight revealed pale white skin and a small tattoo of a flower near her private garden area. Yes, Susan was accurate. Grace was well groomed. In fact, the entire grassland had been mowed. I assume, in part at least, this was to show off the flower tattoo. Her midsection was somewhat flabby but nicely sized breasts made this forgivable. It was tough getting one of those things completely in my mouth but I tried.

Grace took me by the hands and led me onto a mattress on the floor where she pulled me on top of her. Her hands ran wildly over my body leaving tracks left by fingernails. Her breathing became so rapid she sounded out of breath. Reaching the peak of anticipation, she aggressively positioned herself on top of me and began to ride the stick shift. She bounced up and down like a rapid piston. Her boobs flapped wildly against her body.

I began to slip into a state of shock.

Oblivious to my presence except for the part of me inside her, Grace continued to ride me like a wild seesaw. She frantically pounded into my hard flesh like driving a nail into wood. Her face tightened with lustful ecstasy. Suddenly, she grasped her breasts so tightly that her fingernails looked as if they would draw blood. Her head arched back and she climaxed with loud animal grunts while pulling and twisting her nipples. After a moment of catching her breath, her hot sweaty body collapsed on top of me. I could not summon a single muscle to move. Hysterical paralysis I think it is called.

"Mmmm. You are so good," Grace cooed basking with post orgasmic glow.

I did not feel flattered by the compliment. Her aggressiveness and impersonal use of my body to satisfy her needs made me feel she could have accomplished the same thing with a good broom handle.

She rolled off me and got comfortable in bed. I felt an incredible urge to take a shower with a scrub bush to cleanse myself of her bodily fluids. But, I didn't want to insult her by disappearing into the bathroom for a long period of time. Grace soon fell asleep as evidenced by the load snoring sounds next to me.

I laid there in shock, on my back, staring at the ceiling. Despite the alcohol and the late time of night, I did not fall asleep for a long time. My feelings of shock turned into emptiness. Emptiness turned into depression. Depression turned into morning and a nasty hangover.

Sometime in the early morning hours, I finally drifted off. I awoke with a heavy head and a strange warm wet feeling below my waist. Looking down, I found Grace orally helping herself to the early morning automatic arousal of my private parts. Apparently, I had not wakened early enough for her so she decided to take matters into her own mouth.

Noticing me beginning to stir, she skillfully replaced mouth with hand.

"Good morning!" Grace said with lust in her eyes.

Last night's activities were obviously not enough to satisfy her appetite.

"Uh, good morning."

"Did you sleep well?"

"Uh, yeah."

"I hope you like me getting you up like this," she said with a girlish giggle. "Let's see if I can wake the rest of you."

She kissed me on the cheek and ran her hand down my chest. She then eagerly went about exploring my body with her tongue putting it into places that a tongue had no business being. Now that her saliva was all over me, my yearning for a shower became stronger. After covering nearly every inch of my body, she concentrated on her favorite part and strategically positioned her lower half above my face so I could return the favor. I got a close up view of the tattoo. She pressed into me to encourage interaction.

"Uh, excuse me please," I said patting her buttocks to get her attention. "I really need to use the bathroom."

"Hmm, okay, but hurry back," Grace replied with a wicked smile.

I resisted the urge to run, but walked to the bathroom as fast as possible after she got off me. Once in the bathroom, I frantically tried to think of a tactful escape plan as I splashed cold water on my face. When I returned, I found Grace sitting on her knees playfully dangling a pair of handcuffs from one finger.

The nightmare continues.

"Would you like to give them a try?"

"Uh, no, sorry. I have a phobia about being handcuffed," I answered.

"Would you like to use them on me?"

"If you insist."

Using the handcuffs, I secured her to a radiator pipe near the head of the mattress.

"You can do anything to me you like," she lustfully voiced.

Grace rolled over onto her stomach and assumed a position to give me an exaggerated view of her big round buttocks and available points of entry.

"I have some toys in the dresser if you would like to use them on me," she offered as a suggestion.

That sounded like a good idea to me. I would not need to expend as much energy to satisfy her.

The bottom draw of her dresser contained an impressive collection of playthings guaranteed to keep a woman company in the absence of a man.

"What would you like first?" I asked.

"Surprise me! You can use more than one toy at a time if you know what I mean."

"More than one?"

"Oh yeah! I like that double stuff! But first, blindfold me."

"Blindfold?"

"Yeah, do it to me."

I fumbled around her collection of pleasure playthings, found a blindfold, and put it on her.

"How's that?"

"Perfect!"

With her restrained and blindfolded, the opportunity for escape presented itself. My eyes darted around the room for my clothes. The thought flashed through my mind to just run out of there.

"Wait right here," I said while turning on her stereo to drown out the sound of my activity. I scurried to collect my clothes and found everything except my underwear. The hell with it, I thought. I put on everything sans the underwear being careful not to catch the pant's zipper on anything.

"I'm waiting," Grace playfully sang.

"Just a minute," I sang back.

I patted my pockets to check for wallet and keys, tip toed to the front door, and quietly shut it behind me as I made my escape.

When I finally returned home, I took an hour-long shower and threw out the towel when I was done with it. I then flopped into bed and slept deeply for five hours. A blinking light on my answering machine greeted me when I awoke late in the afternoon.

"Hey, this is Grace!" the message on the machine began. I cringed assuming she was angry. I was surprised to even get a call from her because I did not remember giving her my number. "You are a very naughty boy!"

Something was amiss. She did not sound angry. In fact, her voice sounded lustful and heavy as if she were pleasuring herself.

"My God!" the message continued. "When I realized you left me alone with my front door unlocked it made me so hot to think I could be at the mercy of anyone who walked in and found me handcuffed and nude!"

I did not realize it at the time of my escape but in retrospect figured out that the door of Grace's apartment could not be locked from the outside without a key. When Grace realized I had gone, she knew I must have left the door unlocked. Suzan would tell me later that Grace was able to free herself by using her legs and body to slide over the handcuff's key, which was under the mattress on the floor, toward her hands.

Her message concluded with, "You know just how to turn me on! Call me back at…"

I began to laugh in a hysterical fashion that suggested oncoming insanity.

The next Monday at work, Susan inquired about how the date went.

"Hey! I heard you two hit it off," she said.

"I'm sure that whatever you heard is greatly exaggerated."

"Whatever you did really worked because she told me she can't wait to see you again."

"I have no plans to see her again."

Susan looked dumbfounded.

"But she told me you two had a great time together."

"Susan, look, I don't want to get into any details. Suffice it to say I think Grace is probably a nice person but I am not interested in her."

"Why not? She told me you spent the night with her!"

"I would rather not say."

"I don't understand. Why?" Susan continued to press for an answer.

"Okay, okay. I'll tell you why. She is a sex crazed maniac."

"You say that like it's a bad thing!"

"Really, Susan, just tell her my ex-wife called me and there is a chance we may get back together. If you can think of a better lie that will spare her feelings, be my guest to make up something else."

Susan looked disappointed and shook her head in disbelief.

Grace did try to get in touch with me anyway, but I was wise enough to let my answering machine screen all my calls. After her repeated attempts to contact me failed, Grace understood the unwritten etiquette of being ignored and gave up.

After the dismal experience of my first post divorce date, I turned my attention and hopes to the stock I had sunk forty thousand dollars into. "Sunk" was an appropriate word in this case because that damn stock started to head straight down. Thinking that the lower price made it a bargain, some traders purchased additional shares. I probably would have done the same if I had any money left.

Soon, the price was down by one third of what it had been where we first started buying. Rob said it could not go any lower. He was wrong. We hung on but it kept inching down then bounced up and down, mostly down. The whole ordeal made me very frustrated and angry.

That evening, in my small Queens apartment that had only a window view of a wall on the other side of the building, depression slowly gripped my soul like hardening cement. I restlessly paced back and forth like a caged tiger. The disaster of the stock investment and my first post-divorce date were only the latest disappointments in what had been a painful existence for me. Distress steadily grew inside of me overwhelming any sense of rationality. My mind tormented itself with an endless recall of agonizing memories: an abusive childhood, a failed marriage, and a seemingly endless number of other painful experiences.

There seemed to be no end in sight to my miserable existence.

I could not go on like this.

I sat at my desk in the bedroom with my elbows resting on the hard desktop. My fists clenched in anguish covering my eyes.

I pulled out a 22 revolver I kept in my desk drawer. I placed the revolver on the desk and stared at it.

The end of pain is right in front of me. Just one squeeze of the trigger and it will be gone forever.

I picked the weapon up. Studying it, I marveled at how the cold and hardness of the steel mirrored the cold and hardness of life. I placed my finger on the trigger and pressed the nozzle into my temple.

Just one squeeze of the trigger will take away the pain.

I don't want to be in pain anymore. It has been too long - a lifetime.

My mind flashed back to my ex-wife Diane. She loved me more than any man could ask for. Guilt flooded my heart as I recalled how I emotionally distanced myself and made her life as empty as mine.

My finger started to apply pressure to the trigger.

Academic honors, athletic awards, distinguished service in the military; it all meant nothing. In reality, I was a failure. I had accomplished nothing.

I squeezed the trigger a little harder. The revolver's hammer started to back into firing position.

There's no sense in going on with life. No one would even miss me.

Under the pressure of my finger, the trigger moved to the halfway point, just before the hammer would snap back and fire the weapon.

I have been in too much pain. It's time to end it.

I shut my eyes tight and pulled the trigger with all of my strength.

The gun failed to fire. I forgot that the safety was on.

Frustrated, I pounded the desk with my fist, angrily flicked the safety off with my thumb, and firmly pressed the revolver into my temple again.

In the split second before I was ready to discharge the weapon, a few soft notes gently chimed from a music box. On one side of the desk sat a stuffed teddy bear given to me by Diane. Inside the tummy of the fluffy brown bear was a small music box. I rationalized that, by hitting the desk with my fist, I jolted the music box enough so that it played a few notes.

I shut my eyes again ready to pull the trigger. The teddy bear played another three delicate musical notes.

I opened my eyes and looked at it.

Two more musical notes soothingly chimed from the teddy bear.

I fully realize that a person's mental capacity during a suicide attempt is questionable at best, but I truly believe that stupid teddy bear was trying to save my life. I stared at it and it looked back at me with sad eyes. "Please don't do it," it seemed to silently say.

I flicked the safety back on and put the gun down.

I picked the little bear up and wound the music box inside using the small key on its back. The soft music soothed and calmed me. Anguish gave way to a profound sadness. I put my head down on the desk and started to cry.

CHAPTER 2

▼

THE ART OF HUNTING

"Why not be a sheep," she asked, "and enjoy
lazy days grazing grass under a warm sun?"
"Why not be a wolf" I retorted, " and enjoy
the taste of blood?"
from 'The Dark Side of a Warrior', the author.

Leaving for work as I normally did, I entered the courtyard of the icky yellow brick apartment building I lived in. A beautiful sunny autumn day bid me good morning. A few fluffy white clouds floated lazily in the clear blue sky. The crisp air was cool and dry with just a hint of a breeze.

I reached the end of the block heading to the subway and stopped. I took a deep breath enjoying the rush of fresh air in my lungs. My eyes gazed upward. What a shame to have to go to work on such a nice day I thought. The idea crossed my mind to call in sick to the office and play professional hooky. The thought appealed to me. I turned around and went back home. Once inside my apartment, I called the voice mailbox of my boss and announced that I was not feeling well and would be out sick.

Being relieved that I did not have to face work that day, I went back to sleep for a couple of hours. After rising again, feeling infinitely more refreshed; I changed into comfortable clothes and headed outside to my car. Once inside the auto, I pulled out a map from the glove compartment. I looked it over for a good place to take a drive to enjoy the weather. The leaves on the trees were beginning to turn delightful gold and red colors. I decided to venture along the north shore of Long Island to enjoy the scenic foliage.

After an idyllic drive, I ended up at a county park on the North Shore. The beach at the park overlooked the Long Island sound. There were very few people there during the middle of this workday. I enjoyed the solitude and wonderful weather.

An old couple, the two of them hunched over from advanced age, walked at a snail's pace along the beach at the edge of the water. They shuffled on the sand taking small steps holding each other's hand. I sat on a bench admiring how affectionate they seemed to be with each other even at that age. I found myself hoping I would someday be lucky enough to be in a relationship like that. A relationship where I would walk hand in hand with my spouse even when I was too old to do anything else physical to express my love.

Beyond observing the old couple, my mind was unusually clear. I did not think about work, about my ex-wife, the money I lost in the stock market, or that I was sexually mauled on a blind date. I just lay back on the bench admiring the sky. Later, I casually strolled around the park bouncing a rubber ball that I always kept in the back seat of my car. At the moment, I didn't have a care in the world. My mind mirrored the gentle sea breeze caressing me. I felt peaceful and relaxed.

After a few hours, I left the park and drove to a town close by. Upon entering the main street from the east, I passed by a clock tower standing prominently on a grass triangle dividing the roads. A small black cannon silently guarded the entrance of the tower. After parking the car, I strolled down the main street. Several of the quaint houses, built in the 1800s, were designated landmarks. Adjacent to the town library was a sizable park filled with small ponds and a few dozen geese that liberally fed on and fertilized the grass. Across from the clock tower in town was a friendly New Age type of shop called Dreams. For a moment, I stared at its door debating whether to go inside. It seemed to beckon me. For some strange reason, it made me feel welcome. Acting on the impulse, I entered the shop.

Once inside, an old wooden floor creaked beneath my feet. The scents of incense and perfume sticks combined to produce a very pleasant aroma. Relaxing Gothic music filled my ears and calmed my soul. That voice singing! It sounded as if an angel accompanied the music.

"Hello. May I help you?" asked a tall middle-aged gentleman with hair balding into a crown. He stood behind the counter giving me a warm smile.

"I'm just browsing, thank you."

"If you need me, just let me know. My name is George."

I slowly looked around the store being careful to navigate the futon furniture displayed throughout. I noticed a small book section in a back corner. I walked over to it and began to peruse.

"Are you interested in anything particular?"

"Yes," I replied. "I'm interested in finding a new life."

I smiled to indicate I was joking but he looked at me compassionately as if taking my statement seriously.

"Would it be okay if I sat down for a while?" I asked motioning to one of the futon couches. "Certainly," he answered as if he somehow knew I was a troubled soul seeking refuge. "Make yourself at home."

For about twenty minutes, I relaxed on the couch thumbing through a book. It was one of those self-help books, something about how to find your higher self. As I flipped through the pages, I shook my head skeptically. The subject matter struck me as quite whimsical. I put the book back on the shelf.

"George, I love that music playing. Do you have it available on tape or CD?"

"Sure. Just give me a second to find it."

As George searched for the CD on a shelf behind him, I noticed a bearded man sitting at one of the other futon couches toward the front of the store. He was dealing tarot cards on a small black table. However, there was no one seated across from him. Perhaps he is playing solitary tarot, I thought to myself. After locating the CD, George took my twenty-dollar bill and handed me change with a cheery thank you. Out of curiosity, I walked over to the tarot man. I jokingly asked him whose fortune he was reading since no one else was around.

"Yours," he said in a serious manner looking up at me.

"Me? Why would you be reading the cards for me?"

"You are the only one in the store," he said in a matter of fact kind of way.

"And what do the cards tell you?"

"You are about to embark on a new journey."

"I see," I replied skeptically, "What kind of journey?"

"One that has no destination and no end."

"I don't quite understand. What does that mean?"

"It's twenty dollars for a reading."

"No thank you."

I flashed a polite smile and left.

*   *   *

The following day at work, confronted again with the reality of everyday life, my frame of mind returned to a state of gloomy depression. The darkness of my mood was so evident that Tammy, the attractive trading floor manager in the office, became concerned and asked me what was wrong.

"I've been through a lot recently," I sighed. "Let's just say that I'm not happy."

I gave her a weak grin.

"Tony, if you don't mind me making a suggestion, I know a really terrific therapist who helped me a great deal when I was going through a difficult time. You might want to consider seeing him."

"I don't care for therapists. Most of them are just a waste of time and money."

"Trust me. This one is really good. His office is close by too."

"How much does he charge?"

"A hundred dollars a session."

"A hundred dollars a session? That's a lot of money!"

"He's worth it," she said sincerely.

Tammy always impressed me as being a self confident, happy, and successful woman. Heck, maybe I would consider it. She gave me a copy of his business card. For me, to even consider therapy meant I hit a low point in my life.

The next day, Tammy followed up on her suggestion and asked if I made an appointment with the therapist. Still feeling reluctant, I had not done so. At her insistence, I called the fellow up and scheduled a visit the following day after work. His name was Ken. I didn't get any impression, good or bad, from him in the short phone conversation we had.

The next day came and after work I walked down to Ken's office that was located in Greenwich Village about a mile south from the brokerage firm. The building was one of the older ones in the city. I walked up three floors and found the number of the office on a large wooden door. The door was unlocked. I opened it and found a very small waiting area that could at best accommodate four people. There was just enough room for four wooden chairs and a small rectangular table devoid of even a single magazine. There were two doors inside, one leading to an office, the other to the room the therapy sessions were conducted in.

There was no one to greet me so I just sat down in one of the hard wooden chairs. I could hear the muffled sound of a man's voice coming from the other room. After few minutes of waiting, a tall young woman with short black hair came out of the room. She appeared to have been crying. Without acknowledging my presence in any way, she passed by me and exited the office. Behind her was Ken.

My eyes opened wide in surprise. He was what I refer to as a BBG. That is, a Big Black Guy. He was impressively built like a football player - tall, physically imposing, and he had a deep booming voice. He was also completely bald which I guess makes him a BBBG. He greeted me in a friendly way and asked me to fill out a questionnaire. I completed it in a few short minutes. We then went into the other room and I sat down on a large comfortable black leather chair. I noticed a box of tissues on a small table within arms reach of the chair.

"How are you?" he asked politely.

"I've been better." Ken grinned at my reply. "Do you think I'm going to need those?" I asked pointing at the tissue box.

"Well, you never know," he joked. "So, Tony," he said with a deep sing the blues voice, "How can I help you?"

"Well, I've been feeling very depressed lately. When I'm not depressed, I feel anxious most of the time. Everything I do seems to go wrong. I am not happy." I paused.

"Go on," Ken encouraged.

For the next twenty minutes, I spilled out a laundry list of things that bothered me. I mentioned past relationships, my childhood, parents, money, job, and so on. He listened intently only interrupting me a few times to ask for clarification about something I said. Finally, I exhausted my list and looked at him waiting for some words of wisdom.

"Tony, what is it you want?"

The question caught me off guard.

"Well, uh, I don't want to..."

Ken interrupted me. "I am more interested in what you do want rather in what you don't want. After all, you already have what you don't want. If I could wave a magic wand and grant anything you wish, what is it you would ask for?"

My eyes shifted down, then up and to the right as I searched for an answer.

"I am far more aware of what I dislike rather than what I am looking for."

"For the last twenty minutes you spoke about what troubles you. Would it be fair to say you have been focusing on the negative things in your life rather than on the positive?"

"Well, yeah maybe."

"Tony, realize that whatever you consistently focus on you will tend to receive. If you focus on what is wrong with your life that is how you will experience life. If you focus on what is good in your life and direct your attention to achieving what you desire, that will soon become your reality."

"I don't get it. Are you suggesting to me that if I simply think happy thoughts I will start being happy?"

"Something like that," he smiled.

"For this advice I'm paying you a hundred dollars?"

Ken laughed and looked at me, chin resting on hand as if he were trying to figure something out.

"Please close your eyes," he asked. "Good, now hold your right hand up with the palm facing down."

I did so and he placed one of his big hands below my hand just barely touching it.

"Now, Tony…" he said low and softly, "You had been thinking in a way that focused on what made you unhappy…but now…now Tony…you may consider turning your attention to a new direction and focus on what makes you happy and how you can achieve that…that's right. Now let your hand drop only as fast as your mind can rearrange itself to this new and more powerful way of thinking."

My hand, which seemed to be suspended in air with no conscious effort on my part to hold it there, began to descend very slowly. As it did, Ken continued speaking in that deep voice making suggestions for how my mind would now change its focus.

After my hand touched my lap, I opened my eyes feeling very relaxed.

"How do you feel?" Ken asked.

"Wow, that feels strange but good."

"Good. Tony, I would like you to meet someone."

"The attractive woman that left just before me?"

Ken looked at me with a funny face.

"Uh, no. I have a friend who has been a mentor to me. His name is Leo. I think you could benefit greatly from him."

"How much does he charge?"

"You will be happy to know he does not ask for or accept money."

"What's the catch?"

"There is no catch. He just likes helping people."

"He's not going to ask for sexual favors, is he?"

"No!" Ken laughed.

"Well, okay. How do I set up an appointment?"

"He works a little differently than I do. Just let me know if it is okay with you and I will tell him that you are interested in meeting him. He will then contact you."

"He'll contact me?"

"Yes, though more accurately, he will find you."

"That seems strange."

"Trust me."

"Trust you? I don't even know you!" I said half jokingly.

"I realize it is a bit unique. Is it alright with you?"

"Okay," I answered warily.

After writing out a check for a hundred dollars, I left the office a bit perplexed and wondered if the suggestions Ken gave me would really help. I had my doubts but I must admit I felt very relaxed.

The following Friday, as was my habit at the time, I went to a Happy Hour at a bar near the office.

Some people I know from the job would often visit the bar as well. However, on this particular evening, I was on my own. I leaned with my back toward the long wooden bar nursing a drink. My eyes scanned the crowd for pretty woman and familiar faces. I recognized a few people.

However, I did not know any of them well enough for anything more than a polite hello.

While looking around, I became aware of a man who stood near me at the crowded bar. Strange, but I didn't notice him until after he was practically on top of me. He was tall fellow with an athletic looking build and looked to be in his mid fifties. I would guess his nationality was English. However, I could not be certain and he had no discernable accent. He seemed familiar somehow though I could not recall ever seeing him before. I turned toward him and noticed that he was staring at me. He smiled and held his gaze upon my eyes. Normally, I would assume such a gesture might be from a man with a same sex preference seeking the possibility of making a new friend, but something inside told me this was not the case.

"Let me guess," I said, "You're Leo."

"And you are astute!" he laughed heartily. "Ken is a good judge of character," he remarked with a warm ear-to-ear smile.

"I'm Tony."

"I know who you are."

"That's nice. Who are you?"

"Who I am is unimportant. What I am to you is important."

"And what are you to me?"

I began to think he was playing games with me. I quickly started to become agitated.

"What I am depends," he paused, "on you."

"Look, whatever it is you are doing I'm not playing along."

He struck me as strange and I was not about to play mind games with some eccentric shrink.

"From your perspective, I am a teacher. You can learn a great deal from me if you are prepared to."

"And what do you teach?" I asked disinterested.

"I teach how people how to live life as a warrior," he answered with a proud and distinct voice.

"What do you do, show people how to live on wild plants and kill deer with a bow and arrow?"

I was being purposely unpleasant in the hope he would go away.

"No, no, no!" he smiled completely ignoring my attempts to discourage him. "A warrior is one who takes complete responsibility for his or her life. A warrior is concerned with self mastery."

This guy must be a nut.

"Sorry, I'm not interested."

"You are happy with the way you are now?"

"No, but I am still not interested," I repeated in a firmer voice.

He stopped talking and studied me intently with his eyes. Weird, his eyes did not seem focused. It made me feel uncomfortable.

Hoping he would get the message, I turned away from him. My shoulder faced his side and I directed my attention to a table full of young, attractive ladies about twenty feet away. They were engaged in typical girl talk giggling and laughing. My intention was to amuse myself by watching the girls while ignoring Leo and hope he got the hint and went away.

A minute passed by.

"Would you like to meet them?" Leo asked.

"Who? Those girls?" Leo nodded his head affirmatively. "I would love to," I said still staring at the group.

"What's stopping you from going over there and introducing yourself?"

"Oh, yeah, right. I'll just walk over there alone and make a fool out of myself. There are four girls at that table totally engrossed in chit chat and I'm not about to stick my neck out and try to break into that."

"That's one of the problems with you. You lack courage. Its safer for you to complain and do nothing than to take action and risk failing."

Leo was starting to irritate me but he continued before I could defend myself.

"Watch me. I'm going to go over to that table and within two minutes I'll know all their names and be engaged in conversation with them. When I scratch my head that will be the signal for you to come over."

"Wait a minute!" I objected.

"Watch a pro!" he said with a confident smile as he headed toward the young women.

Now this should be worth a laugh, I thought.

Leo sauntered to the table in an exaggerated way that was, I assume, for my amusement. He leaned over with his hands resting on the table and started talking to them. The place was too loud for me to hear what he said.

His directness in entering their circle mildly startled the young ladies. They stopped talking. Their attention focused completely on him. He finished a sentence and I saw the smiling girls dart glances at each other and then they all broke out laughing. Leo pulled up an unused chair from an adjacent table and sat with them. A lively conversation followed and I could tell he was making the rounds finding out each woman's name. More good-natured laughing followed.

"Son of a gun!" I said out loud. "How did he do that?"

Leo started to scratch his head. That was my signal but I froze in place. He scratched his head in an even more conspicuous manner. My stomach tightened as I headed toward them.

"Hi!" I said with my best smile while taking in all the pretty faces.

"Hi!" they said in almost musical chorus.

"This is my godson Tony" Leo introduced.

"I guess that makes you the Godfather," the ladies giggled.

God, these ladies are nice looking I thought to myself. I took a quick inventory. Two had engagement rings and two did not. The names were Laura (ring), Susan (ring), Jennifer, and Christine.

Leo directed the verbal interaction among the six of us like a fine composer directs an orchestra. He listened intently when someone else spoke, smiled, had a great sense of humor, and divided his attention evenly. The girls loved him. He had them in the palm of his hand. We all engaged in lively conversation for about an hour. Christine and I eventually branched off into a separate conversation. Leo nudged me with his elbow.

"Tony," he said pointing to his watch, "we have to go soon. So, if you have enough good taste to ask this lovely young lady for a her phone number, I suggest you do so now."

I was a bit surprised and embarrassed by Leo's bluntness.

"Uh, yes!" I turned to Christine. Her friends looked on with girlish delight. "I think it would be nice if we could get together."

"Sure!" Christine said putting her pocketbook on the table. She produced a small piece of paper and scribbled her number on it.

"Great! I'll give you a call."

My heart pounded with boyish excitement. I folded the little piece of paper and put it in my shirt pocket. Leo stood up. He said goodbye to the women as if they were all princesses of some magical kingdom. I was impressed. We then walked out of the place.

"So," Leo began to ask when we reached the sidewalk, "what do you think?"

"You're hired." I replied.

*　　　　　　*　　　　　　*

The next Monday after work I went to see Leo at the same building Ken operated out of.

Apparently, they shared the office.

"In your path to becoming a warrior I have decided to teach you how to be a hunter first." Leo began.

"Wait a second. I am still not clear what you mean by a warrior let alone a hunter."

"A warrior takes responsibility and control of his life. There is more, but that definition will suffice for now."

"And you are going to teach me to become a warrior?"

"Yes. I am going to convert you from a wimp to a warrior."

"Me? A wimp? You have got to be kidding!"

"Whether you care to admit it or not that is how you have lived most of your life. The very fact that you are so easily offended is testimony to it."

"I'll have you know I…"

Leo cut off my sentence with a wave of his hand.

"I have read your long list of honors and accomplishments on the questionnaire you filled out for Ken. All that means is that you excelled in being a follower.

"You have never taken responsibility for your own life. That makes you a wimp by my definition."

I fumed and shook my head disapprovingly though I somehow felt inclined to hear him out.

"What is this hunting stuff about?" I asked gruffly with my arms folded in front of me.

"A hunter learns keen awareness and develops skills to obtain what he desires. In the true sense of the term, a hunter learns to act in harmony with nature and take only what he needs. This is where we will start with you."

"What are you going to teach me to hunt? Women?" I asked jokingly.

"Exactly."

"You must be joking."

"No, I am serious. It is clear to me that you have strong desires to, shall we say, interact with the opposite sex. Therefore, I will instruct you on how to seduce just about any woman you desire."

This guy has to be the weirdest therapist on the planet.

"If you don't mind me saying so, that seems to me to be a strange way to start what you call the path of a warrior."

"I did not choose it. You did."

"I did? What do you mean?"

"In order to motivate you, I need to teach you something you strongly desire. Testosterone induced urges seem to be high on your priority list at the moment. Therefore, I will teach you the skills required to obtain what you desire. In time, you shall find those skills have practical application in other areas of your life as well. I am also using this instruction as an avenue to get you to take control of a part of your life that you have, up to now, left to chance."

"You're going to teach me how to be a Don Juan?"

"In a sense, yes."

"Alright!"

"We shall start with the basics. Both your breathing and posture are poor."

"What's wrong with my breathing and posture?" I asked defensively.

"The two are related. You do not maintain a properly aligned back when you stand or walk. Stand up for a moment."

I did as he asked.

"Now put you back on the wall." Leo placed me so that the back of my shoulders and buttocks touched the wall. "You walk hunched over as if beaten down by life. Keep your back straight in a comfortable manner. Your posture should be like that of a general on horseback ready to lead troops into battle. Be proud. Your posture is a reflection of your state of mind. People sense your disposition merely from how you carry yourself."

"Like this?" I attempted to stand as he described.

"You look like you have a pole up your backside! Be relaxed." After I maintained the standing posture long enough for his approval, he took me out into the hall outside the small waiting room.

"This is an old trick I learned in beauty school." He gave me a weird smile then broke out laughing. Leo then placed a hard cover book on my head. "Try walking without the book falling off." I did so slowly but the book fell off after just two steps. "Graceful, aren't you? Try it again." I repeated the attempt three times, each time walking one or two steps further before the book fell off my head.

"Are you kidding me with this stuff?" I asked losing my patience.

"No I am not. Master how to stand and walk and you will present yourself a thousand times better than you are now.

"Practice at home and become aware of your posture throughout the day. Correct it when required which for you is all the time. This will begin to teach you how to walk with balance and grace."

We then went back inside and he asked me to get comfortable in the leather chair.

"Let's work on your breathing, Tony."

"For heaven's sake, how can a person breathe wrong?"

"What you learn may surprise you."

Leo asked me to place one hand on my chest and the other on my stomach. "Your breathing is too shallow and high in the chest. It is a reflection of the anxiousness of your rushed life style. Breathe in so that the air reaches and fills the bottom of your stomach. For practice, breathe out slowly and completely so that no air is in the lungs."

With my hands in place, Leo had me practice this type of breathing for ten minutes. I was pleasantly surprised by how much less tense I felt.

"Good", Leo said, "Practice this at home as well for at least ten minutes every day. Make sure your body is comfortable and your back is straight during the exercise."

"Will do."

"Now, let us begin the to learn the art of hunting," Leo exclaimed with exaggerated fanfare waving his arms as if introducing a stage act. He started to laugh at his own antics.

"Why do you laugh so much?"

"Because you are so damn depressed I figure it might rub off on you."

He smiled and then continued, "Now, I am going to teach you a very powerful way of learning. Some people call it modeling. That is a fancy term but academicians are like that.

"The premise of modeling is simple. When you want to learn how to do something exceptionally well, you study people who are already extremely good at it. Then, you inventory what they all have in common and copy it. You practice to do what they do. When you get good at whatever it is you are practicing, you will begin to develop your own style. Understand?"

"I think so," I replied hesitantly.

"We shall do an exercise in modeling together and you will learn exactly how it is done."

"Okay."

"Do you have any friends or acquaintances now or in the past who excelled at meeting women?"

"Yes, I do."

From my days at the defense contractor, I had come to know a number of fellows who were particularly successful at meeting and dating numerous women. These men were the type who walk into a nightclub and leave with at least a woman's telephone number, if not the woman herself, almost every time they go out.

One fellow, John, would regularly leave a bar with a newly acquired female friend he just met. He was in the habit of immediately taking her to a secluded spot in the back lot of a home improvement store. There he would take advantage of the privacy and enjoy her in the most intimate of ways. Although I personally did not care to meet women who were that promiscuous, it made me jealous that he had such success consistently.

Mike, another guy, averaged two or more new sexual conquests a month. I did not even date that much. After satisfying himself with a new partner, he would soon label her as a slut and dump her. He hated his mother so maybe it was a psychological revenge thing.

Another fellow, Lenny, could attract women without even speaking to them. He moved on a dance floor like an erotic male dancer. I personally witnessed, on more than one occasion, a female across the dance floor pointing to Lenny with a finger that indicated, "Come here big boy!" Once I tried to imitate the way he danced and split my pants.

Leo continued our Don Juan lesson, "Think about what they all had in common. Just close your eyes, relax, and think about the characteristics of their behavior that enable them to be so successful with women. That's right…good. Now tell me the first item that comes to mind."

"Well, they all dressed well when they went out. Usually they would wear a suit."

"Okay. Next item?"

"Hmm…they were fairly alert to what was going on around them. They would scope out the place for available women."

"Good. Keep going."

"They would usually approach a women subtly though not always. They often compliment a lady in some way or say something to get her to laugh."

"What about their demeanor? How did they present themselves?"

"They came across as friendly, confident, enjoying themselves."

"Okay," Leo said, "That is a decent start. Let's develop a prototype Don Juan as you put it.

"First, he dresses well to blend in with the environment and be pleasing to the eye. Second, he stalks the area for viable opportunities. Third, he attempts to approach a woman in a non-threatening way. Fourth, he baits the woman by giving her what seem to be sincere compliments and by using his sense of humor to get her laughing. And finally, the Don Juan's state of mind is one of having fun and being confident."

It felt as if a light bulb flicked on in my head. "Yes," I said beginning to spark with enthusiasm.

"If they were rejected after an approach, how did they react?"

"They would often utter some kind of derogatory comment related to the female gender and then move on."

"They would continue pursuing females undeterred. Correct?"

"Yes."

"Good. Now we have some basics."

Leo had me close my eyes, recline back in the leather chair, and breathe deep into the stomach as he just taught me earlier. He started to speak in a slow deliberate manner.

"Just breathe easily and relax. There's no place you have to be; nothing you have to do. That's right, just relax.

"What I would like you to do each evening is to find some quiet time. Get comfortable just like you are now. Concentrate on your breathing for ten minutes. Then, in your mind's eye, picture yourself as if watching a movie. Picture yourself in a popular place to meet women. Watch yourself act like a perfect Don Juan prototype. You are comfortable and relaxed. You are charming and confident. You brush off rejection and move on to females who are more receptive. That's right; watch the whole scene as if it was on a movie screen. When the scene has developed to the point where you feel very comfortable and confident, replay it but this time step into your own body and experience it as if it was really happening. Use your all your senses; see, hear, feel everything. Perform this visualization every evening. Think of the words as you do this—Don Juan."

He touched the side of my temple firmly with two of his fingers. After a moment or two, Leo asked me to open my eyes and sit up.

"What we are doing is programming you, Tony. You have already been programmed in your life. Unfortunately, it has been in ways that do not serve your best interests. A warrior takes control of his life. In order to accomplish this, I will teach you how to reprogram the tangled mess that is now in your head."

"Does this stuff really work Leo?"

"What do you have to lose?" he smiled. "The worst that can happen is that you remain a mindless sheep in the human herd."

"All right. I'll give it a try."

"Practice the visualization. Next week, I will teach you powerful techniques to greatly enhance your appeal to the opposite sex."

The idea of mastering such knowledge intrigued me. I began to eagerly anticipate Leo's next lesson.

The following week I went to Leo's office as scheduled. Like a masterful professor who captures the intense interest and imagination of his students, Leo taught me what he called the art of persuasion. For three straight hours, he instructed me how to determine a person's state of mind and how to move it to the state I desired. This education included how to read body language, paying attention to eye cues, voice tone, and the pace of speech. Leo also taught me how to be aware of and decipher a person's language patterns to find out how they think and how to best communicate with them. The material was involved but I found it fascinating despite my natural skepticism.

"Does this really work?" I asked.

"Yes, it does. What do you think sales professionals learn at seminars? The same skills as I am teaching you."

I stated an objection saying that to intentionally try to influence the state of mind in another person was manipulative.

"Of course it is manipulative!" he replied.

"Isn't that wrong?"

Leo laughed loudly.

"There is nothing inherently right or wrong with manipulating other people. It is your intention that determines the action's morality."

"Is it immoral to use these techniques to improve my sex life?"

Leo broke out laughing again.

"No, that's biological!"

Leo then turned serious and said, "Learn your lessons well because next week we are going on a field trip."

"A field trip?"

"A field trip," he repeated. "We are going to practice hunting."

"I don't know if that's a good idea."

Leo laughed.

"You are used to school where you simply memorized concepts without any attempt at practical application. Of course, the great majority of the things you learned had no practical application anyway!

"To truly learn, you have to do! That is the purpose of our field trip."

The next Tuesday evening, Leo arrived at my apartment as arranged beforehand. I was apprehensive about this so-called field trip and what it might entail. Though I found Leo interesting, his sanity was still a question mark to me. There was no telling what he had in mind.

"Where are we going?" I inquired.

"To the mall."

"To the mall? Why the mall?"

"Why does a lion stalk a water hole? That is where the prey are!"

Leo had double-parked on the street in front of the icky yellow apartment building. The vehicle was a sleek, shiny, black German sports car.

"Nice! Is it yours?"

"Of course it is mine," he answered.

"Can you get me one?"

Leo laughed and said, "This possession is part of the reward of being a warrior. You shall find that good things come to you once you learn to act in harmony with the universe."

"Could I lease one meanwhile?"

Leo smiled but did not reply. Then, for some unknown reason, he asked me to drive. I happily took the driver's seat. As we headed to our destination, I enjoyed the smoothness and precision handling of the sports car.

As directed by Leo, I took us to a mall in Nassau County, just east of Queens. It is one of the largest malls in the United States and recently renovated. The inside is a pleasing combination of white marble, glass, waterfalls, and attractive women of various ages.

"What's the plan?" I inquired as we were walking inside.

"This is your mission," Leo said with a humorously exaggerated expression of seriousness. "You are to initiate a conversation with every attractive woman between the ages of twenty to thirty we happen to come upon."

"What! That's crazy! I can't do that!"

"What is stopping you Tony?"

"I would be embarrassed as hell Leo! I would feel like an idiot trying to talk to every woman I came across!"

"Ah," Leo said, "Remember that a hunter sneaks up on its prey before pouncing. You will not be obvious but casual. You will make the conversation natural and spontaneous as if you hadn't planned it at all."

"You are a nut. You know that, don't you?"

"Perhaps, but I am a happy nut."

I shook my head wondering what I had gotten myself into.

With Leo leading the way, we walked to the jewelry section in a large department store.

"Big water hole," he smiled with his eyebrows raised.

I spied a young lady browsing the glass case where the women's watches were displayed. She was a very attractive brunette; wearing jeans whose snugness was modest enough not to generate undue attention but still revealed the fact that a very fine body occupied the denim. The length of her shirt did not quite make it to her jeans exposing a thin line of flesh at the midsection. I tried to sneak a peek at her bellybutton.

"It is time for you to confront your fears and put into practice what I have been teaching you," Leo said gesturing to the girl.

My stomach immediately tightened as if tied into a knot.

"No way!" I shook my head vigorously. "I can't do it."

"Okay. If you cannot do it, pretend you are someone who can and go over there."

"No way! You were right. I'm a wimp. Let's go home."

"You are not a wimp. You are a hunter! Your nationality has a colorful history of great lovers. Pretend to be one of them! Fake it if you have to! Think," he paused, "of Don Juan". He touched the side of my temple firmly with two of his fingers. "Take a deep breath and go!" Leo grabbed me by the shoulders and pointed me in the direction of the woman.

"What should I say?"

"Don't think about it! Just do what I taught you!"

I started towards the prey, I mean female.

"And remember Tony," Leo whispered, "Old Master say, 'He who hesitates masturbates'!" He broke out into stifled laughter.

I must be crazy listening to this guy.

As nonchalantly as possible, I moseyed over to the long glass display case a few feet away from the young woman. I pretended to be browsing while slowly heading in her direction. I stealthily watched her from the corner of my eye. She was younger than I was, maybe twenty years old, and even prettier than her rear profile first suggested. I eased my way closer until I entered inside her personal space. Leo taught me that, under normal conditions, a person would take notice of you once you enter their personal space. Supposedly, this is an automatic survival response programmed into the genes.

The brunette and I briefly made eye contact. I smiled casually and said hello.

"Hi," she said briefly with a quick short smile. She then turned her attention back to the jewelry.

"If it is okay for me to ask, I was wondering if I could get your opinion about gifts from a female perspective." I kept my voice tone and demeanor purposely low key.

"What would that be?" she asked slightly puzzled.

"Assuming you have a boyfriend, would you prefer to simply tell him what you would like for a gift or would you rather he pick out something on his own and surprise you?"

"Well," she thought for a moment, "I would rather be surprised."

"You would rather be surprised?"

"Yes," she said with a slight but noticeable increased interest, "It's more fun that way."

Her body was now facing me instead of being turned to the side. She was smiling. Leo taught me to be aware of this nonverbal feedback and to quickly exploit in the conversation anything that created a positive response in the other person.

"And what was the nicest surprise you ever had?" I asked with an engaging smile.

The purpose of this type of question is to get the woman to access a pleasant memory. The recall of the memory transitions her to the identical state of mind generated by the actual past event. The end result is that she feels happy and excited just like she did when she was pleasantly surprised.

"When I was a little girl, I had a birthday party and my father gave me the most beautiful bracelet."

She went on to tell me a little about the party and I encouraged her to talk by asking open-ended questions. Just like Leo taught me, I paid careful attention to her body language, what she was saying, and how she was saying it. This experiment was working out better than I expected.

The conversation came to a pause. She looked at me intently with a smile on her face as if waiting for me to say something.

"What's your name?" I asked.

"Danielle."

She said her name in such a sweet, nice way that my heart started to melt.

"Hi Danielle. I'm Tony. Were you looking around to give your boyfriend some hints for what you like?"

As one would reasonably guess, I asked this to find out if she even had a boyfriend. Leo suggested this tactic as a way to avoid pursuing women already involved.

"Oh, I'm not seeing anyone now. I recently broke up with someone."

Her demeanor changed to a slightly sad one.

"Well, judging from your looks and personality you must have broke up with him."

She laughed and then said with one hand on her hip and a half grin, "Believe it or not he broke up with me."

"That fool!" I half shouted in a humorous way. "Well, Danielle, perhaps your boyfriend was just not smart enough to appreciate you."

She sighed and appeared almost relieved.

It was time to pounce.

"I would love to talk to you more but my Godfather is waiting for me."

I motioned to the area Leo was. She turned around.

"I don't see anyone."

"Oh," I said looking around for him, "He must have wandered off. I'll have to find him."

I paused for a moment then continued, "I realize this is a bit unusual for me to ask just after meeting you for a couple of minutes but you seem like a person worth getting to know better. May I have your phone number? That way we can talk and perhaps get to know each other."

She hesitated for a moment and then said with a smile and a little shrug of the shoulders, "Sure. Why not?"

After taking her number, I went to look for Leo. I found him in the soap and fragrance section a short distance away.

The astounding initial success with Danielle made me giddy.

Leo frowned.

"What's wrong?"

"The worst possible thing happened to you!" Leo exclaimed.

"What? What do you mean Leo?"

"You were successful on your first try. That's the worst thing that could have happened!"

"Why?" I asked bewildered.

"You didn't learn anything! A warrior learns from his mistakes not his successes. Mistakes force a warrior to try different approaches, to persevere, to learn new lessons. Mistakes encourage humility and patience.

"It is far better for you to fail and stumble in your early endeavors! It is bad luck if you should succeed on your first attempts. That experience will incline you to mistakenly think you have mastered the art and inflate your ego."

"I thought the whole purpose was to succeed."

"No, no, no! The purpose is for you to learn how to live like a warrior. Once you achieve that, the outcome of any action is inconsequential."

I was confused but did not know what to say or ask next.

"Let's go," Leo said, "our mission tonight is not yet over."

We walked through the mall. Leo had me attempt to initiate conversations with other women. Some responded to me pleasantly; others ignored me the best they could.

"Boy, she was not friendly," I commented about one woman who gave me the cold shoulder.

"She rejected your approach," Leo added.

"Yes."

"And you survived - yes? You have feared rejection in the past as if it would kill you. Now, perhaps you find yourself understanding that rejection is harmless to your well being as an adult. As a warrior, you shall conquer that biological fear."

"Biological fear?"

"Yes. The fear of rejection is genetically inherited. Children naturally fear the rejection of their caretakers. This is biological programming. In nature, if parents ignore a child, that child will not survive. Therefore, a child will do anything it can to gain the attention of its parents. The child fears rejection because rejection means death.

"You are now an adult, but you still carry that fear of rejection. That is why your stomach goes into knots when you approach a woman you have an interest in. To conquer the fear, you must confront it. By confronting it and surviving, you demonstrate to your subconscious that its fear is unwarranted. The fear of rejection then begins to disappear."

As Leo and I made our way through the mall, I became better at selecting women who were friendlier. As directed by Leo, I did not try to acquire any more phone numbers.

"One step at a time," he said.

While in a bookstore, we came upon a particularly stunning woman. Long blonde hair adorned a lovely figure clad in black pants and a white shirt. Leo pointed to her with his eyes.

"I can't," I said.

Leo frowned.

"What is stopping you?"

"That's big game. I'm not ready for that."

"The more beautiful a woman is, the more your are intimidated. That is why you have only dated average looking woman in the past."

I gave him a "what do you mean" look.

Leo continued, "You lacked self confidence in the past so you would only date plain looking women. They made you feel safe." I started to protest, but Leo cut me off. "Your parents were not kind to you when you were young. Were they?"

The statement itself and its deviation from the immediately preceding topic brought me to a complete mental stop.

"How do you know that?" I asked bemused.

"You told me, Tony."

"I never said a word to you about my parents!"

"Words are the least effective form of communication. You did not use words but you told me just the same. Part of the consequence of the mistreatment you suffered as a child is a lack of self confidence."

I reacted to his observation by feeling sorry for myself.

"Stop!" Leo commanded sharply snapping his fingers in my face. Like magic, the sadness instantaneously vanished.

During this exchange, the woman we noticed had walked away.

"Come," Leo said looking at his watch, "It is still early."

"Where are we going now?"

"We need to work on eliminating your feeling of intimidation with beautiful women."

"And how are we going to do that?"

"Two ways. One, by building self-confidence. Two, by going to a topless bar."

"A topless bar?" I loudly spurted out with amusement.

"Yes. You need to get used to being around scantily clad beautiful women with big boobs."

"What?" I laughed.

Leo smiled.

"I'm serious! Let's go!"

We walked out of the mall into the night air and the parking lot. When we got to Leo's sleek German auto, he popped open the rear trunk and took out a charcoal gray sport coat. He put it on.

"Always prepared I see," I said in wonderment.

"Yes, and this one is for you."

He pulled out a black sport coat. It fit fairly well.

Leo decided to drive this time. I settled into the passenger seat and looked at him suspiciously.

"Do you do this often?" I asked half jokingly.

Leo broke out into a good-natured laugh slapping the car's dashboard.

We drove back to Queens and went to a popular upscale topless bar. The crowd consisted of a typical mix of men of varying seediness and young women of varying breast sizes though the general disposition was towards large.

I ordered a beer and Leo got a club soda. We positioned ourselves by a wall just across from the center bar, which was shaped like a square. In the center of the square were a raised stage with three poles and a half dozen girls dancing. To our far right was a stage. Small tables with seated patrons were scattered about the place. Some of the girls circled the bar mixing with the men. The music was loud and the men mostly silent. One of the girls dancing on the stage had ridiculously augmented breasts that overwhelmed her otherwise lean frame.

"Wow. Those are huge!" I commented gawking at her.

"She could knock you out with those things," Leo added.

One of the roaming ladies looking for victims to buy her a drink or pay for a lap dance headed toward us. She looked very young, perhaps a teenager eighteen or nineteen years old. She had brown hair, brown eyes, and denim shorts cut along the bottom to reveal the lower part of her derriere and cut randomly along the sides to reveal she wore no under garments. Her top was covered, just barely, with a cut off white tee shirt that failed to hide the bottom part of her smallish but perky breasts. Her nipples pressed against the shirt like two pencil erasers and a gold belly button ring wonderfully highlighted her perfectly flat stomach.

"I think we are now the hunted," I remarked to Leo.

"Turn the tables on her," he suggested slyly. "Remember the lesson on eliciting values?"

"Yes?"

"Practice." He motioned with his chin toward the approaching girl.

Leo taught me that to gain deep rapport with a person one had to determine their values. Eliciting values is simply finding out what is important to a person.

"Hello," the young girl said with a smile as perky as her breasts.

"Hello," I replied.

"My name is Scorpio. What's your name?"

"Aries and this is Leo," I joked. "No, I'm just kidding. My name is Tony. This is my godfather Leo. Leo is his real name." I pointed to Leo who was standing by my side near my elbow.

"Hi! So how are you gentlemen tonight?"

"Fine. We were on our way home but decided to take the scenic route," I said.

"Good. Do you enjoy the scenery right in front of you?" she asked looking down as if checking out her own body. She then looked me seductively in the eyes as if she was attempting to suck my very soul out of me.

"Very much so. May I ask you a question?"

"Sure."

"You obviously meet a lot of men here. I am sure you are very skillful at ultimately keeping them at a distance despite appearances. But, what I am interested in finding out is if you ever meet a man you find very attractive? You know, someone you would like to get to know personally?"

"Every once in a while that happens."

"When that does happen, what is it you find attractive about a man that makes you interested in him?"

"Well, some of guys I meet are very good looking. Or I can just tell they have something going for them."

"How can you tell that?"

"They have this air of confidence like they know what they want and they know they were going to get it. I like a man who can take control!"

"Ah," I said, "You like a take control kind of guy."

As I made my last statement, I inconspicuously placed my hand on my chest as if pointing to myself just like Leo had taught me. This is supposed to subconsciously get her to identify me as the take control kind of man she desires. Don't ask me if this really works. I don't know.

"Yeah," she said smiling her eyes shifting down and to the right.

According to Leo, that type of eye movement meant she was thinking in feelings. If her eyes had shifted upward, that would have meant she was thinking in pictures.

Leo taught that I should observe a person's thought process by watching their eyes and carefully listen to how they structure their language. The idea is then to communicate back in the same fashion to gain rapport. For example, if someone says they have a bright idea, they are thinking in pictures so you would respond by saying something like "yeah, I see". If someone says, "I feel this is a good idea," you would respond, "That feels right to me too." Or, a person may ask, "Do you hear what I am saying?" To match, you would respond, "That sounds good to me," and so on.

"I can understand how a girl like you desires a self-confident man who is not afraid to take control," I told the dancer. "You seem a little wild and probably want someone man enough to handle you. Someone," I said looking into her eyes, "that can match your intensity."

"Yeah!" she enthusiastically answered. "Would you like a lap dance?"

"No thank you. That would be like smelling a big juicy steak under my nose but not being able to eat it."

She laughed.

"You're so cute! I'll see you later!" She lightly touched my shoulder with her hand and moved on.

"Pretty good for a beginner," Leo commented.

For the next hour, other girls came by and I spoke to them as well. At times, I actually became more absorbed in the verbal interaction than the jiggling breasts. Leo told me that to really understand people you have to be a good listener.

It started to get late. Leo and I made our way to the exit. Scorpio, the young girl with the denim shorts, came up and kissed me on the cheek.

"It was so nice to meet you!" Her arms circled my waist and lower back. One of her hands found its way into my back pocket.

"It was nice meeting you too," I said enjoying the physical closeness to her. A warm sensual heat radiated from her body.

When Leo and I were in the parking lot, I pulled out a business card from my back pocket. Her phone number was hastily scribbled on the back of it.

"Look at this!" I shouted to Leo.

"Congratulations."

"That's two in one night! I tied a personal record!"

Leo laughed.

"You know," I said holding up the card, "This is like striking oil!"

"Just be sure to protect your equipment before you start drilling!"

We broke out laughing.

"Temper your enthusiasm," Leo cautioned, "Your journey has just begun."

The next day I called Scorpio in the afternoon from my desk at work. I found out that her real name was Angela. After a minute or two of exchanging pleasantries, I asked if she would like to get together.

"Sure! What did you have in mind?"

"You," I answered. She giggled. "I suspect that a lot of men take you out for dinner and all that other trivial stuff. Why don't you and I forget the ceremonial nonsense? What would you say if I suggested that I come over to your place with a couple of bottles of champagne; one for drinking and one for pouring on each other?"

This degree of bluntness was quite unusual for me. However, I reasoned that she was the type of girl who appreciated the direct approach.

"Hmmm, if you asked me that, I guess I would say what time will you be over?"

Direct hit.

Impulsively, I loudly slapped the top of my desk in delight. The sound caught the attention of my desk neighbor, Rob, who wondered what was going on.

Angela and I made plans to see each other the next Monday night; one of the few evenings she did not work as an erotic dancer.

Anticipating an action filled evening; I began to take Ginseng tablets every day starting that same day. I swallowed four extra tablets that Monday morning. A fellow at work mentioned that taking Ginseng in this manner enabled his soldier to stay at attention even after giving the final salute. It had been a while since my pleasure-seeking appendage had any real action. Therefore, I wanted to do everything possible to insure peak performance.

The much-awaited Monday night arrived. I headed to Angela's apartment with two bottles of champagne. She shared the apartment with her roommate, another dancer, but had her own bedroom. Soon after the romantic activities began, champagne wasn't the only thing flowing. As I suspected, Angela was wild in bed. The action was so hot and heavy that I frequently checked the protective rubber armor on my spear to make sure it did not pierce during the repeated lancing. In the throes of passion, Angela repeatedly hit the wall on the side of the bed with one of her legs and verbalized her pleasures loudly. Her roommate had to hear us. I guess she didn't care or perhaps she was just used to it.

I left late that night a little weak in the knees but well satisfied. A pair of skimpy panties courtesy of Angela stuffed in my pocket as a souvenir. I called Leo the next day and gleefully told him the news.

"Leo! You are a genius!"

"Congratulations on your first kill."

"Does that mean I'm a hunter now?"

"No, it does not. You have only learned the techniques which, to your credit, you have done well. However, you do not have the attitude of a hunter. You have not yet learned responsibility."

"Responsibility?"

"To use an analogy, I have taught you how to aim and fire your weapon but you do not have the sense of responsibility that should accompany that power. You are like a young boy that learns how to use a rifle and then gets so excited at mastering the skill that he runs into the woods and shoots at everything that moves. As you acquire skills and become a more powerful person you must develop a profound sense of responsibility."

"I'm not sure I understand how that applies to me."

"It is simple," Leo explained. "If you do not learn temperance and responsibility, the power you come to possess will soon possess you."

CHAPTER 3

▼

CRUSHING ENEMIES

"I can protect you from everyone except
yourself," the old man cautioned.
from 'How I Got Lucky and Bumped into God'—the author

Leo announced that he would be travelling out of state for the next few weeks. When I asked him where he was going, he evaded the question. I thought it prudent not to inquire any further. During his absence, I continued to pursue women using the techniques he taught. My favorite places to hunt were bars at Happy Hours and bookstores during my lunch break. As a result, my social life with the opposite sex improved dramatically. However, despite my romantic successes, I still felt lonely. None of the encounters resulted in any potential long-term relationships. I did not feel ready for one in any case.

Even with the turnaround in my social life, I continued to be plagued with a general sense of unhappiness. I did not care for my job and I was still losing money in the stock market. Feelings of depression soon invaded my temperament again until I reached the point of not wanting to do much of anything, even socializing with the opposite sex.

Shortly after Leo returned from his trip, he gave me a call. My tone of voice betrayed my state of mind.

"You sound blue," Leo observed.

"Yeah, I've been feeling a bit down."

"That," said Leo pausing for emphasis, "is one of your greatest enemies."

"What is?"

"You like to indulge in feeling sorry for yourself. That horrible habit cripples you. You muddle through life hunched over, complaining, and feeling sorry for yourself. A warrior rids himself of all such nonsense. He takes responsibility for his life. If he is not happy, he takes action to change."

"But not everything is within a person's control," I pointed out defensively.

"You have far more control than you think! You relinquish your power to others. Rather than be a warrior, you have been a sheep in a herd blaming the shepherd for anything you don't like.

"That mentality is a carry over from your childhood. When you were a young boy, your parents were cruel to you so you felt like a helpless victim. At that time in your life that was true but you are an adult now. You are no longer helpless. There are no more excuses to be a victim. If you still are, you and only you are responsible."

"You don't know what my parents did to me."

I was becoming despondent and irritated.

"I know more than you think," Leo said in a low slow voice, "For example, I know about the time your father beat you mercilessly with a leather belt until you passed out."

"How in the world do you know about that?" I was stunned. I never told Leo about that incident.

When I was a young boy, I had dropped an easy fly ball playing the outfield during a championship little league baseball game. That error resulted in the eventual game winning run by the other team. My father's idea of providing motivation so that I would never make a similar mistake again was to discipline me harshly. After we returned home from the game, he secured me to a pole in the garage and lashed my bare back with a leather belt until I collapsed in a heap on the cold cement floor.

"You still carry scars inside," Leo said. "That is how I know. You need to crush your internal enemies and reclaim the power rightfully yours. That shall be your greatest victory. It shall be your entry to the path of a warrior."

"Those words are all high and mighty Leo, but it's not so easy in real life. Life is difficult."

"You make life far more difficult than it is. You are your greatest enemy. The enemy from within! The old master said, 'He who has control over others is powerful. He who has control over himself is the most powerful of all.' "

"I understand what you are trying to say, but it has little meaning for me in real life."

"Yes, I agree with you. My words are only words to you. You have not taken the lesson to heart. It is time to rectify that. I think it is time for - can you guess?"

"I'm almost afraid to ask."

"Field trip!"

"Field trip? Again?"

"Yes. My lessons are not like the ones you learned in school where you filled your head with words from a book and little more. My lessons are lessons of life and must be practiced in daily life to be mastered."

"Where are we going now, a nudist colony?"

"No," Leo replied with a grin on his face. "This field trip will be far less pleasant than the last one."

The ominous nature of his statement made me cringe inside.

The next day, after work, Leo met me outside of my office building. I asked him where we would be going.

"Your inclination to feel sorry for yourself is strong. Therefore, I am seeking the aid of a very powerful teacher."

"Who?"

"It is not a who but a what."

"Then what?"

"Death."

"Death? Are you kidding?"

"No. I am serious."

"Where are we going - a cemetery?"

"No."

"Where then?"

"Patience Tony. You shall see."

Leo waved down a cab and we headed uptown. He directed the driver to take us to a large hospital in the city well known for treating cancer patients.

Ugh. I hated hospitals - especially the antiseptic smell.

"Why are we going there?" I asked.

"That is where our teacher resides."

"Leo, you are without a doubt the strangest damn therapist I ever heard of."

The cab pulled up to the front entrance of the hospital. We paid the driver and entered the hospital's main entrance. Inside stood a security guard checking for patient visitor passes and hospital ids before allowing anyone to enter the hospital beyond the front lobby.

"We don't know anyone to visit," I whispered to Leo.

"That is alright. Clear your mind just as you do when practicing your breathing. Do not look directly at any of the hospital staff. Pretend you are invisible. Think invisible. Follow right behind me."

Though skeptical of Leo's plan, I did as he instructed. To my amazement, we walked right past the guard who had been otherwise diligently checking everyone for id or passes. Looking out the corner of my eye it seemed that the guard did not even notice us.

"How did you do that?" I whispered.

"Quiet!" Leo admonished. "I'll tell you later."

We reached an elevator and took it up, way up. "They keep the most critical patients on the higher floors," Leo mentioned.

"Why do they do that?"

"I don't know," he shrugged. "Perhaps it is to keep them as close as possible to heaven to shorten the trip."

Leo snickered at his own light-hearted hypothesis.

The elevator door opened. A long corridor took us to what I assume was a geriatric ward judging from the advanced age of the patients inside the rooms. The nurses and other people in the ward seemed completely oblivious to our presence.

"This one will serve our purposes." Leo motioned me to enter a patient's room. The door was half opened. I slipped into the room quietly with Leo following close behind. In the bed lay an old shriveled up man; his face wrinkled like a prune. Tubes and monitors crisscrossed his frail thin frame. His body looked like a dried out leaf. The man's gray eyes were half-shut and unblinking.

"Death is stalking him," Leo said in a low voice. "Soon, it will snatch him from this earth.

The sight of the helpless dying man disgusted me. Though I felt pity for him, his helplessness and weakness repulsed me.

"Touch the old man lightly at the top of his wrist."

I hesitated at first but then did so. Immediately, I experienced a strange sensation in the pit of my stomach.

"Now, Tony. Close your eyes and imagine for the moment that you are that old man. That's right. Pretend to step out of your body and into his. Good. Now, feel as he feels. You cannot move under your own power. You cannot so much as lift an eyebrow or go to the bathroom on your own. This is all that is left of your life. Your time has come to an end. The only thing you can do is wait for Death to take you."

Leo placed two fingers at the base of the back of my neck.

"Now as that old man, gaze up and look at yourself. You see this young man looking down at you. He has an entire life ahead of him. He is healthy and capable of doing anything he wants."

Leo's fingers pressed more firmly but gently into the back of my neck. "Now," Leo said quickly, "imagine a miracle has occurred and you, the old man, suddenly find yourself in the young man's body! You are young again. There is no pain, you can move freely! You are capable of doing anything you wish! How do you feel?" He removed the fingers from my neck.

It took a moment for me to orient myself and then I said, "I feel ecstatic to be alive and well. I have the urge to want to run down the hall wildly shouting for joy!"

"And if that old man could have your body now, what do you think he would do?"

"I imagine he would want to see and experience all those things he had always wanted to in his life, but never seemed to find the time to do. He probably would worry a lot less, not care so much what other people think, and live his life the way that makes him the happiest."

"So what is your excuse, Tony? What do you think this old man would say to you if he could speak and see how you walk around feeling sorry for yourself?"

"He would probably want to kick me in the butt and tell me how fortunate I really am."

We remained silent a few moments, my eyes fixated on the deep crevices of the old man's face. I felt a tremendous surge of energy coursing through my body.

"This," Leo said pointing to the man, "is the lesson of Death. You are not immortal. Someday you will pass from this earth. A warrior realizes that his time is the most precious resource he has and acts accordingly."

I stood silent and unmoving until Leo broke me out of my transfixed state.

"Come, we have another visit to make."

We left the room. Leo reminded me to keep my mind free from thoughts, to not look directly at anyone, and follow unswervingly behind him. This time, we traveled down to a lower floor to a children's ward. As we walked down the hall and glanced inside of rooms, I noticed that many of the young patients were bald from chemotherapy treatments.

Leo quietly led me to a room with two children in it. There was a nurse tending to the child in the bed furthest away from the door, which gave me a pause, but Leo seemed unconcerned.

In the bed nearest the entrance, was a little girl; her head covered with a small white cap. Perhaps she was three years old. The girl loosely held a little stuffed animal, a black penguin with a big white nose. An IV protruded from her tiny arm. I moved close to the bed. The girl stared blankly into my eyes. Her face displayed no expression. I touched her lightly on the arm and turned around to Leo.

"She's not going to make it, is she?"

"No," Leo said as he again placed two fingers on the back of my neck, "You are correct, she is not going to make it. She will never know what it is to grow up. Imagine all the wonderful things she will never experience. Think of how great a tragedy it is that she will not even have an opportunity to live life." I felt tears coming to my eyes.

"She doesn't have a chance, Tony. Death will soon take her from this world."

Leo released his fingers from my neck and turned me around looking straight into my eyes. "Unlike her, you have a chance. You have the glorious gift of opportunity that life provides but you disregard the gift as if it were nothing. Fate shall soon snatch the gift of life from that girl. However, you still have it in your possession. Now, what are you going to do with it?"

I did not answer his rhetorical question.

"Ask yourself Tony; what is the lesson of Death?"

I turned back and looked down at the girl. Her pale stone-like face remained expressionless as she clung to the funny looking big nosed penguin

"It is time for us to leave," Leo whispered.

I left the room with Leo feeling I was in some kind of trance. It was like my mind was rewiring itself at a rapid pace and I was incapable of any focused attention during the process.

Leo and I vacated the building just as unnoticed as when we entered. On the way to the subway station Leo advised, "Anytime you experience the temptation to wallow in self pity, remember our visit to the hospital this day and the lesson of Death. If necessary, visit the hospital yourself again.

"You now know how to defeat your worst enemy. When we face our inevitable death, the trivial things that encourage self pity quickly disappear."

He stopped talking for a minute, and then continued. "A warrior is ruthless and calculating when crushing his enemies whether they be internal or external. Like a hunter, stalk and strike down your weaknesses. Each time you do so, you evolve further and grow more powerful."

*   *   *

The lack of any genuine motivation for my alleged career began to take its toll. The number of calls I conducted per day to solicit potential clients dropped below what the management deemed acceptable. During our session that week, Leo explained that it was my subconscious sabotaging my sales efforts.

"You aren't happy with the job. That is no secret. There is a part of you operating at the subconscious level hoping to get fired so you will not have to endure the emotional pain of being in an unrewarding job any longer."

"But I don't want to get fired."

"Therein lies the conflict!" Leo laughed.

I did not share his perceived humor of the situation.

"Seriously now, what do you mean?"

"Ask yourself, what is the positive intention of the part of you trying to get you fired?"

"Positive intention?"

"Yes," Leo said, "Behind every behavior is some sort of positive intention no matter how negative it may seem on the surface. "

"I find that hard to believe."

"Trust me. Think for a moment. You are unhappy with your job, but like a sheep, you have not done anything about it. So, you just go on feeling miserable. Since you failed to rectify the situation, another hidden part of you has decided to take action."

"What do you mean?" I was having difficulty following his line of reasoning.

"Quiet your mind for a moment. Ask yourself, what is the intention of the part of you causing your poor performance on the job?"

I fell silent for a moment while internally asking myself the question. An answer immediately presented itself. "This job is just not for me, Leo. I can't stand it. I just stick with it because I need the money."

"Then," Leo went on, "satisfy the intention on your own terms. Proceed strategically as a warrior instead of haphazardly at the mercy of external circumstances. Satisfy the intention of the hidden part in a favorable way and the conflict will be resolved."

I did not understand completely what Leo said but I reflected on it and thought back to my marriage.

I was unhappy in my marriage with Diane. But I failed to act to rectify the situation either to make the relationship better or to end it. As time went on, I became increasingly distant and unpleasant toward her. In hindsight, there was a subconscious part of me that wanted the relationship to end. That part began to sabotage the marriage. After almost a year enduring me being cold and distant, Diane could tolerate it no longer and initiated the divorce. When confronted by Diane, I offered only token resistance to the idea of ending the marriage and we soon separated.

"Yes," Leo said after I told him of my self-observation, "making your ex-wife's life disagreeable was the behavior caused by a part of you that realized you were unhappily married. The positive intention of the part was to get you out of the marriage to end your unhappiness.

Unfortunately, as often happens, the behavioral actions of an uncontrolled part may produce undesirable or even destructive behavior. The subconscious does not know any better on its own.

"As a warrior, you can use the internal feelings of conflict as a signal that something is wrong. Your conscious and subconscious desires are not in harmony at that time. Your task is then to determine what is causing the conflict and to resolve it on your own terms. If you do not, your behavior will be determined by impulsive emotions instead of purposeful action."

My now consistently poor performance on the job began to be noticed. Rob warned me that he heard I was being monitored and may be fired unless my call numbers improved. I suspect that his friendly warning originated from a senior person hoping I would get the message without direct management involvement. One day, an order originating from management directed us to recommend a particular stock to both new and existing clients. I knew from experience that this meant the brokerage house owned the stock itself and they were trying to get rid of it. In other words, they were trying to get their customers to buy a stock they did not want to own themselves. When the word came around to start making the calls I sat at my desk staring at the telephone.

"You better get going," Rob said in a concerned way. "At least make it look like you're trying."

"I can't do this nonsense anymore."

"What are you going to do? Quit?"

"No. I have something more advantageous in mind."

"What?"

"It's a secret," I smiled coyly.

Rob looked at me perplexed. When I did not elaborate further, he went back to his business. I continued to sit at my desk off the phone. The inevitable happened and my manager, an older gruff looking three-martini lunch fellow, came up to my desk.

"Why aren't you making any calls?" he huffed.

"I've been asked to recommend for purchase a stock that this company is attempting to eliminate from its own inventory. Is that correct?"

"Yeah. So what?"

"Recommending a stock to my client based on this brokerage firm's financial interests instead of my client's financial interests is a violation of my fiduciary responsibility to that client."

The manager and Rob, who was in earshot at the adjacent desk, both looked at each other puzzled. Rob shrugged his shoulders at the manager to indicate ignorance about what was going on.

"You sound like a God damned lawyer. What are you talking about?" the gruff one shouted. "Get on that phone!"

"No."

"No?"

"No. To do so would be unethical."

He started to fume. His head began to take on a red angry glow as if someone turned the heat on high in his skull.

"Look you arrogant guinea. This is your last warning. Get on that phone or I'll fire you right on the spot!"

"I am not getting on the phone and you are not going to fire me. You will lay me off so I can collect unemployment benefits."

"What?" His head now looked as if it was ready to explode like a squeezed ripe tomato. "You have some nerve! You're fired! Pack up your stuff and get the hell out now!"

I stood up from my desk chair and faced him directly.

"I strongly suggest that you go back to your office and fill out the paper work indicating that I have been laid off. You will explain that there are too many brokers for the current level of business the firm has. If you don't do this, I'll see to it you lose your job."

"And just how are you going to do that?" he snarled.

"If you fire me, I will still file for unemployment. If this firm claims I was fired and that I am not entitled to benefits there will be, as required by law, a hearing with the unemployment office. I will claim that I was instructed to conduct business of an unethical nature and was fired when I refused."

"Who is going to believe you?" he smiled smugly, "We'll just claim you are a disgruntled employee and that you were fired for incompetence."

"They'll believe this."

I reached into the inside pocket of my suit jacket, which hung on the back of my chair, and pulled out a micro-cassette recorder. A little red light indicating a recording mode was clearly visible. I held up the recorder and pointed to it with my free hand.

"If I produce this tape at an unemployment hearing, the firm will claim it knew nothing about your orders and that you acted without their knowledge. They will then fire you to cover themselves."

The pressure continued to build in his skull. Veins bulged predominantly on his forehead. I suspected he might experience a stroke on the spot. His body language indicated that he knew I had him.

"Pack your things and get the hell out!"

"With pleasure."

Having prepared in advance for my imminent departure, I packed the few personal items left in the desk into my briefcase.

I said my good byes to Rob, Susan, Tammy, and a few other people I had been friendly with. They were caught off guard by my sudden dismissal but all of them wished me well. When I stepped outside of the building, it felt like I had been released from a self-imposed prison. My mood immediately lightened. The commute home was a quiet time of reflection to plan my next step. I had a college degree in Computer Science. Therefore, I decided to take computer classes in those business areas where a strong demand existed.

As I planned, I filed for unemployment two weeks after my departure from the brokerage firm. They never challenged it. An added bonus was that the unemployment benefits would pay for the computer classes.

Leo found out what happened from Ken who apparently spoke to Tammy. He gave me a call at home and congratulated me for beginning to take control of my life.

"Your journey has begun," Leo proclaimed. "Each step you take on the path of a warrior brings you closer to controlling your destiny."

"You wouldn't happen to know the destination?" I asked.

He laughed. "The path of a warrior is just that, a path. There is no destination. Any road we take ultimately leads to death. That is our lot as human beings. What matters is how you intend to experience life."

"You can be very philosophical when you want to be."

"Yes, I suppose I can," he chuckled. "Come into the city tomorrow night and meet me at my office. We'll go out and celebrate the beginning of your personal freedom."

As he suggested, Leo and I went out that next night. We wound up in a cozy neighborhood bar to have a few drinks. He asked me to retell the story of how I set my boss up to incriminate himself on tape so that I could quit the job but still receive unemployment benefits.

"Ah," Leo replied, "You are developing the cunning of a hunter! Beware however of thinking you are smarter than you really are. Ego is an enemy to the warrior. Ego drains tremendous energy from us when we endeavor to defend it."

To my surprise, Leo joined me with an alcoholic beverage instead of a club soda.

"You drink?" I inquired.

"Yes, on occasion. A warrior can do anything as long as it does not become a habit."

"I'm curious. Are you married?"

"My wife passed away some time ago."

"I'm sorry to hear that."

"Your polite condolences are wasted on me. There is nothing to be sorry about. She had a full and happy life. One day, her spirit returned to the heavens and her body returned to the earth. The same fate befalls us all. To find sorrow in that is an indulgence in self pity."

"You don't miss her?"

Leo smiled and pointed to his heart, "She is still here. My point to you is that it is foolish to mourn death. If anything, people should mourn the miserable life they lead.

"I think that is enough serious discussion," he grinned, "You need to learn to have more fun. Having fun increases power, it gives us more energy!"

We spent the rest of the night drinking, telling jokes, laughing, and generally having a grand time.

I found myself feeling fond of Leo. When I was a child, I never had an adult or parent I could look up to for guidance. My mother and father's idea of having me grow up well adjusted was to beat me into submission.

A few hours passed and we left the bar. Leo escorted me to a subway station where I could catch a train back to Queens. I felt a bit drunk but he seemed to be unaffected by the alcohol.

On our way to the subway, we went down a dark narrow street. Pulled down steel gates in front of stores gave the street the look of an outdoor prison block. Loitering restlessly on the side of the street were three young men probably in their late teens or early twenties. The scent of marijuana lingered in the air.

Leo slowed his pace so that he followed two or three steps behind me. Despite the fact I was not in my normal work attire that included the briefcase, tear gas, and knife pen, the alcohol provided me with foolish bravado. As we started to pass by, I kept my eye on the group of teenagers but I made the mistake of making eye contact. That prompted a hostile reaction.

"Hey! What you looking at?" one remarked as he lifted up his chin in my direction.

"Not much," I responded in a derogatory tone. While passing him, I turned around and walked backwards so that I remained facing him. Somehow, Leo navigated himself to stay behind me even after I turned. My offensive posture encouraged a confrontation.

"You got a f—ing problem?" He headed in my direction with his finger pointed menacingly at my nose.

"Yes. I have a short temper," I snapped back.

"F—ing wise ass!" He closed the distance separating us and tried to shove me backward. I eluded the attempt by stepping to the side and parrying his nearest arm away from me. His momentum and outstretched arms left him situated close to me; his side precariously exposed to attack. I took advantage of the situation by smashing my knee into his rib cage.

Seven years of studying karate finally came in handy.

Attempting to exploit the fact that he was momentarily stunned, I swung at his face. My knuckles slammed into his head instead. A follow up right hook with the other hand found its mark on his nose. There was a sickening cracking sound on impact. Blood splattered in the air staining his face and my hand. He let out a muffled yell and doubled over holding his nose.

Looking around me for other possible attackers, I saw Leo holding a knife in his hand and one of the other teenagers on the ground. Apparently, Leo disarmed the young man of the knife. The teenager got up unharmed and ran away along with the third fellow who did not enter the fray.

Leo grabbed me under my right arm and led me away from the scene at a fast pace.

"Time to make a quick exit," he said.

We hurried away from the scene and Leo threw the knife down a sewer we passed. After quickly walking ten or twelve city blocks in a zigzag pattern, we slowed down to a normal pace.

"I am disappointed with the way you handled the situation. You did not act like a warrior back there," Leo said sternly.

"What do you mean? I wasn't about to take any garbage from some punk."

Leo shook his head as if trying to find patience.

"A warrior does not act from anger even in battle. You were violent and, in being so, you harmed another human being and almost brought great harm to yourself.

"You are a violent man, mostly to yourself, but violent none-the-less. The other young man is also violent. That is why you two attracted each other."

Leo's words confused me.

"What do you mean by attracted each other?" I asked.

"Violence attracts violence. You are a black belt in karate so you think you know how to defend yourself but you do not. You only know how to cause harm."

"How do you know I'm a black belt?"

"You listed that on the questionnaire you filled out for Ken when you first came to the office. You learned some very bad habits training in that style of the martial arts."

"What do you mean? What bad habits?"

"It teaches one to confront violence with violence. Your movements in defense and offense tend to be linear and one-dimensional. We shall explore the topic in depth at a latter time. What is important now is that you develop the attitude of a warrior. A warrior would have easily avoided trouble in that situation. You, on the other hand, welcomed the opportunity of combat. You saw it as another opportunity for you to prove yourself."

"Prove myself?"

"Yes. You are constantly trying to prove yourself. That is another enemy you must crush mercilessly on your path."

His statement made me think back to the time when I was a little boy not even in kindergarten yet. An older bully lived up the block from me. At that young age, this older bully was significantly bigger than I was. The bully, who obviously had his own set of personal problems, picked a fight with me every time I played near his house. I used to fight back but, since I was younger and smaller, I would get the worst of it. After one such scuffle, I returned home crying. My father asked what happened. I told him the bully up the block beat me up. My father then smacked me sharply in the face.

"Why are you hitting me?" I cried.

"Because you aren't good enough to beat him," my father yelled at me.

"But he's bigger than me!"

"That doesn't matter," he shouted whacking me in the face again.

"Tony," Leo said softly putting his hand gently on my lower back. I snapped back from the dream of recalling the past into the present reality. "Go home and put your hand in ice. I'll speak to you soon." I looked down at my hand. The knuckles began to swell from hitting the teenager in the head.

Leo waved down a cab, carefully guided me into it, and handed the driver a twenty-dollar bill.

The next morning, I awoke with a headache and a sore hand. At least my hand wasn't broken—just swollen. More than anything, I felt embarrassed about my behavior the previous night. I called Leo to apologize.

"Your apology is not required," he said in a kind voice. "Your redemption is to learn to live like a warrior.

"Come see me next week. A warrior needs weapons in battle and I shall outfit you with a very powerful one. Also, I have an associate I want to introduce you to. So, come an hour earlier than usual."

"An associate? Is he a short Chinese guy with the long chin beard?"

"No," Leo laughed, "You shall see."

Now free from the shackles of a thankless job, I spent my time attending the computer classes I registered for. On the days no classes were held, I practiced in the lab of the school and studied in preparation for certification exams as a network engineer. As was my habit for many years, I would go to my gym in the evenings and lift weights for an hour and a half. During my spare time, I looked through the help wanted and real estate sections of the newspaper. The six story icky yellow apartment house in Queens I lived in continued to deteriorate from age and poor maintenance. The surrounding neighborhood had also become unbearably overcrowded in recent years.

A change of scenery was in order.I began to consider moving east to nearby Nassau County on Long Island.

With changes in career and residence imminent, and the new direction Leo pointed me toward, I became aware that my life was entering a transitional phase. Though I felt hopeful, at times I experienced a sense of anxious doubtfulness. Like someone who decides to pack up and leave town but does not know what lies in store for him elsewhere, I pondered my future.

On the day of my appointment with Leo, I purposely left home early and arrived in the city well ahead of schedule. I decided to spend the extra time exploring a large city bookstore for potential female companions.

The bookstore consisted of two stories, a coffee shop, and a huge magazine rack. From experience, I knew that the magazine rack is the best place to meet single women. A distant second best is the astrology section followed by the self-help section.

A number of females ranking well above edible wandered about the store. My developing hunter instincts switched on. I stopped the internal dialog inside my head. Leo taught me this as a way of becoming extremely aware of my surroundings.

It took less than a minute for my radar to lock onto a potential target standing in the crowded magazine area. She was a very beautiful twenty-something young woman adorned with naturally blue tinted long jet-black hair. Light blue jeans showed off an impressive derrière and curvy hips.

I observed her from a distance for a while. She stood by the magazine rack flipping the pages of some woman's periodical. Leo taught that you could learn a great deal about people by just watching them if you keep your mind clear and free from judgements. He called this part of stalking.

"A hunter does not attempt a kill immediately after sighting prey," Leo explained. "He observes habits, patterns, and any weakness to be potentially exploited."

The body language and demeanor of this desirable young lady clearly conveyed that she had no real interest in the magazine she idly held in her hands. She barely looked at it and glanced around frequently. Translation —she was hoping to meet someone.

Target acquired. I began my approach.

She moved from the magazine racks and sat down on the ledge of a nearby windowsill. Patrons commonly used the ledge as a place to sit down while leafing through magazines and newspapers. Next to her was a pile of books left behind by someone. I grabbed a magazine off the rack to blend in and walked over next to her.

"Hi. Are these your books?" I asked knowing they were not.

"No," she answered softly looking up at me.

I picked up the books, moved them, and sat next to her. She didn't say anything else and turned her attention to the magazine she held in her hands. Looking in her direction, I noticed various ads in the magazine that featured ultra thin female models that appeared no older than thirteen.

"Why do they use such skinny girls in those ads?" I asked to get her attention. "Does the average woman really want to look like a bulimic thirteen-year-old girl?"

She smiled a little. I continued, "Personally, I prefer a woman who is more curvy. You know, someone who I can tell is a woman even in the dark when I run my hands over them."

Her smile became a little bigger.

"I don't know why," she said finally turning her head toward me. Her voice sounded like soft velvet, if velvet could make a sound. Her pretty face rivaled the mythical beauty of a Greek Goddess. "Speaking for myself, I prefer young, but mature, attractive women with pleasing curves, shiny long black hair, and hazelnut eyes." This was a transparent description of her of course. She tried to suppress a smile.

"What are you reading?" she asked.

I turned over the magazine cover so she could see it. The magazine contained a collection of photographs that portrayed expensive luxury homes. She looked on with interest.

"Now, this is a nice one", I said pointing to a photograph of a Spanish ranch home with a large pool overlooking mountains in the distance.

"Yes, that is nice," she nodded in agreement.

"If you were to describe the perfect house for you, what would it be?"

"Well," she thought, "I would like a spacious, but not too big a house, with a lot of windows to let the sun in. A backyard with enough space for a garden would be nice too."

"What colors would you paint the inside with?"

"Hmm, something bright and cheery."

Her face lit up and I could tell she was creating an imaginary picture in her mind by the way her eyes shifted up and to her right. Her eyes then shifted down and to her left. According to Leo, that meant she was experiencing a feeling. This interpretation of eye directions assumes she is right handed. The lateral direction of the eyes for the same cues in a left-handed person is the opposite. Judging by her use of the hands, I determined she was indeed right handed. Therefore, her eye movements meant that she made a picture in her head of this nice house and then experienced the pleasant feelings associated with living in it. I purposely matched the structure of my next sentence to her thought process—visual image, then feeling. Leo claimed that verbally matching a person's internal mental process in this fashion quickly builds rapport and trust. It makes a person feel that you understand them.

"So, you would like a house that is sunny and cheery looking? One that you could walk into and just feel warm and wonderful!"

"Yes!" she enthusiastically replied.   ,

The last part of my sentence, "…feel warm and wonderful" is what Leo called an embedded command. The embedded command is contained in the context of a larger sentence. The part of the sentence considered an embedded command is spoken with a slight change of tonality from the rest of the sentence. Theoretically, her subconscious is supposed to notice the shift in tonality and interpret "…feel warm and wonderful" as a command separate from the rest of the sentence. To be honest, I am not certain if this really works. However, judging from this beautiful woman's reaction, something was going right. She was now animated with the biggest you could die for smile on her face. I knew immediately that she was mine.

"And if you had a pet, or maybe you already do", I continued, "what would it be?"

"Oh, I would have a cute puppy!"

"Really? You know, many women would say they like cats as pets better. Why would you prefer a dog?"

"Cats are too cold and aloof. I'd rather have a dog. They are much more affectionate and friendly."

"So, you would like a puppy to cuddle and be affectionate with?" I smiled.

"Yeah!" Her eyes were open wide accompanied by an ear-to-ear grin.

The purpose of asking her what pet she prefers is to determine what qualities in another person she values and what emotional states she desires. As mentioned earlier, this allows you to discover what is important to another person, that is, what he or she values. All you have to do is ask the right questions and then shut up and listen. Once you know their values, you can make a person feel wonderful by matching those values in your speech and behavior, or you can make a person feel completely violated by purposely mismatching. Of course, the way into a woman's heart is by matching.

"What's your name?" I asked.

"Helen."

"Ah, so you are appropriately named after a beautiful princess who launched a thousand ships to rescue her." Her face broke out into another big grin. "My name is Tony."

"Hi Tony," she said with a sweet smile that hinted of shyness.

"You know, I would love to talk to you longer but I have an appointment to keep this afternoon. I get the impression that you are a person who is worth getting to know better. That is, if you think it would be a good idea."

Notice the embedded suggestion; "…think it would be a good idea."

"Sure," she said with a nod of her head.

"May I have your number?"

She opened her small black pocketbook, produced a pen and a piece of paper, and wrote down her name and number.

"Thanks," I said when she handed it to me. "I'll give you a call tomorrow evening."

I found from experience that women tend to like it when a man mentions when he plans to call instead of leaving them to guess. Another advantage of this tactic is that, if they are interested in you, they will usually delay making weekend plans until you call.

Skipping ahead a little bit in our story, Helen and I went out the following weekend. Five wonderful hours into that first date, she eagerly offered the Mediterranean delights of her flesh. No more pleasurable a conquest could any ancient Greek army hope for. She may have been the most beautiful woman I ever had the pleasure of intimately enjoying.

CHAPTER 4

▼

INCREASING POWER

"Power can be possessed, or possessive,"
I whispered while eyeing her pierced bellybutton.
from 'The Belly Dancing Witches of New Jersey', the author

After I left the bookstore where I met Helen, I made my way to the down-town address that Leo gave me. Soon, I arrived at the address; an old building dedicated in part to an athletic club.

"What the hell is this?" I asked myself.

The suite number Leo gave me was a ballet studio. What did Leo have in mind? Was he going to have me take ballet lessons?

The large wooden floor room had long mirrors the entire length of two opposite walls. A handrail lined the mirrors. I noticed Leo in the room and, to my pleasant surprise; an attractive twenty-something-year-old Asian woman was with him.

She stood about five foot two tall. Tight lycra shorts offered a nice view of round and firm cantaloupe-size buttocks. A sport top left her hard flat midsection exposed. She had a pretty face and round hazelnut eyes.

Perhaps my conquests have a chance to expand eastward I thought to myself.

"Hello," I said looking directly at her wearing my best smile. My eyes involuntarily scanned up and down her firm body.

"Don't even think about it," she responded with a slight shake of her head.

"What? What do you mean?" I asked innocently pretending to not know what she meant.

"Leo has warned me about you. I suggest you keep your eyes in your head and your frankfurter in your pants."

Her abrupt rebuff caused my frankfurter to retreat like a turtle going into its shell.

"Ahem," Leo interrupted, "Tony, this is Tara."

"Hi Tara."

"Hi," she said with her hands on her hips. I got the sense she was sizing me up.

"Tara will be your instructor."

"Huh?" I uttered, "What will she be instructing me in?"

"She will be teaching you many things, Tony. But to keep it simple for you, she will be teaching you Tai Chi."

"Tai Chi?"

"Tai Chi."

"That's the slow moving Chinese forms I see on TV occasionally, correct? You know, where a number of people are moving in unison?"

"Yes," Leo answered.

"Why would I want to learn that? I already know how to defend myself."

"Because," Leo explained, "You acquired bad habits training in the hard martial arts. Now, you must unlearn them."

"Why? I find it hard to believe a person can defend themselves by practicing that slow moving Chinese stuff." I looked at Tara. "No offense meant."

"None taken," she jeered with hands still on hips.

"If I can demonstrate to your satisfaction, Tony, that what you learn can make you a more powerful person, would you be willing to give it a try?"

I was skeptical of the whole affair and felt it would be a waste of time. I did not voice my objection verbally but responded by making a face expressing my doubt.

"Do you think you are stronger than Tara?"

"Of course I do. I'm probably three times her strength," I said without exaggeration.

"Do you think you could push her backwards?"

"Of course!" I scoffed.

"Let's give it a try, shall we?"

Leo gestured toward Tara. I really didn't want to be bothered with the whole matter. Then Leo whispered in my ear, "This is a good excuse to get your hands on her body." That convinced me.

Tara moved into what looked like a semi forward stance that I learned in conventional Karate. Her feet were slightly beyond shoulder width apart with her left foot forward and right foot back. Three quarters of her weight appeared to be on the rear leg.

"Now," Leo said to me, "Place your hands on her waist and try to push her back any way you can."

"She's not going to pull some judo move on me and send me to the floor, is she?" I suspiciously asked.

"No, no, no. She will simply stand her ground."

"Okay," I said still not totally convinced.

I got into a good, almost football lineman, stance and placed my hands on her waist just below the ribcage. She placed one hand on my midsection. I couldn't help but notice how nice her haired smelled.

"Are you ready?" I asked Tara.

"Yes, I'm ready."

I pushed suddenly and powerfully. Not only did I fail to move her; she also forced me to take half a step back. Dumbfounded, I stepped back trying to figure out how she accomplished that. Tara smiled smugly. Before I could say anything, Leo placed his hand on my shoulder to get my attention.

"Fair is fair," he said, "Now, she will try to push you."

"Okay," I replied still bewildered.

I dug into a deep stance. Tara and I placed our hands on each other just as before. Seemingly without any overt effort, she pushed me back a step. That dumbfounded look came over me again.

"What do you think now?" Leo asked.

Tara stood, hand on hips, looking at me.

"Oh, come on. It has to be some trick of leverage. I still don't see this as being of any practical use in a real fight."

I glared back at Tara. She gave me a look as if she was sticking her tongue out at me only without the tongue. I somehow surmised that meant she liked me. In a begrudging kind of way, I sort of liked her too. Tara and Leo looked at each other.

"He's a hard one to convince, isn't he?" Leo said to Tara with a smile.

"Gee," Tara replied back to Leo, "I thought this tight outfit would be enough to convince him to take lessons from me."

They both laughed and seemingly pretended I didn't exist for the moment.

"Look," I protested, "I just don't see how a person could defend themselves with this stuff!"

Leo turned toward me.

"Would you like a more practical demonstration?"

"Yes. In fact, I would."

I placed my hands on my hips and faced Tara who mockingly mirrored my posture. Leo rolled his eyes at the sight of us acting like two children bent on annoying and showing each other up. Leo then had us square off much like two fighters ready to box.

"Try throwing a punch or one of the fancy kicks you learned in Karate as fast as you are able to."

"Are you sure Leo? She might get hurt."

"Trust me Tony. I'm sure."

I moved into a fighting stance.

"Are you ready?" I asked Tara.

"Ready," she said.

Despite my imminent offensive move, her arms remained at her side. She stood like a western gunslinger ready to draw her six shooters. With my lead leg, I threw a quick roundhouse kick at her face.

In a blur of the split second that followed, I found myself spinning to the floor. The best I can surmise is that she stepped in on me twisting counter clockwise from my perspective so that her body moved in the same direction as my approaching leg. She deflected the kick and grabbed my ankle with her right hand while simultaneously using her left hand to apply force to my upper chest area. What really baffled me was the almost complete lack of any impact when my leg made contact with her. She threw me to the floor in a guided, almost gentle way.

I sprang to my feet and faced Tara again.

"One more time," I challenged.

"My, my, my. Are we a glutton for embarrassment?" she teased.

We faced off again but before she was fully set, I tried to surprise her with a fast thrusting front kick aimed at her midsection. In a flash, Tara parried the kick, and moved to the inside. With one hand at the small of my back and the other under my chin, she sent my body sailing backward slamming me into the hard wooden floor. The impact with the floor knocked the wind out of my lungs. I picked my ego and myself off the floor. As my lungs began to fill with air again, I noticed Leo looking at Tara in a disapproving kind of way.

"Play nice," he told her.

"Okay, I'm convinced," I conceded. "Can you teach me how to do that?"

"In time," Leo answered. "Tara will first teach you the basics which will take a while to master." Leo glanced at both of us. "Can I trust you two to behave yourselves?" he joked.

We nodded our heads.

"Tara, please come with me for a moment." Leo and her walked to the far part of the room by the door. He spoke to her in a calm but serious demeanor. I couldn't overhear the conversation but I assumed it had something to do with me. She nodded apologetically in response.

Leo walked back to me and said, "I leave you in her capable hands. She will teach you well." He started to leave but then looked back at me. With a glint in his eye he said, "Oh, yes. I made Tara promise not to beat you up anymore."

"Thanks," I replied sarcastically.

Leo said goodbye to Tara with a quick hug and then left.

"What is your relationship to Leo?" I asked.

"None of your business."

"Well, how did you meet him?"

"That's not relevant. Let's just concentrate on training. Okay?"

Despite her rebuff to my questions, her tone of voice was kind in contrast to before.

"Sure, that's okay," I said not wanting to cause any friction between us.

Over the next hour, Tara showed me some basic Tai Chi warm-up exercises. She emphasized for me to breathe deeply into my stomach and to keep my back straight. Despite the fact that I could lift over three hundred pounds with my legs working out in a gym, the Tai Chi exercises tired out my thighs after only a few minutes. I had to periodically stand up straight to rest my legs.

"After some practice, you'll get stronger," Tara commented after noticing my fatigue.

"Stronger? My legs are already very strong!"

"Not for this," she said.

Tara conducted herself in a very business like way as if she were my personal trainer. After an hour, I noticed both my body and mental disposition felt better.

"Thank you," I said sincerely.

"You're welcome."

She smiled and peered into my eyes but then quickly disengaged. We arranged to meet the following week and walked out into the corridor together. Tara went in the direction of the woman's locker room and I headed the opposite way toward the building exit. As she walked away, I stole a glance at the perfect rear view afforded by the tight shorts she wore. Halfway down the hall, she turned around and noticed me watching her. Tara flashed a quick smile and continued to walk away with an exaggerated sway of the hips.

I think she likes me.

*   *   *

In the ensuing weeks, a new routine took shape in my life. Unburdened from the demands of a full time job, I concentrated on training for my new career. I attended computer classes on some weekday evenings and the weekend. When not in class, I honed my technical skills in the school's computer lab.

Taking advantage of free time early in the day, I regularly visited the gym to pit flesh against iron. As I took steps to gain control over my life, a renewed sense of purpose strengthened my mind and body.

Once a week I sat in session with Leo who continued educating me in the esoteric ways of a warrior. I also began to see Tara regularly once a week for Tai Chi lessons.

November of that year arrived and the weather became seasonably cooler. My desire to move out of the increasingly overcrowded and rundown neighborhood intensified when I discovered my car missing its entire rear bumper. Late night thieves doing auto parts shopping made me their latest victim.

Disgust motivated me to begin looking in earnest for a new place to live. My plan was to move to western Nassau County. I became familiar with the area during the time I worked in the defense industry on Long Island. There are nice neighborhoods in that section and New York City is easily accessible by rail.

After thumbing through the newspaper, I found a real estate agent in the area by the name of Tom. A big Irish man in his fifties with gray hair and a raspy voice; Tom would drive us around in his big old tan Cadillac to look at different apartments. Most of the rentals in the area were in the second floor or basement of private houses. There were a few single level garden apartments as well.

During my time with Tom, I noticed something curious. Whenever he took me somewhere, I had an immediate feeling as soon as we arrived, before I even saw the inside of the apartment, of whether I was going to like it or not.

A few weeks into my search, Tom took me to a large brick house on a corner. The moment I stepped out of the car, I sensed it was the place for me. When I expressed interest after touring the inside of the rental, Tom took me to meet the landlord - a middle aged short Italian fellow with a heavy accent that reminded me of my late grandfather. The monthly rent was negotiated and the second floor apartment in the house was mine. Excited about it, I called Leo soon afterward to tell him the news.

"Leo!" I beamed over the phone, "I found a new place to live."

"Congratulations! Be sure to give me your new number when you move."

"Yes, of course. I'll probably move in the next two weeks. Hey, do you have a minute for a question?"

"Yes. What it is?"

"When I was looking at apartments, I somehow knew if I was going to be interested in a place even before seeing the inside."

"Ah," said Leo, "The best way to describe it to you is that it is your intuition."

"Intuition?"

"Yes, in a way." Leo started to chuckle.

"Why are you laughing?"

"I find it amusing."

"Why?"

"You are a good student, practicing daily the breathing exercises and other things I taught you."

"Yes. But, what does that have to do with it?"

"One of the benefits of training to be a warrior is that you have significantly increased your awareness. Part of your awareness is what some people call intuition. For example, when you are looking for, shall we put it politely, female companionship, you now have a greater sense if the woman will be receptive even before you speak to her. Correct?"

I thought about it for a moment and Leo was right. After putting into practice Leo's lessons, I was far better at selecting women with the greatest probability of a successful encounter.

"So, you are saying I am more intuitive?"

"It would be more accurate to say your awareness has increased. This is part of your training as a hunter and warrior. A hunter must be keenly aware. Each human being has what we are calling intuition to at least some degree. However, people's noisy minds and mental disharmony cut them off from it. They may not notice it, ignore it, or rationalize it away." Leo paused to allow me a question but I did not ask one. "I believe it is time to bring you to the next level Tony."

"The next level?"

"Yes. You are progressing quite satisfactorily in part because you are so damn predictable!" He chuckled again, which made me feel uneasy. "I'll see you next Wednesday as planned. Goodbye," he said ending the conversation.

The next few days, I spent most of my time packing in preparation for the move. While emptying out dresser draws, I discovered a stack of greeting cards from my ex-wife Diane. Indulging in sentimentality, I saved every card, note, and gift she ever gave me. The cards were stacked in order with the most recent one at the top, and the oldest one at the bottom. I slipped the oldest card out from the bottom of the stack and opened it. Diane gave me the card on our six-month anniversary of the first day we met - April 15th. The cover of the card had a cute little teddy bear clutching a red heart. Inside the card, she wrote,

"Dear Tony, I can't tell you how happy I am we found each other. You are the best! My love for you grows stronger every day. I hope we will be happy together for a very long time! Love, Diane."

Following her signature were numerous X's and O's.

I sighed and experienced conflicting emotions of fond memories, guilt, and heartache. The emotions commingled in my stomach like some sickening soup. I looked at the inside of the card again and recalled the very last thing Diane said to me during our final telephone conversation,

"Please don't ever call me again!"

My eyes sunk down as I asked myself how things could have gone so terribly wrong. The intermingled emotions transformed into a deep sadness. Leo would tell me I was feeling sorry for myself again and he would be right. I could not help it though.

Mixed in with the cards were a few photographs of Diane. I stared at them looking into her eyes and imagining the way she felt when I held her. I then stretched out on the floor and stared blankly at the white ceiling of the bedroom. My mind went empty and numb until the loud roar of a low flying jet brought me back to reality. I inserted the card back in the bottom of the stack, placed a rubber band around it, and put it into a cardboard box for safe keeping.

The day of my personal exodus arrived. An old dust covered dirty white van with two Russian-speaking men I hired pulled in front of the icky yellow building I so eagerly looked forward to leaving.

It took the hired men only a couple of hours to move the few pieces of furniture and other items into the van. I packed my more personal and valuable belongings in my own car.

I took one last look at the now empty apartment. Paint on the water stained ceiling peeled off the wall. Dust balls rolled freely along the cracked and aged wooden floors like tumbleweed in a desert.

Good riddance. I never did like this lousy place.

I walked down the courtyard and turned around to look at the six-story yellow brick building I spent the last two years in. The bottoms of the corner walls at the entrance were decayed from years of dogs urinating on them. Lines ran through the cracked glass of the heavy twin front doors. The outside locks were visibly in need of repair. Random graffiti marked both the inside and outside of the building. With disdain, I spit in the courtyard. If allowed the privacy, I would have urinated on the front steps to better express my contempt.

The movers, who started out to the new place prior to my departure, arrived there ahead of me. The two men, one older and the other a teenager, went about the task of unloading the van. Due to the difference in our native languages, they communicated with me in broken English and simple hand signals.

While unloading the van of my belongings, the younger fellow expressed an interest in my two Samurai swords. He turned over the longer sword of the collection in his hands to study it. I motioned to him that it was okay to unsheathe the sword so he could get a better look. He pulled the sword from its holder. His eyes opened widely at the sight of the shiny blade glistening in the sunlight.

Years ago, I kept the sword in my car for protection. I reasoned that the three-foot sword would immediately discourage any attacker from another vehicle armed with a tire iron or baseball bat. More recently, I stored the blade in a closet, only using it occasionally to practice weapon martial art forms. After accidentally decapitating the ceiling fan when practicing, the sword was relegated to mostly collecting dust.

In the traditional sense, the sword would be considered unwieldy. The light wooden handle failed to balance the heavier steel blade.

The young man slowly slid the sword back into its holder.

"Wow," I think he said in Russian.

His reaction amused me. After years of training with martial art weapons, the sight of them ceased to impress me.

The teenager and the older gray bearded fellow went about their task. In a little under two hours, they had moved everything into the second floor apartment except for the items I packed in my own car. I handed each of them a generous gratuity. They started to clean up some left over packing tape on the sidewalk before leaving.

I went inside and upstairs into my new home and noticed the Samurai sword leaning against the wall. Heck, I was just going to stash it in a closet again never to see the light of day. I grabbed it and went back outside. The young man looked up at me. I held out the sword with the handle facing him. My gesture initially confused him. I motioned with my free hand first pointing to the blade then to him to indicate he could have it. Slowly, with his two hands, he took it and thanked me with an expression of disbelief. He ran back to the van. I could see him in the front passenger seat looking at the sword as they pulled away. I smiled. His face had the expression of a little kid who just got a brand new awesome toy.

After I unpacked my car, I decided to take a bike ride around the neighborhood to get more familiar with the area. The weather was still mild despite it being mid November.

I hopped on my twelve-speed bike and headed off in no particular direction. The rush of cool air on my face felt refreshing while cycling.

The streets were very quiet with hardly a soul to be found. I ended riding in a random pattern and headed to the town's park. Like the surrounding streets, it too was deserted. I stopped for a while to relax but soon became restless and started home.

While streaking past a row of houses on one block, I noticed a hunched over little old lady pushing a shopping cart. She moved slowly with small steps. I slowed down and tried to determine if she was homeless. However, I didn't think that to be the case since it was an upper middle-class neighborhood.

The old lady's gait caught my attention. Her movement appeared to be purposeful and strong despite the slowness of her pace and the fragility of her crooked body. Her attire consisted of dark clothing and a black scarf wrapped around her head. Something inside made me feel suspicious so I watched her carefully. I cycled by slowly. She either ignored me or was totally unaware of my presence when I passed traveling in the opposite direction of her path. The momentum of my bike carried me to the end of the block. The old lady rounded the corner out of my line of sight. Impulsively, I executed a fast U-turn and quickly pedaled around the block to follow her. To my bewilderment, she was nowhere to be found. I came to a full stop and visually scanned in all directions. The air was still and quiet. Not a single human being appeared in my field of vision. Only a shiny black crow fluttering in the treetops disturbed the peace.

It was practically impossible for her to have disappeared in such a short time even if she entered the nearest house. I sped through the surrounding blocks almost frantically to find her to no avail. I gave up the search. For some odd reason, I felt inclined to mention the incident to Leo.

"Describe the woman in detail," Leo requested. As well as memory served, I told him what she was wearing and how she walked. "That was no old lady," he concluded.

"What do you mean that was no old lady?"

"That was no old lady," he repeated. He seemed amused and then said, "Apparently, you have been discovered."

"You lost me," I said genuinely confused.

"What you mistook for an old woman is really a scout."

"A scout? A scout for what? For who? What are you talking about?"

Leo laughed at my agitation.

"You must have crossed paths with a female who sensed your evolving personal energy. The energy transformation you are undergoing is quite unusual for an ordinary person living an ordinary life. So, you were scouted." He paused.

I became concerned not because I believed Leo but that he might be crazier than I already thought.

"I'm sorry," I said shaking my head, "I don't understand."

"Your evolution from an ordinary human being to a warrior involves both an increase and change in the quality of your personal energy. You are not yet aware of it but the transformation is already taking place in you. All living things have an energy field. With the proper training and discipline, a warrior can improve the quality of the energy as well as increase the quantity of energy.

"Think of a radio. The volume would be analogous to the quantity of energy, the tuning, that is how clear the sound is, would be analogous to the quality of energy. Some people make the mistake of increasing their power, the amount of energy, without the corresponding capacity to control it. This leads to disaster and self destruction."

"Okay," I said, "I think I understand that. But what does this have to do with the old lady or scout as you call her?"

"A female with an advanced awareness has sensed your energy shift. She is attempting to discern what you are. The purpose of the disguise is to get in close proximity to you."

Leo started laughing heartily as if he just heard a good joke.

"Why are you laughing?"

"Because you must have terrified her!"

"Terrified? What did I do?"

Leo laughed even harder at my questions.

"Not only did your intuition sense the female was not an old lady, but then you chased her!" Leo was nearly crying from laughter and slapped his thigh repeatedly. "Imagine the panic of the scout! First it is discovered then pursued by a violent young man!"

"Violent? I'm not violent!" I protested.

"You are a very violent young man. Because you do not usually direct your violence toward others, you do not consider yourself so. However, your violence is directed inward. The scout must have sensed your violence but it would have no idea of how you direct it. That is one reason why it fled so quickly. You do know how it escaped, don't you?"

I shrugged my shoulders and shook my head no.

"Your conscious mind lags far behind your intuitive powers of perception!" Leo said. You mentioned you noticed a crow high up in the trees after you turned the corner on your bike."

"Yeah, so?"

Leo shook his head with a smile of disbelief. "That was the scout! Did you stop to think why you remembered such a small detail? Intuitively you already knew."

"Leo, be honest with me. Have you ever been institutionalized in a mental hospital? No offense but I don't believe any of this nonsense."

Leo shook his head again with a smile.

"You are a difficult one to convince! It does not matter much though. The incident you experienced, as fantastic as my description may seem, is really a minor one. I doubt the scout will return. Or perhaps she will observe only at a distance next time."

"Why is that?" I asked feigning interest.

"She will be afraid of being discovered again. She may also fear the possibility that you are an apprentice."

"An apprentice of what?"

"As I said, energy shifts do not normally happen to ordinary people unless they experience a traumatic event of some kind. The scout may suspect you are an apprentice of a wizard."

"A wizard?" I eyed Leo suspiciously, "Is that what you are?"

Leo chuckled. 'No, no, no. Not the way you understand the term. I am a warrior above all else though I do have what you could call some special talents."

"Like what?"

"Like enough to know this conversation is not productive and our time is short. We have arrived at a point in your training where I shall teach you how to heal yourself and dramatically increase your personal energy. After you learn this, you will be more powerful than ninety-nine percent of the human population."

Leo asked me to get comfortable in the large leather chair. "The first thing we are going to do is teach you how to meditate," he began.

"Meditate?"

"Yes."

"Are you kidding me? It seems to be a waste of time just sitting around doing nothing like some bald headed monk on a mountain." Leo laughed at my response. "Why are you laughing?" I asked.

"I am laughing because you are already practicing a form of meditation and don't even realize it. Remember the breathing exercises where I instructed you to position yourself comfortably with your back straight and concentrate on breathing deeply into your lower belly? That is a one type of meditation."

I started to say something but he waved his hand to indicate to not interrupt him.

"Meditation serves a number of purposes, all of which will make you a much more powerful human being. First, it clears and calms the mind. Once that mental state is achieved, you will notice your anxiety dissipating. Another benefit is that your awareness and intuition shall increase. Second, meditation is a pathway to healing and programming the mind. Once the mind is in a relaxed state, we can intervene to rewire it. I could continue to explain, but you would only grasp a small portion of what I wish to communicate. Rather, I will demonstrate by example."

"What are we going to do?"

"First, I am going to teach you how to achieve what I refer to as a meditative state. Once you accomplish that I am going to take advantage of that state and heal one of your most severe emotional wounds."

"Emotional wound?" I asked with a tone indicating I wished a more detailed explanation.

"When a person experiences an emotional trauma, he or she often reacts by burying and repressing the emotion to avoid experiencing the pain. These repressed emotions remain inside the body forever until they are allowed expression in some way.

"It's like a pot of boiling water. If one is unwilling to lift the lid, they will have to press down harder to keep it from boiling over. Eventually the pressure becomes too great, and the water spills out.

"Buried emotional wounds drain us of valuable energy. At times of stress, they often erupt to the surface uncontrolled. Whenever you witness a person grossly overreacting to a minor annoyance, they are experiencing an uncontrolled expression of unresolved issues."

"So," I asked, "what's the trick?"

"The trick, as you put it, is to allow the repressed emotion to be expressed in a safe way that does no harm to yourself or others. Once the repressed emotion is acknowledged and allowed expression, it is released. Once released, the energy once used to repress it is free to return into our being. The knot disappears allowing a better flow of our life force." Leo pointed to the middle of my upper torso, just under the breastplate. "You have a large knot right here. It is not the only one in you but it is the one draining you the most of your energy. Shall we begin?"

"I guess so." I took a deep breath to prepare myself. Leo asked me to close my eyes.

"Take two more deep breaths and let the air out very slowly each time," he instructed. "Just relax and concentrate on your breathing. When you are comfortable doing so, expand your awareness to your body and then to your surroundings. Let your mind begin to clear."

After trying this for about five minutes, I commented to Leo that I found it very difficult to clear my mind. A constant stream of thoughts paraded through my head. It seemed impossible to stop. I began to feel restless.

"Don't try to stop any thoughts nor dwell upon them. Just observe the thoughts floating by and let them go. Observe the activity of the mind with detachment."

Another five minutes went by but my mind was just as active.

"This is not working Leo."

"Patience my dear apprentice. If your mind is busy, just let it be without interference. Detach and observe it as if watching a movie."

It seemed paradoxical to me that relaxing could require such great effort.

"Patience, Tony. You are learning a new skill. You may just find," his voice getting lower and slower, "that little by little the stream of thoughts just disappear into space and you find yourself slipping into a deeper and deeper state of relaxation. That's right," he said almost in a whisper, "let your mind find the quiet peace it so deserves. There is no place you have to be. There is nothing you have to do. That's right. Just relax."

In a few minutes, my breathing and heart rate slowed. I felt more peaceful and at ease.

"Good," Leo said, "See? You are good at this after all. Please nod your head if you can hear my voice." I nodded my head. "Good. You are now so relaxed that you cannot even open your eyes. They are very heavy. So heavy that when you try to open them, they stay shut. Try to open them now and find that you cannot."

I tried to open my eyes. They fluttered a little bit but my eyelids remained closed.

"Good. You are doing just fine. Now, Tony, there is a part of you protecting you from pain. You've experienced much pain in the past. And this part has been there to protect you. I would like to speak to that part. When I have the part's permission to communicate with it, please nod your head."

My head nodded with no conscious effort that I was aware of. I felt a very subtle jolt in my body originating around the midsection.

"Good. Speaking to that part, Tony and I would like to thank you for protecting him all these years. Yes, I know, you have not really been appreciated until now. He has been hurt in the past, hasn't he? That is one of the reasons why you so loyally protect him. You have done well to protect him from harm and now we need you to help him heal. Would you be willing to do that in a way you find agreeable?"

My head, temporarily operating as an independent unit from my consciousness, nodded yes.

"Good. We would like to begin to release those emotions repressed for so long. Emotions locked away that drain Tony of his energy. The events that caused these emotions have no doubt given you valuable experience. We shall preserve such lessons in that special place inside that you reserve for such lessons.

"Are you willing to allow us to start releasing these emotions in the very safe environment we have created?" My head nodded yes. "Very good. I thank you. Now, I would like to speak to you again Tony. Please nod your head when ready." I did. "Tony, you have been carrying a great pain inside of you. That's right. You have carried that pain for years."

As Leo spoke, tears began to well in my eyes.

"You are safe now, safe from all harm both present and past. Its time to - let - it - go - and separate those lessons you learned from the pain and put them in that special place you reserve for such lessons. That's right. Tell me Tony, what is the origin of the pain?"

As tears flowed freely from my eyes, I barely gasped, "Diane."

"Remember," Leo said in a gentle voice, "those memories with Diane that cause you pain when you recall them. Observe those memories as if you were watching a movie on the big screen."

I did as Leo suggested.

Diane was a very kind hearted person. She was also a very sensitive woman. I began to recall the many times I carelessly hurt her feelings because of my thoughtless or callous behavior. The events crossed the screen in my mind like a newsreel. Leo patted away tears on my face with a tissue. After I internally viewed all the events I could remember, Leo asked me to do it again. After the second time he asked that I repeat it yet another time. This process continued until my crying subsided, my breathing slowed, and I started to relax again.

"Now," Leo started to speak again, "imagine Diane is right in front of you. Ask for her forgiveness."

An image of Diane appeared in my mind. Her face was clear, beautiful, and kind, just as I remembered it. I looked into her eyes and asked for forgiveness. A broken dam of tears fell down my cheeks.

"I forgive you," Diane said.

"Now look at her Tony and tell her that you forgive her for any offense, real or imagined, that she may have done to you. Then embrace her."

I imagined saying, "I forgive you," then hugging her tightly. I sobbed almost uncontrollably. Leo said nothing for a while. He continued to pat my face with tissues to absorb the tears. After a few minutes, the tears subsided and I began to experience a profound peace and relaxation.

"Tony, to test what we just did, I would like you to recall those once painful memories again."

I brought up the same memories as before. To my amazement, the negative feelings once attached to those memories was now gone."

"Good, you are clear!" Leo declared.

"My hands and feet are tingling."

"That is a combination of the increased flow of energy in your body now that the obstruction has been removed and the release of energy that was used to repress the emotions."

I stood up out of the chair and stretched my arms. My body had a pleasant feeling of lightness.

"I feel different," I commented.

"That is to be expected. It is a good sign," Leo explained. "It is like having a splinter stuck in your finger for years where you learn to live with the pain. Suddenly, it is removed and you feel relief. In time, the wound closes and the initial feeling of relief transforms itself into general well being."

After a few moments of silence, I turned to Leo and said sincerely, "Thank you."

He smiled. "You're welcome." He continued to smile and I looked at him quizzically as if to ask why. "That is the first time you have expressed any genuine appreciation," he answered.

"Does this mean I am healed?"

"We have indeed healed a deep emotional wound. But you have many others; most of which originate from childhood. I will help you to heal and I will also teach you how to heal yourself. If you think about the procedure we just followed, you can probably clear repressed emotions on your own.

"A warrior is a master of his emotions whereas most other people are a slave to them. Many repress their emotions until they fall sick and die. Or they will express the emotions in an uncontrolled destructive manner.

"Controlling emotions is not ignoring and burying them deep inside so they can fester and poison your being. Controlling emotions is to acknowledge and give them expression in a safe and harmless way. When you evolve further into a warrior, you will be able to use and direct the energy from even the most negative emotions in a way that best serves you."

"How do I do that?"

Leo smiled. "That is for another time. Go home now and rest. We have accomplished much today."

My mind felt incredibly centered and clear for the remainder of the day. Sleep that night was dreamless and peaceful instead of my usual tossing and turning half the night. The next day I continued to experience a peaceful sense of calm. My body felt lighter as if a great weight had been removed from my shoulders.

The experience and resulting sense of well being convinced me that
Leo's philosophy had merit. I consciously committed myself to learning as
much as possible from him even if he was eccentric.

CHAPTER 5

▼

RICHES

"Measure your wealth by
love, not by dollars."
from 'How I Got Lucky and Bumped into God'—the author

The weather turned cooler in late November. Trees stood bare and early sunsets brought the night in quickly. The pleasant scent of crisp drying leaves filled the air.

I took a deep relaxing breath and evaluated my personal progress. Two thirds of the computer classes were completed. I passed the first of seven certification exams.

Though nature approached its winter slumber, my social life with the opposite sex bloomed. On average, I dated two or three different women a week. A few months earlier, if some fellow told me he dated two or three times a week, I would have assumed he was grossly exaggerating to impress me. Never would I have imagined back then such success on my own.

The attention I received from females boosted my ego and confidence. However, at those times I was without companionship, I felt empty and alone. Interestingly, those feelings were most intense immediately after an otherwise satisfying sexual encounter.

This pattern continued until one night, while hunting for intimate female companionship, I met a petite woman in her early thirties. Her name was Tina. Recently separated from her husband, she was emotionally ripe for the taking; the equivalent of a crippled antelope limping on the plain at the mercy of the first predator that laid eyes on it.

Soon after meeting her, it became obvious that she craved attention. Her emotional state was a consequence of her soon to be ex-husband abruptly ending the marriage. Without warning, he moved out of their apartment while Tina was at work. She returned home to half empty rooms thinking they were robbed until she found the note her husband left.

Leo instilled upon me that a hunter is ruthless without mercy or compassion. When he taught me this, it was not in the context of meeting women. However, I misinterpreted his words to believe that the philosophy applied to all aspects of life including romantic conquests. I would later learn that Leo's true meaning was to be ruthless in hunting down my own weaknesses. Unfortunately, I was not so evolved yet to fully understand his sometimes metaphorical wisdom.

By utilizing the "Casanova" techniques I learned, I quickly removed what little resistance Tina had in her vulnerable state. She was an easy mark and I knew it.

The first night I met her in a dance club, she asked me to escort her home. When we arrived, she invited me in. Later, I would find out she was, at that time, in the habit of inviting strange men into her apartment to spend the night. However, I did not know it then. For the moment, I simply assumed I was about to experience another intimate encounter with a woman I barely knew.

After offering me a glass of wine, Tina and I talked for some time. More accurately, she talked and I listened with varying degrees of interest. She sat close to me on her couch with a collection of photo albums and paged through them giving me a personal history of her life. She flipped over one page of the album that revealed a stunning wedding portrait of her.

"My God," I commented, "You were a beautiful bride!"

She seemed briefly complimented. But then her faced turned sad. I found myself feeling sorry for her.

We stayed up until four in the morning going through her photos and memories. Since it was late, or early depending on your perspective, I politely announced I should get going. I stood up and put on my jacket. I was tired and gave up the idea of engaging in any intimate activities that night. Tina remained on the couch, eyes downcast, staring at the floor.

"Aren't you going to see me out?"

She remained silent, only briefly glancing up at me when I asked the question.

"Are you alright?" I asked gently putting one hand on her shoulder.

Tina finally stood up and looked at me. With a mix of loneliness and shyness she asked in a soft voice, "Would you please spend the night with me?"

It was only natural for me to be tempted to take advantage of such an offer from an attractive woman. But I didn't have the heart to use her for just physical gratification.

Taking a deep breath to compose myself I said, "Tina, I find you very attractive. If I stay I will be irresistibly tempted to be with you passionately. However, I think it is best that we not rush into anything."

It is hard to believe I turned down a prime opportunity but I genuinely liked her. I wished to demonstrate that she meant more to me than just a one-night tryst.

Without saying a word, she hugged me tightly for a long time. We then said good night and I went home.

After having acted like a gentleman to my satisfaction at our first meeting, I eagerly anticipated a more physically intimate date with Tina the next weekend. Unfortunately, reality fell short of my expectations.

While at her apartment, we looked over a movie schedule in the newspaper. The next show we decided to go to did not start for an hour. To pass the time before we left, Tina treated me to wine and a cheese platter. As I enjoyed the snack, her telephone rang and she disappeared into the bedroom to answer it.

"Oh my God!" I overheard her cry from the next room. "What happened?"

I caught pieces of the conversation but did not hear enough to figure out what was going on. When I heard her crying loudly I peeked my head into the bedroom.

"What's wrong Tina?" I asked.

"It's Joe!" Joe was the name of her estranged husband. "He tried to kill himself! I knew this was going to happen! I just knew it!"

She cried while holding on the phone to speak to a nurse in the emergency room. Joe and Tina were not legally separated or divorced. Technically, she was still his wife and therefore responsible for any medical decisions to be made if he was incapacitated.

Tina elected to remain on the phone instead of going to the hospital. She wished to avoid Joe's girlfriend who she assumed would soon be there. She held on the phone for almost an hour, but nobody came back on the line. Someone in the emergency room must have put down the phone and forgot about it.

"You can go home," Tina told me after an hour passed. "I'm sorry for ruining your night."

"It's not your fault," I assured her. "I'll keep you company if you like." I sat beside her on the side of the bed.

Accompanied by a steady flow of tears, Tina kept repeating in a loud voice, "I knew he would do something like this! He was so unhappy! He was so depressed the last time I spoke to him! His stupid mother didn't even pay attention. She kept saying that Joe was feeling down only because his business went bad. What a stupid woman!"

Another hour passed and Tina finally spoke to a doctor in the emergency room who told her that Joe was in stable condition. Relieved, Tina hung up the phone. After a few minutes, I asked if she would like to go out to unwind. She nodded her head yes and we went to a small restaurant and sipped a couple of glasses of wine together. The conversation was sparse. The look on her face told me she was lost in her thoughts.

"Thank you for staying with me," she said with her face nuzzled into my neck. "It's very nice of you."

"You're welcome," I replied holding her close to me.

A couple of weeks later I found out from Tina that Joe's mother never even went to visit him in the hospital. His girlfriend broke up with him shortly after the suicide attempt because she was embarrassed by the incident. Though he ruined my much-anticipated night with Tina, I could not help but feel sorry for the guy.

To demonstrate her appreciation for my company the night her husband tried to end it all, Tina took me to an upscale seafood restaurant overlooking Long Island's north shore.

We enjoyed a delightful dinner together. When we left the restaurant, the sun was setting below the water line. Soft red rays from the sun crossed the beach giving it a warm orange glow. The water sparkled like diamonds as the last of the sunlight danced across it. It was a cold early December day. The wind blew strongly off the water sending a chill through us. Standing shoulder to shoulder, we tolerated the elements to admire the sun painted sky and ocean.

"I love sunsets," Tina said. "If you ever come back here without me and watch the sun set, please remember me."

I looked at her curious as to why she would make such a comment. She just stared in the direction of the sun without saying anything further.

Upon returning to her apartment, we made ourselves comfortable on the couch. Tina sat quietly next to me hugging a small black couch pillow in her lap. She looked straight ahead rather than at me.

Her body language was not as inviting as I had hoped for. However, despite the defensive nature of her posture, I decided to find out how receptive she would be to romantic advances.

I started to kiss her gently on the cheek. My tongue gracefully glided down the side of her neck followed by another soft kiss. I lightly nibbled on her ear lobe and let my tongue gently trace the outer portion of the ear just before it glided back down her neck and up again applying just the right degree of pressure to illicit arousal. Though she did not move or respond in any overt way, her breathing began to get deeper. Encouraged, I undid the top button of her shirt. Still, she did not explicitly respond. But she did not resist either. I undid the next shirt button. My tongue continued to explore the contours of her neck with slightly more pressure on the more sensitive spots I could discover. My hand unbuttoned the rest of her shirt. I began to caress her small breasts through the bra.

Surprisingly, she did not return the physical attention in any way or even look directly at me.

Tina's breathing continued to get noticeably deeper. Since that was the only feedback available, I used it to gauge her response to my advances.

I removed her shirt. My right hand then unclasped the bra in the back and my left hand pushed the straps off her shoulders. I began to stroke the soft flesh of her breasts by just barely touching them with the back of my hand. I then turned my wrist and cupped one of her breasts in my palm massaging it while gently manipulating the nipple with two of my fingers. My own breathing quickened while I pondered how far she would allow me to go.

I unbuckled the belt on her black jeans and unsnapped the top button of the pants. My left hand pulled down the zipper as far as it would go in her seated position. I knelt down in front of Tina with her legs to one side of me, let my tongue circle and gently suck her nipples while my hands slipped into the sides of her pants by the waist. I assertively began to tug the jeans downward. Though Tina still refrained from any reaction beyond her increasingly heavy breathing, she obediently raised her hips so her buttocks were off the couch enabling me to pull the jeans down to her ankles. She then lifted her feet so I could take them off entirely. My hands then grasped each side of the black lace panties she was wearing and quickly removed them as well. Wanting to be thorough, I removed her white socks while my eyes took in her nude body in the fully lit room.

I sat next to her on the couch. She finally responded by returning my kisses and running her hands through my hair. It was a special, erotic, thrill to french kiss her while she was completely in the nude and I was still fully dressed. She enthusiastically explored the inside of my mouth sucking my tongue and encircling it wildly with hers. By this time, my flag had risen to full staff. I took Tina by the hand and led her into the bedroom. Beyond her return kisses, she was just as passive in bed as on the couch. Taking the initiative, I decided to find out just how far she was willing to let me have my way with her.

The totality of her capitulation astonished me. For two hours, I took complete advantage of her passive submission. I penetrated her physical being using all available avenues, some of which are illegal in certain states, in a variety of creative angles. Low groans and sporadic spasms suggested that Tina reached peaks of pleasure multiple times and my own fireworks erupted on more than one occasion.

Even at the heights of her passion, Tina never voiced encouragement or objection during our intimate encounter. Considering she was a medical nurse by profession, her complete disregard for risk of disease or pregnancy astounded me. Her surrender was so total that it gave me a chilling sense of power over her.

After enjoying each other, we drifted off to sleep. Not long afterward, I was abruptly awakened to a horrible realization. Tina snored like an elephant.

$$* \qquad * \qquad *$$

The next Monday following the delightful weekend encounter with Tina, I went downtown into the city for my continuing Tai Chi lessons.

As usual at that time of day, the large building was nearly empty. I would pass by only one or two people on my way to the ballet studio. As I entered the room, Tara was already there gracefully performing some forms. I stood silently marveling at how fluid and cat-like she moved. Secretly, I wondered how good she would be in bed.

"Hello," Tara said breaking me out of my trance. "You are right on time as usual."

She stopped the form and walked across the room toward me.

"Hello Tara," I said in my best Don Juan voice.

She stood close to me square to my shoulders as if studying me.

"My, my, my. Did you have a busy weekend?"

"Why do you say that?" I innocently asked.

"You appear to be very satisfied," she said with a knowing smile. "I hope you at least used a condom?"

I was taken back by the accuracy of her observation as well as the directness of her question.

"Of course I did," I said seriously. That was a lie though. I was in the bad habit of not using one unless specifically requested by the other party.

"Hmm, I don't think you are being honest with me."

Tara slowly moved her left hand with the palm facing me across my chest and midsection. Her hand stayed about two inches away from touching me directly. "Considering your recklessness, you are lucky. So far, you are free of any communicable diseases. But I wouldn't take that for granted."

"How could you possibly tell?" I asked skeptically.

"If disease or injury is present, I can feel it."

"How? How could you know?"

"Your energy patterns would be abnormally weak or disrupted if you were not healthy," she explained. "Part of your problem," she added changing the subject, "is that you waste a tremendous amount of your energy. A warrior uses his or her available energy wisely."

"How do I waste energy?"

"You squander your energy in many ways. For example, you think too much without any benefit. You worry excessively. You feel enormous guilt. You have a great deal of repressed anger that you use a tremendous amount of energy to keep from erupting. You expend your sexual energy wantonly without discrimination. You work out too frequently."

Tara paused intently looking at me. "Shall I go on?" she asked hands on hips.

Her mannerism gave me the impression that she was angry with me. Her inventory of my energy wasting habits made me feel gloomy. I did not respond to her question.

"Tai Chi will help you. It quiets the mind, allows your life force to flow more freely. It makes you better aware of tension in the body so you can release it. That is why Leo has you taking lessons with me."

"I don't like being criticized," I said in a delayed reaction to her earlier comments.

"I'm just trying to help you."

I looked her over. She was wearing baggy gray sweatpants and an over-sized thick white tee shirt. "Gee, you are not even wearing the tight outfit you had on last time. Now I can't check out your body in the mirrors when you are not looking."

Her eyes rolled up and she smiled.

"You have such a one track mind!" she exclaimed. "Let's get started."

She began the lesson by teaching me an exercise called "push hands". I liked it because I at least got to touch her.

We stood square to each other about a foot apart. One hand is placed behind the other's lower back and the other hand on the center of the opponent's chest. The idea is then to push with the body pivoting but feet still on the ground. Whoever had the stronger "root", as she called it, would be able to push the other. Despite my overwhelming advantage in size and strength, she won the pushing contest every time. Unlike the annoyed reaction I had the first time I met her and tried unsuccessfully to push her back, I was now sincerely interested in learning the trick.

Tara taught in a very patient and kind manner. This was in stark contrast to our verbal exchanges outside the Tai Chi instruction. After the push hands exercise, she taught me the next four movements of the Tai Chi short form. She moved with a grace that was almost hypnotic. Something inside of me was growing very fond of her.

"Would you like to get a cup of coffee or something?" I asked after the lesson.

"I don't fraternize with students," she joked.

"No, really. Let me buy you lunch."

"I don't think that would be a good idea."

"Why? What's stopping you?"

"I wish to keep our relationship one of instructor and student."

"That's okay. I just want to thank you in some way for the lessons."

"There's no need to thank me," she said picking up her sweatshirt from the floor.

"I can't convince you to have lunch with me?" I said in a feigned tone of defeat.

"No," she answered as nicely as possible.

"Rejection," I thought to myself. "Are you going to take a shower now?" I asked aborting the lunch date attempt.

"Yes."

She looked at me quizzically.

"Could I at least watch?"

"There you go again!" she said throwing her arms up in the air. She started to walk out of the room.

I intercepted her path and moved almost nose to nose with her. "I have a feeling...that you can tell...I am skilled in the arts of pleasure," I whispered. "I could make you feel more like a woman than any other man you have been with."

"And I can make you feel a knee in the groin more than any other woman you have been with."

"Message received," I conceded and backed off.

She vacated the studio and made her way down the hall to the women's locker room. I watched her as she walked away. I wasn't looking to admire her figure now obscured by baggy sweats. There was something else about Tara I found very intriguing.

*   *   *

The weather turned colder. The first snowfall lightly dusted the earth with a soft white coating. The Christmas and New Year holidays were just a couple of weeks away. Houses in my town were wonderfully decorated with bright colored lights and shiny ornaments.

Even though the holiday season is supposed to be a festive time of year, I instead felt an impending sadness. It would be my first Christmas without Diane. True, I was still seeing Tina. But in getting to know her, I realized we were not compatible for a long-term relationship. She lacked a sense of humor, tended to be moody, and our personalities were frictionally different. I considered breaking up with her but decided to wait until after the New Year. I didn't want to ruin the holidays for her. Besides, she adored me and I found the attention and her sexual availability difficult to give up.

By late December, I had passed all but one of the network engineer certification exams. I started to compose my resume and look through the help wanted ads.

Having most of the day to myself, I spent a lot of time studying the stock market and trying to make money in it. I reasoned that if I got good at playing the market I wouldn't have to work for a living. Unfortunately, all I did was lose money. It became painfully apparent to me that intelligence and education is no guarantee of success in the financial markets. During one of my weekly visits with Leo in the office in downtown Manhattan, I mentioned to him my growing frustration with losing money in the market.

"Why do you dabble in the stock market?" he inquired.

"To make money of course."

"And why do you want to make money?"

"Well, so I don't have to work for someone else."

"And why do you not want to work for someone else?"

"So I have the freedom and independence of making a living on my own. Say, you are determining my values aren't you?"

Leo smiled. "You are perceptive. What is ultimately important to you is freedom and independence. For this, you ascertain you need money. The method you have chosen in your attempt to accomplish this is the stock market. Is that correct?"

"Yes."

Leo paused to think for a moment as if he were trying to find the right words.

"Has it ever occurred to you that your endeavors in the stock market are another way of you trying to prove yourself?" I was about to interrupt but he continued. "The stock market, like many other things for you, has become a battleground. You try to prove yourself but instead fail and become angry and depressed. You are not objective in your efforts but act emotionally. That is why success has alluded you."

"I'm not quite sure I understand."

"What you really seek," Leo explained, "is to feel like you are a success. You have a need to feel worthy. You also wish to achieve freedom from the white-collar rat race. You would probably not even dabble in the stock market if these core needs were satisfied. Still, you are stubborn and I would venture to guess you will not give up until you feel you've been successful."

"So, you can help me?" I asked.

"I know little about the market but perhaps I can assist you. What makes you decide whether or not you buy a stock?"

"That's easy. I buy if I think it is going to go up in price."

Leo made a face as if that should have been obvious to him. "Okay, how do you know when to sell?"

"That depends. If it goes up, I'll sell at a certain level."

"And what do you do if the price goes down?"

"I'll usually hold on to it until it comes back up and I can at least get even."

"But what if it keeps going down?"

"If it sinks too much, I'll give up on it after a while and just sell."

"Aha." Leo said sounding as if he discovered some flaw to my method. "Allow me to confirm if I understand this correctly. You buy a stock. If it goes up, you sell it at a certain point for a profit. If it goes down, you just hold on to it unless it goes so low you give up."

"Yes, that is pretty much it," I verified.

"First, what you are doing does not make sense mathematically. If a stock drops and you hold on to it you may lose a great deal of money. If a stock goes up you sell it fairly quickly which means you cut your potential profit short if the stock keeps going up. Second, you are more concerned with being correct with your stock selection than making money."

"What makes you say that?" I asked puzzled.

"You take a quick profit if a stock goes up to prove you were correct but hold on to a stock going down hoping it will turnaround so you can still prove you were right. You are more concerned with your ego than making money."

My mind went into a loop to find objections to Leo's hypothesis. I responded to his observations. "But Leo, a lot of times a stock will go down, then come back. If I do what you say, I may sell it just as it falls and be out when it goes back up. Or, a stock that goes up may start down and then I would lose the profit in it."

"Yes, I am certain that happens sometimes. But cutting your losses on a falling stock that eventually rebounds would be a small price compared to not protecting yourself if a stock keeps going down. And, risking a down turn in a stock that is rising is favorable compared to taking a profit quickly in those cases where the stock continues to go up."

"I don't know if that will work," I said skeptically.

"Well, like I said, I don't have much knowledge about the market," Leo replied. "I suggest you go over all your transactions in the last year. Calculate what would have happened if you sold a stock only if it declined a certain percent from when you purchased it or, if it went up, from its highest price after you purchased it."

"Okay, I'll try it." Later that evening I did as Leo suggested. I reviewed all my transactions in the past year and electronically collected the stocks' price history on my computer to compare how I would have done following Leo's advice. To my surprise, instead of losing half my life savings like I did, I would have eked out a modest gain. Though the results of my testing were not overly profitable, Leo's method would have at least saved me from losing a great deal of money. Unfortunately for my financial health, it would not be until years later that I took his advice to heart.

"You know, Leo, I naively thought that since I have a masters degree in finance and I did so well in school, it would be fairly easy for me to learn how to play the market. Boy, was I wrong!"

Leo smiled.

"The reason for that is simple. The stock market is not governed by logic but the mass emotions of the crowd. Your intellect is useless. Your emotions blind you. You may not like to hear this, but you do not yet have the mental discipline to succeed in such a hazardous endeavor.

"If you are serious about mastering the market, I suggest you utilize the modeling technique I taught you."

"The one where we modeled a so called Don Juan type?"

"Yes. Investigate and study those who have consistently excelled at profiting from the financial markets. Discover what they all have in common. Use that as a guide and attempt to emulate."

"I don't have the time for that."

"Then you should stop trading in the market. Or give your money to somebody with a profitable long term track record and let them invest for you."

I frowned not really happy about any of his suggestions.

"How do you earn a living, Leo?" I asked. "You've never asked me for money."

Leo laughed. "In my present situation, I do not need to work for income unless I choose to."

"Are you rich?"

"Beyond your wildest dreams," he smiled.

"Really! How much are you worth?"

Leo continued to laugh while answering me. "I'm worth more than you can imagine!"

"How much? A few million?"

He put his hand on my shoulder and said with his laughter subsiding, "A warrior measures his wealth by his heart. You are still superficial and emphasize what society has conditioned you to value rather than on what brings true happiness."

"Are you saying money is not important?"

"No, Tony. Money is very important. Anyone who tells you otherwise is lying. If money were not important, people would not spend most of their lives working for it.

"Money can enslave a person either by the possessive pursuit of it or from being heavily in debt. Take the typical American for example. He or she graduates college with student loans to pay. Then they take out a car loan. Perhaps they pay rent or live at home. They take on credit card debt. Later in life, he or she may get married and spend an exorbitant sum on a wedding. Then the final nails in the financial coffin are a mortgage and children. Many people live from paycheck to paycheck hoping just to survive and live up to society's expectations. They work themselves to death fearful of losing their job. When their children grow up, the cycle repeats itself.

"A warrior seeks to achieve freedom in all respects, including financial. That is part of your quest, your evolution, your revolution."

I absorbed his words then asked, "How does a warrior free himself?"

"A number of ways," Leo answered. He waited as if to prompt another question from me.

"What makes a person a warrior Leo? You have spoken to me about various characteristics but you never have given me a comprehensive description."

Leo sighed in seeming preparation to supply an answer he felt he already gave.

"I have purposely avoided giving, as you put it, a comprehensive description. You are used to thinking in a way best suited for an academic environment where a subject is broken down and categorized. Being a warrior is a state of mind, not a subject to be memorized. One cannot intellectualize it; at least not to any real purpose. It must be felt in the heart. A warrior does not pretend to really know anything for certain. He uses only what is practical. He believes in only that which empowers him with disregard to theory or intellectual analysis."

We sat in silence for a few moments while I pondered his answer.

"Perhaps if you gave me a broad description of what you consider to be a warrior I would at least have a road map for what you are teaching me."

Leo thought for a moment and then said, "Fair enough." He took a deep breath and began his explanation. "As I have mentioned to you before, a warrior is one who takes complete responsibility and control of their life."

"But that is impossible," I retorted.

"It is true that a warrior does not have full control of every event that occurs in his life. But he has far more control than ordinary people do. A warrior's mastery is attained when he is able to control his response to external events."

Leo paused to allow a question but I remained silent. He continued. "A warrior frees himself from the petty expectations of society whether it be from the government, religion, or culture. He rids himself of ego. That is his revolution.

"A warrior directs all his outward and inward behavior to increase his power as far as possible while attaining ultimate integrity and morality. That is his evolution.

"A warrior," he said with his speech slowing and voice lowering, "is patient and kind to others." Leo leaned forward in his chair and raised his hand to the side of my head lightly touching my right temple with two of his fingers. His voice became even slower and deeper. "A warrior is also patient and kind to himself."

He retracted his hand and sat back in the chair. His speech returned to normal.

"I have given you something of a check list as you requested but it is meaningless to try to intellectualize or memorize it. Knowing what to do is not the same as doing. Knowing what to be is not the same as being."

I felt as if I entered a profound, deep, but fully aware trance during Leo's description. "How," I started to ask, "How will I know when I am a warrior?"

"Understand that being a warrior is not a destination. Our ultimate destination is death. That is our lot as human beings. Our freedom lies in what path we choose during our lives. Being a warrior is a path, a state of mind."

"How will I know I have achieved that state of mind?"

"When your actions and thoughts lead you to harmony with yourself, others, and the universe, you are acting as a warrior. When your actions or thoughts lead to harming yourself or others or result in disharmony, then you are acting like a jackass. In your life, you will find yourself wavering from warrior to jackass and back again. Your degree of evolution is determined by how much time you are one and not the other."

Leo stopped talking and looked at me as if waiting for a comment. For some reason his explanation made me smile. I also felt a little tired but in a comfortable way. "I think that is enough for today," Leo said. We stood up from the chairs.

"Thank you Leo."

"Hey," Leo joked, "This is the second time you are thanking me! You may actually turn out well after all!" We both laughed.

I walked out of the room and noticed Ken, the therapist who set up the introduction to Leo, fingering through some paper work in the adjacent office. Leo did not follow me but remained in the room we were just in.

"Ken! How are you?" I greeted shaking his hand.

"Hey, Tony! How are you doing?" he responded with a big white tooth smile.

"Good thank you. What have you been up to?" I asked to make polite conversation.

"I have an appointment so I will be using the room next."

Ken gestured to the small waiting area visible to us. There was a tall young woman with short black hair seated in one of the old hard wooden chairs. Her head was down and she seemed absorbed.

"It was nice bumping into you Ken," I said.

"You too Tony," he smiled.

Ken addressed the young woman by the name of Eileen and told her she could go inside. The wide open door of the room allowed me to view its entirety. Strangely, I did not see Leo and yet I had not observed him leaving. It was impossible for him to have left without passing me.

Impulsively, I became frightened. There were no other exits save for the one door. There were no closets or large furniture to hide his view. Eileen went in. I followed her looking around the office. Ken came in right behind me.

"Did you forget something?" Ken asked in a friendly way.

"Leo was just in here."

"Yes?"

"And now he is not," I said with mild panic if there is such a thing.

"Yes? So?" Ken responded in a matter of fact way.

"Did you see him leave?"

"No, but I wasn't paying attention. Would you excuse us?" he asked with a polite smile. He shut the door after I stepped out. I looked around the small waiting area and the other office. There was just no way Leo could have left without me noticing. I ran down the building stairs to the outside reasoning that I might catch up with him if he did leave. Leo was nowhere to be found.

CHAPTER 6

▼

DISCOVERING THE HEART

"Please tell me you love me," she whispered in my ear with
warm moist breath. "And if you don't love me, please
deceive me so that I shall never know."
from 'The Belly Dancing Witches of New Jersey' - the author

Christmas Eve arrived but I was far from a holiday mood. My religious
convictions had long disappeared. I held bitter memories of spending
Christmas Eve alone as a young boy living with my father after my parents
divorced. Because of the night shifts he worked as a police officer, he was
often on duty that night. Feeling desolate and abandoned, I would pass
the time listening to Christmas music on a small radio until very late at
night. After a number of years of spending the holiday in this fashion,
loneliness and depression turned into a conditioned emotional numbness.

I would often walk the cold streets this time of year jealously witnessing
lovers and families sharing the joy of the holiday. Sometimes, I would
come across the other loners like me. On one Christmas day, since I had

nothing else to do, I went to a video store to rent some movies. I noticed at least three other men at the store obviously in the same lonely situation as myself.

This Christmas, I was not alone per say. But one can be lonely even in the midst of other people. I spent part of Christmas with a friend, Andy, and his family. Later in the day, I met Tina at her parent's house. It felt strange being with her and her family. I didn't love her and I planned to stop seeing her shortly after the New Year. For her sake, I went through the motions of being a boyfriend, at least until the holidays were over. The two of us also spent New Year's Eve together. I rang in the year with a person I knew I wouldn't be with next year. I was happy in a relieved sense when the holidays ended. I no longer had to be reminded just how empty my life had become.

"You are distracted," Tara commented during our weekly Tai Chi lesson.

"Yes, I am," I coldly replied. I was in a patented foul mood.

"You must be," she said lightly. "You have been here a half hour and haven't yet made a single joke or remark about my body and how you wish you could devour it."

Her remarks forced me to smile though I tried to repress it.

"I just have some things on my mind."

What I had on my mind was how I would go about breaking up with Tina. Over the last few months, Tina had become extremely attached to me. It was not going to be easy.

"You are troubled," Tara said in a genuinely concerned way while studying me with her eyes.

"What else is new?" I responded despondently.

"May I offer you some advice?"

"Advice? You don't even know what is bothering me."

"True," Tara replied refusing to react to my negative attitude. "But I can give you a suggestion particularly appropriate to times when you are troubled and another person is involved."

"And what would that be?" I asked not really expecting any practical advice.

"Follow the heart," she simply stated.

"Follow the heart? Oh gee," I went on with my best sarcastic voice, "follow the heart. That will solve everything. How cute! Let's solve all our problems now. Just follow the heart!"

Tara put her hands on her hips—her trademark—and said, "You know, you can be very charming when you want to be. You can also be a big pain in the ass when you want to be."

"Well, at least I'm talented."

She walked over to me. Poking her finger into my chest for emphasis she said, "Follow—the—Heart!"

I poked her back. "What—does—that—mean? What am I supposed to do? Throw reason and rationality out the window and just do what my emotions dictate?" My voice grew louder. "Typical woman! Let's think with our heart, not with our head!"

"If you stop ranting for a moment I can explain."

"Please do," I said with a wave of my hand to give her the floor.

"A warrior follows her heart. That does not mean blindly following our emotional desires or attachments. It means doing what we know in our heart to be right even if it conflicts with what we desire."

"What do you mean by attachment?"

"Attachment is becoming emotionally dependent to some desire. For example, you may find yourself very attached to a beautiful woman, like me." She smiled warmly holding her hands in front of her heart. "But perhaps you know deep inside she doesn't love you or that the two of you are not compatible. Your emotional impulse caused by the attachment will lead you to try to make the relationship work no matter what. But your heart will tell you different. Your heart will tell you to let her go."

"I'm not sure I understand."

"You may not now, but you will. You will find that when you deal with people from the heart instead of selfishness or emotional impulses, you will be far better off. Attachment weakens a person. Following the heart makes you strong."

"You sound a lot like Leo sometimes," I said to her. At the time though, I didn't believe her words of wisdom had any practical bearing on my current predicament.

"Seriously, Tony," Tara said coming very close to me, "When you feel everything is going wrong or you are all mixed up and you don't know what to say or do just take a deep breath and think to yourself—follow the heart."

"Yeah, okay. I'll do that," I said not really meaning it.

*   *   *

My dreaded self-imposed deadline to break up with Tina arrived. As I mulled over my options for how to approach the situation, I considered the usual collection of break up techniques at my disposal:

- I could act like a complete jerk and hope she initiates a break up with me.
- I could not call her or take her calls and hope she gets the message.
- I could provoke an argument and escalate it into a break up.
- I could tell her I met someone else.
- I could give her the "you are a nice girl but…" routine.
- I could make a false confession that I am bisexual and found a boyfriend.

After some deliberation, I decided to be gently honest with her and just explain how I felt. After all, she was very nice to me and I did not want to cause her unnecessary pain.

One weekday night I stopped by her apartment. I started the conversation while we were seated on the couch together. I told her sincerely that while I was fond of her I also believed our personalities were incompatible.

Therefore, I did not see a future together in a long-term relationship. Tears quickly welled up in her eyes as she became overcome with grief and anger. In the middle of one of my sentences, Tina abruptly stood up and headed off to the bathroom; I assumed to get some facial tissues. On the way, she grabbed my jacket hanging from a hook near the front door and angrily flung it to the floor.

"Please don't take it out on my jacket," I said weakly trying in vain to diffuse the situation with humor.

Tina stormed back from the bathroom. "How could you do this to me!" she screamed in between tears. "I don't deserve this! I don't deserve to be treated like this!"

"I'm sorry," I said with both voice and persona shrinking.

"Why are you doing this to me?" She started to punch my chest with both her fists. I tried grabbing her hands but she pulled loose. "I thought you were different! But you just used me and now you are throwing me away! I love you and you are throwing me away just like Joe did! What did I do wrong? Why are you treating me like this?"

She sat down sobbing on the couch. Tears streamed freely down her face. She made no attempt to wipe the tears away with a tissue or her hands. I sat there watching her with a sickening feeling in my stomach. I didn't know what to say or what to do. If a rock were nearby, I would have crawled under it. After a few minutes of awkward silence passed, I thought it wise to just leave.

"Where are you going?" Tina snapped at me when I picked up my jacket off the floor.

"You are understandably upset. I am going to go home," I answered.

"You are just going to leave me? How could you leave me like this?"

I sighed and said in a low voice laced with guilt, "I don't know what else to do." I slipped into my jacket and headed out.

"How can you do this to me?" she screamed.

Tina followed me out into the cold January night with bare feet and no coat. I opened the driver side door to my car. "How can you leave me?" she cried with her voice turning from angry to sad. "Please don't go."

"I'm sorry Tina." My voice now turning hard and cold. "If I thought staying with you or doing anything else would help, I would do it."

I entered the car, engaged the ignition, and drove off. Glancing in the rear view mirror, I could see Tina standing in the middle of the street crying while she watched me drive away.

When I returned home, I felt sick to my stomach with guilt. My mind shut down and turned numb in an attempt to repress the pain. That night, sleep came to me empty and dark. I didn't even care if I woke up the next morning. However, the universe was not so merciful to end my life and take away the pain. I awoke the next day to heavy feelings of anguish and guilt.

Tina phoned me at work. She told me that she was so heartbroken she didn't sleep that night and called in sick to work. Besides an "I'm sorry", I really didn't know what else to say. I made some excuse to hurriedly end the conversation.

The following Saturday Tina showed up at my apartment unannounced. She knocked on the ground floor door of the house where I rented out the second floor. I knew it was Tina but I didn't answer. She knocked again on and off for about ten minutes. She must have known I was home because my car was parked right in front. Finally, she gave up and left. I breathed a sigh of relief. About an hour later, I pulled into my health club's parking lot to find her waiting there for me. She was calmer but still distraught and questioning why I broke up with her. Instead of trying to be kind and rational, which she certainly deserved, I instead resorted to being cruel. I spewed off a long list of things I didn't like about her and basically told her in different words to get lost and leave me alone. I left her standing alone in the parking lot.

Leo sat with uncharacteristic silence during our session while I recounted the events with Tina. When I finished speaking, he just looked at me.

"Aren't you going to say something?" I asked getting impatient.

He waited a few seconds to answer and then said, "What is it you want?"

His question seemed out of context. Why he asked it confused me. After a moment of thought, I answered, "I want to not feel so guilty and angry."

"Sorry," he said, "But I can't help you with that right now."

"Why not?" I asked bewildered and a little irritated.

"Because," he started to explain, "You should feel guilty and angry at yourself."

"Why?"

"Because you are responsible for creating the situation and you suffered the consequences for your actions. And still, you have not learned your lesson. Unfortunately, you emotionally injured an innocent person in the process."

I was beginning to seethe with anger but I stayed quiet for the time being.

"When I first met you Tony, you were disinterested in learning the ways of a warrior. I had to appeal to your selfish sexual ambitions to hook you into learning. I taught you techniques to build rapport and trust with other people. I taught you how to make a person feel understood, how to skillfully move a person to a positive state of mind. And what did you use these skills for? You did not use them to build healthy relationships. You used the skills to satisfy your pecker and ego.

"It would not have been so bad if you bothered to choose your subjects well by picking out women who were only interested in casual sex like you. However, you were wanton and indiscriminate. You used women carelessly with disregard. Tina was not the only one whose feelings you hurt though she was the worst. Now that you suffer from your actions you complain and feel sorry for yourself instead of taking responsibility."

"But you are the one who taught me how to pick up women!" I protested.

"Teaching you skills to help you enhance your social life with the opposite sex was just the bait at the end of a hook I used to point you in the right direction—the path of a warrior. What I was really teaching you is how you can take control of your life. You learned well how to attract women but you never assumed responsibility for your actions. It was inevitable that your irresponsibility would cause you and others harm."

"Why then didn't you stop or warn me? You knew what I was doing!"

"Tony," he said with a tone of trying to find patience, "I have spoken many times about a warrior taking full responsibility for his life. However, you are thick headed and arrogant just as I was in my youth. Sadly, you needed to fall on your face and suffer consequences to fully realize what it means to be responsible."

We sat silent for a few seconds as conflicting thoughts raced through my mind.

"You set me up! Damn it! You knew just what you were doing by teaching me all those seduction techniques and then letting me loose."

In a low and steady voice Leo responded, "My task as an instructor is to present the material in a way the student will come to understand it. I cannot help it if the student is self-centered, egotistical, and more interested in satisfying his physical desires than in the welfare of the people he chooses to use."

Leo's last statement was the final straw for me.

"Well, just thank you!" I yelled at him sarcastically as I rose from my chair and grabbed my black leather jacket. "Thank you for all your so called help! Be happy you didn't charge me because I would be suing you for my money back!"

I headed out of the office and yelled behind me as I slammed the door, "Goodbye!"

Seated in the waiting area was that same young lady with the short black hair I saw once before in the office. She looked at me quizzically wondering what was going on.

"He's nuts," I said in answer to her silent question pointing at the door of the room, "and I'm having a bad day." I forced a smile and said, "Have a nice life."

I left the building fuming. The cold January air helped cool my angry overheated body.

"F—ing old man," I muttered to myself as I walked the streets. I had no intention of ever seeing Leo again or his cohort Tara for that matter.

*   *   *

The phone at the other end of the line rang more than ten times. I thought it strange that an answering machine didn't at least pick up. This was the first time I attempted calling Tara at the number she gave me in case I could not keep an appointment. Without success, I called several times at different hours during the course of two days to inform her I was ending our Tai Chi lessons.

The scheduled day for our lesson came. I decided to go rather than just not show up. I brought my small gym bag with a towel and change of clothes like I usually did.

The ballet studio room was empty when I arrived. Strange. In the past, she was always there before me. After a minute or two of waiting, Tara showed up.

"Hi there," she said warmly with bright eyes and a nice smile. To my very pleasant surprise, she wore an incredibly tight thong leotard workout outfit that left little to the imagination. Every delightful contour of her body was evident. With that outfit on, her silhouette in the dark would appear as if she were entirely in the nude. Perhaps I should reconsider ending the lessons.

"Hi," I smiled back. I wondered if Leo had told her about what transpired during our last session.

"Are you ready to get started?" Tara asked.

"Yeah, sure." I figured it would be worth the lesson just to secretly ogle her body with my eyes. The wall length mirrors in the studio were great for that.

In the previous lesson, Tara showed me the last three movements of the Tai Chi short form. She now had me perform the entire form by myself and made corrections as we went along. Her manner was more friendly and less business like than usual.

After forty-five minutes or so of her making technical corrections to my movements, we performed the short form together standing side by side a few feet apart. The beauty of perfect synchronicity and harmonious motion of our bodies awed me. The experience had a very centering and calming effect.

"You are doing very well," she commented after we finished the form.

"Thank you," I said looking at her and thinking how desirable she looked in that leotard outfit. "You know, I'm not sure how much longer I will be taking lessons."

"Oh?" she replied nonchalantly.

"I just passed my last certification exam and I have started to circulate my resume. It's only a matter of time before I find a job and I don't intend to work in the city." I paused waiting for her to respond but she did not. "So, I am not going to be able to come into the city like I am now."

"Well, Tony," she said with a shrug of her shoulders, "Do whatever it is you want to."

"I wish it was that easy," I commented half jokingly.

"What is it you really want?" she asked me with a serious tone of voice.

"Hmm," I began trying to sound humorous, "What I really want is to be a rich young man on a yacht cruising the Caribbean with a half dozen centerfold models all tanning themselves in the nude on the boat's deck."

Apparently, she did not find my answer funny. "What is it you really want?" she asked again with the same serious tone.

"Okay. What I really want," I said, "is you."

She hesitated for a moment and then answered with a sly smile, "Be careful of what you ask for. You might just get it."

With that last remark, she casually left the studio.

I went to the men's locker room and undressed to take a quick shower. Tai Chi is not physically strenuous. However, I liked to feel fresh and change clothes afterward.

As usual for that time of day, the place was empty except for me. The locker room was old but typical with narrow wooden benches in front of rows of metallic light gray lockers. At one end of the room was a large blue tiled communal shower area with a dozen or so showerheads.

I turned on the water and held one hand under the stream to test the temperature. When my hand was satisfied with the water temperature, I moved my body under the cascading shower and enjoyed the feeling of being enveloped with the wet heat of the steamy water. I turned around, facing the shower nozzle, with my arms up and hands resting on the tiled wall to gently stretch my shoulders as the hot water sprayed down on them. While enjoying the feeling of relaxation this provided, I suddenly heard a soft but clear "hello" reverberating in the shower area. Startled, I quickly turned toward the shower room entrance about ten feet away. Tara!

In profound shock, with my eyes ready to pop out of my head and onto the floor, I watched Tara enter the showers completely in the nude. She moved slowly toward me with a feline grace that exuded power and sexuality. Her hazel round eyes, seductive and deep, peered hypnotically into mine. My heart began to pound hard in my chest. Adrenaline and testosterone flooded into my veins giving me an incredible rush. I froze in place.

"Is it okay for me to join you?" Tara teasingly asked.

I could not speak. My eyes drunk in her beauty now bared completely to me. She turned on the shower nozzle located just a few feet away on the wall to my left. Facing me, she tilted her head back into the water. She ran her hands through her now wet hair then down the front of her body starting just below her neck and travelling slowly and sensually over her breasts, midsection, and upper thighs. Her eyes locked on mine.

"This is what you want. Isn't it? You said so yourself. I have decided to grant your wish. You can have me."

I tried to speak, but I was incapable of producing any audible sound.

"Come on," she encouraged, "I'm yours."

Tara slowly twirled around so that her back faced me. She assumed a position, with hands on the wall and feet spread slightly more than shoulder width apart, like someone who was about to be frisked by a law officer.

"Take me!" she commanded with a sinister smile. "Or, do I have to pleasure myself?" One of her hands slid down the length of her slender body stopping between her luscious thighs. Her beautifully round and taut derriere jutted invitingly toward me.

My heart and mind raced at a maddening speed.

Was this an elaborate bluff? It had to be! Should I call her bluff? Should I find out how far she will go? Should I run out of the shower screaming?

My periscope hovered at the half way point as if waiting for me to make up my mind so it could decisively choose what direction to move in. What should I do? A multitude of erotic thoughts fired inside my head. My mental confusion suddenly climaxed. My mind erupted, no pun intended, leaving me abruptly clear headed and centered.

"You win," I said resignedly with a sigh. "You win."

I turned off the water and headed out of the shower. Using the white towel I had hung on a hook just outside the shower area, I started to dry myself off. Glancing over, I noticed Tara gazing at me with a slightly puzzled look on her face. She stepped out of the shower area and stood shoulder to shoulder with me not more than a foot away. Tara stared at me with kind twinkling eyes that so captivated me I momentarily forgot the wonderful view below her neck.

"Turn around," I said softly. She looked perplexed at the request but complied.

I moved behind her and used the towel to gently dry her hair and then delicately pat the water off her magnificent body. She remained still. I lightly kissed her on the back of her neck and draped the towel over her shoulders. Without saying a word, I left her and walked into the adjoining locker room.

After I dressed, I sat on the hard wooden bench in front of the locker. My elbows rested on my thighs and my hands covered my eyes. Unexpectedly, a profound feeling of sadness accompanied by tears overcame me. I felt a hand on my shoulder. Out of the corner of my eye I saw Tara who was now dressed modestly in a black sweat suit. She sat next to me straddling the bench and put one arm around my shoulders and her other arm around my waist. She held me until the sadness passed and then left just as silently as she had come.

*   *   *

The weeks passed into February. I had stopped going into the city to see Leo or Tara. I didn't even try to call them, nor did either of them attempt to contact me.

During this time, I temporarily stopped dating preferring instead to emotionally regroup and rest.

The circulation of my resume and replies to help wanted ads resulted in numerous job interviews. My advanced interviewing skills, thanks to Leo's lessons on how to build rapport and lead peoples' minds in the direction you desire, produced effective results. Ultimately, a number of positions were offered to me.

I selected to work for a small but fast growing software company on Long Island. It was not the most lucrative offer. But the commute was only ten minutes from my home and the hours were straightforward and not overly demanding. Time, I realized, was the most precious commodity, not money. Curiously, I experienced a cognitive intuition of knowing if I wanted to work for a company as soon as I arrived at the office even before the actual interview. This was similar to the time I was apartment hunting and experienced a feeling of knowing if I would like an apartment before I even saw it.

I was hired as a member of the technical support group. It turned out to be a great department to work in. The majority of people were in the early twenties. Just about everyone was supportive and friendly despite the hectic pace of the workday. An attitude of teamwork spontaneously transpired in the department.

My workday ended at 4:30 p.m. The relatively short day, combined with only a ten-minute commute, left me plenty of leisure time to pursue personal interests. Each day, I had enough time to work out in the gym, meditate, and practice Tai Chi.

One day after I had returned home from work, my doorbell rang. I did not expect anyone. So, I opened the second floor window and peered down to see who it might be.

"Leo! What are you doing here?"

"Hello Tony," he said looking up. His voice was friendly and polite. "I apologize for the unannounced visit. May I see you?"

I would not have admitted it to Leo but I was happy to see him.

"Wait just a minute. I'll come down to let you in."

"Nice place," Leo said with a smile as I gave him the ten-second tour of my three room apartment. "You keep it very neat."

"Thanks, I try to."

Leo studied my large collection of athletic trophies displayed atop a large bookcase in the living room.

"Impressive," he commented.

"I guess that is the overachiever in me."

He looked at another smaller bookcase filled with numerous stuffed animals including the teddy bear that convinced me not to shoot myself in the head. He turned to me with a facial expression indicating that stuffed animals seemed inconsistent with my personality.

"They keep me company," I explained to his silent question. "And they don't eat much."

"Ah," he responded nodding his head. "May I sit down?" he asked pointing to my futon couch.

"Sure, go ahead. Can I get you something? I have an assortment pack of herbal tea."

"I would rather have a beer instead. Do you have any?"

"Uh, yes I do," I answered a little surprised. I went into the kitchen and got him one.

"Are you joining me?"

"Yeah, okay." I went back into the kitchen and got a beer for myself as well.

I popped open the green bottles for us.

"German," Leo remarked as he read the label on the bottle. "You have good taste." I laughed and then we sat in silence for a while enjoying the brew.

"Are you still angry at me Tony?" Leo asked me jokingly with a kind smile.

I sighed and said, "No, I'm not angry at you. I suppose that I was angry with myself. I have to say though, your tactics are at times questionable."

"You needed some time alone. That is understandable. How have you been?"

Leo stated his question with such sincerity that I found myself wishing I had a father like him.

I told Leo the news about my new job.

"Excellent," he remarked. "You are now living where you want to live and working where you want to work. That is a vast improvement in the state of your life from when I first met you."

"I guess so," I said with a shrug of my shoulders.

"Any lady friends?" he inquired.

Leo must have noticed the Valentine's Day card standing atop my TV. Tina, despite how upset she was with me, was nice enough to mail one to me. Inside the card, she wrote that she loved and missed me.

"No, not at the moment. I have taken a short vacation," I said with a forced grin.

"I know someone who misses you dearly," Leo mysteriously commented.

"Who?" I asked excitedly. "Tara?"

"Tara," he confirmed.

My eyes opened wide wondering if he knew about the shower scene.

"It's okay," he said with a wave of his hand, "She told me what happened. It's really quite funny actually."

"What's so funny about it?"

Leo started to chuckle.

"Her maneuver was brilliant but it backfired on her!"

Leo started to laugh harder. He slapped his thigh a few times in obvious delight.

"I don't get it," I said befuddled.

"You guessed correctly. It was a bluff! She initiated the event quite confident that you would not engage in any physical interaction with her even when tempted. However, she gravely miscalculated part of your response!"

Leo nearly doubled over with laughter. It was contagious and I started to laugh too.

"What? Tell me what!"

"Tara," Leo struggled to say between laughter, "...it was a brilliant move to get you to see past your superficial impulses and discover your heart! She is aware that you are fond of her. When faced with an opportunity to have meaningless sex with a person you have true feelings for, you realized that sex is not all you really want!"

"Yes," I said joining his laughter, "It's like eating a big bag of potato chips for dinner. It satisfies you for a while but you really want a more meaningful meal!"

We both roared with laughter. If anybody saw us, they would have assumed we were drinking for hours while reveling each other with jokes.

"But Leo, I don't understand what you mean when you say she miscalculated."

"In a way, it worked too well. You experienced an instantaneous revelation. You wept because you rediscovered a lost part of yourself."

"But what was the miscalculation?"

Leo quieted down a bit and said, "She did not expect such a complete shift in you so suddenly. Your reaction caught her off guard and left her vulnerable. When you treated her with profound unselfish kindness, she unexpectedly experienced feelings of attachment for you!"

Leo started to laugh loudly again. I, however, fell quiet.

"She started to feel attached to me?" I said in a low voice.

"Yes! And that is not an easy thing to do! Tara is a warrior. She is not given to attachment. You..." Leo could barely speak the words with his laughing, "You found her weak spot! You are truly a mighty hunter! No other man has penetrated her emotionally since she became a warrior!"

"But I wasn't even trying!"

"That's the whole point!" Leo slapped me on the shoulder. "Your discovery of the heart makes you more powerful than you can imagine!"

"I don't feel very powerful," I said sincerely.

Leo calmed down and started to speak more seriously.

"I did not know in advance what Tara intended to do. Her actions were spontaneous, unplanned. To me, you are an open book. Your responses are predictable. I could have told her how you would react. She thought too that she could easily predict your behavior. However, she was wrong. She is a warrior after all, not a sorceress. She miscalculated the extent of your response and furthered her predicament by experiencing feelings of affection for you."

I sat without talking for a minute considering what Leo was telling me.

"What should I do? Should I see her?" I asked not really knowing what to do about the situation.

"Oh, no," Leo said. "That would be a mistake. In any case, she will avoid you like the plague."

"Why? That doesn't make any sense!"

Leo explained kindly. "First, she needs to explore her own heart. It has been a very long time since she felt touched by a man. In some ways, she considers her feelings a weakness, which would be true if her feelings are one of attachment. In other ways, she feels her emotional confusion is caused by fear, which is true if she denies herself genuine love. Tara needs to resolve these matters."

"I wish her luck because I have no idea what you are talking about," I said.

Leo grinned. "Second, despite your progress, you are not a warrior yet. If you entered into a relationship with Tara, you would bring violence and chaos into her world."

"Whoa! Thanks for the compliment!"

"Please understand me. You and Tara are simply on a different evolutionary scale at the moment."

"But I do like her," I said.

"Do you care for her enough to leave her be if that is the best thing to do?"

"Yes," I reluctantly replied. "Will I ever see her again?"

"Perhaps," was the only answer Leo would provide. He walked over to the TV and picked up the Valentine's Day card from Tina. "There is something about you," he said to me.

"What is there about me?"

Leo smiled. "I am repeating what is written in the card and what women have told you over the years."

"Yes, you are right," I said deep in thought, "All of my long term girlfriends said there was something about me they were very attracted to. But they could never put their finger on it."

"Exactly," Leo said, "That is one of the reasons why I chose you."

After we finished our beers, Leo and I arranged to continue our sessions on a biweekly basis. He wrote out a long list of instructions for me. "Homework" he called it.

"You have passed a critical juncture," he announced. "It is time to accelerate your training."

Normally I would ask for further clarification when he made a mysterious sounding statement like that. However, I was mentally tired and just wanted to rest.

"Whatever you say," I replied to humor him.

*   *   *

On Friday night, three days after Leo's surprise visit, I found myself restless and mulled over the idea of going out. The thought of being in a loud smoke filled nightclub did not appeal to me. So, I instead decided to go to a large bookstore not too far away from where I lived. I reasoned that it would be smoke free and relatively quiet while still offering the possibility of social interaction with the opposite sex. The establishment had numerous long magazine racks and a café to encourage such activity.

The bookstore was rather crowded that evening. I learned from an employee that early Friday evenings were the busiest time for the store.

My mind was unusually clear of its typical endless internal dialogue. I reasoned that this lucidity was due to mental fatigue and that I simply did not have the energy for the relentless banter that normally filled my head.

While casually browsing through the busy main floor, I passed by a middle-aged woman. Suddenly, I became instantaneously aware of her state of mind: slightly agitated and sad. Perplexed by the experience of immediate cognition of another person's mental state, I stealthily observed her for a minute. She then walked out of my sight and I questioned the validity of the event.

Soon, I had occasion to notice an attractive blonde woman who looked my age. She wore faded blue jeans with fashionable holes just above the knees. Immediately, I became aware that she felt uncertain and hurried. I caught a glimpse of a face of a man who passed me. I sensed that he felt resigned, yet relaxed.

Fascinated, I roamed the store armed with this heightened awareness. Unfortunately, the majority of individuals I observed were mired in a negative emotional state. Because of this, I found the experience mildly disturbing. And yet, I also felt a sense of elation as if a vial had been lifted from my eyes and I could see again.

Satiated with the experience, I ceased my observations and turned my attention in earnest to browsing books of potential interest. After I skimmed through a few titles on the shelves, I looked around again and noticed I lost the awareness. I consciously cleared my mind and scanned the area with my eyes. The awareness returned. I realized then I could turn it on and off at will. That knowledge gave me a daunting sense of power.

I walked down a flight of stairs to the first floor near the exit. Just before the exit were large square displays of newly released books and best-sellers. A very attractive young Indian woman of the eastern variety slowly perused one of the displays. I found myself transfixed by the exotic beauty of her face. Immediately, I sensed loneliness and vulnerability. This young lady was another crippled antelope just waiting to fall prey to a hunter. A charming and attentive man would quickly dissolve what little resistance she may have.

I slowed my pace to circle clockwise in the same direction she moved around the display. Instinctively, I readied myself to close the distance between us. She had no idea that a stalking hunter was almost upon her.

In an instant before I attempted verbal contact, my perspective shifted. Instead of seeing her as another potential conquest, I saw her as a lonely person desiring companionship. I indulged in feeling sorry for her. Having felt so alone for so much of my life, I sympathized with her predicament. I didn't have the heart to use her as just another sexual coup. Without any further consideration about whether or not I should approach her, I left the store inconspicuously.

CHAPTER 7

▼

HARMONY

"Your destiny is not a gift. It must be earned."
from 'How I Got Lucky and Bumped Into God'—the author

"A hunter learns to blend in with the world around him," Leo said beginning his instruction during our biweekly session.

"Why do you use the hunter analogy so much?"

"That is a good question. There are many characteristics of a true hunter that serve well as an allegory for how to live one's life.

"A hunter depends on no one. He takes only what he needs and wastes nothing. He does not kill for sport. He is careful to maintain the balance of nature and has the utmost respect for all living things. His skills depend on patience, awareness, and action at the correct moment."

"What do you mean by blend in?"

"Blending in is a way of being in harmony with your surroundings."

"I'm not so sure I understand," I said trying to make sense of it.

"Being in harmony with the universe is like going with the flow of a river. If your efforts are in the same direction as the force of the flow, you will be more powerful. If you go against the flow, you will quickly tire and weaken."

"That is like the old saying, 'Go with the flow,'" I commented.

"Not quite," Leo said. "People misinterpret that saying to take a lazy approach to life. It implies they have no power. A warrior is very active in achieving the life he or she desires. The key is that a warrior learns to work with the universe instead of against it."

Leo sensed that I was mentally searching for examples in real life.

"Tony, remember when I introduced you to Tara and asked you to attempt to strike her?"

"Yes."

"She did not try to defend herself using force against force as you were taught. If she did, you would have hurt her. After all, you are far stronger than she is and just as fast. What Tara did was simply use the force you generated to her own advantage by redirecting it instead of resisting it. To accomplish that feat requires awareness and appropriate action." Leo paused. "The same principles work in other aspects of life."

"How is she?" I asked changing the subject.

Leo sighed with a hint of a smile on the corners of his mouth. "She is fine," he answered.

"Does she ask about me?"

"No."

Somehow, I expected that answer.

"What about my Tai Chi lessons?"

"There are numerous academic institutions in your area that have Tai Chi classes in the evenings. I suggest you continue studying the art in one of them."

"Why don't you teach me?"

"I prefer to use our time together to teach you what others cannot. Many other people can teach you Tai Chi."

"Alright," I replied disappointed.

"How would you like to try something totally new that may help you gain personal insight?" Leo asked.

"Does it involve smoking anything?"

"No," he laughed. "Do you believe in past lives?"

"I am really not sure. I don't have a firm opinion."

"That's alright," Leo said, "Remember that a warrior is not concerned with intellectual proofs but rather with what is of practical use. I have found from experience, that personal issues sometimes have their origin in a past life; whether that past life is real or perceived. Would you like to experiment?"

"Sure. Why not?"

Following Leo's instructions, I closed my eyes and leaned back into the soft leather chair. Leo guided me through what he called progressive relaxation. After completing the steps, he lifted up my arm by the wrist and let it fall to test if my body did indeed achieve a complete state of relaxation. The arm fell like a limp noodle.

Leo asked me to imagine what he referred to as my life line.

"Float above your personal life line," he directed, "where all the events of your life, past, present, and future reside. Nod your head when you have done this." I nodded my head. "What direction is the past?"

"My left," I answered.

"What direction is your future?"

"To my right"

"And where is your present?"

"Directly in front of me."

"Plant a big yellow flag on your life line at your present. This is your marker to return to the present."

I did as he instructed.

"Now, go to the very beginning of the life line and drop down into it," he said.

When I followed the instruction, I felt a very strange shift in both my body and consciousness. "We wish to travel to a time of a past life; one that will benefit or be of value to us to recall. Look toward the direction before you were born in this life and imagine a tunnel. This is your link to the past life. Enter the tunnel and walk through it to the other side."

I tried to do what Leo said but I suddenly became very frightened and hesitated.

"I can't do it," I told him.

"What is stopping you?"

"I'm scared. I don't want to go."

"You are perfectly safe," he reassured. "No harm shall come to you and you can return at any time to the yellow marker we set."

My body began to shiver.

"Conquer your fear and enter with the full knowledge that you are perfectly safe," Leo continued.

With enormous effort and anxiety, I entered the tunnel and traveled through it to the other side. Leo then guided me in detail to explore my surroundings.

"Look down at your feet. What kind of shoes are you wearing?"

"Sandals," I answered.

A marble floor lay beneath my feet.

"How are you dressed?"

I told Leo I was dressed in a white robe.

Observing my other surroundings with the guidance of Leo, I realized I was in a large palace of what appeared to be of ancient Roman origin. Apparently, in this past life, I was a member of royalty during the time of the Roman Empire. Too bad I didn't have the same esteemed status in this life.

My lovely wife and I held hands and walked along long open corridors with a splendid view of outside gardens. We had a young son three or four years old. Though I loved my wife and child, my attitude was snobbish and aloof. I suppose being royalty will do that to a person. My family and I enjoyed a life of luxury with many servants at our disposal.

"Now," Leo instructed, "Go to the end of that previous life to your death."

A chilling sense of fear gripped me.

I imagined myself still as a young man. While on one of our regular palace ground strolls, a half dozen guards suddenly surrounded me and my wife. Unarmed and panicking with the realization I was about to be assassinated, one of the guards thrust his short sword into the left side of my lower back. Mortally wounded, I collapsed to my knees. I looked up at my wife being restrained by two other guards. She cried and shouted for me as she struggled vainly to break the hold of the guards. I stared into her eyes and was overcome with remorse that I was helpless to defend myself. I felt as if I was responsible for abandoning her.

Leo touched my forehead and brought me back to present reality. Tears ran down my face.

He let me be for a while until the emotional response to the recall subsided. He then asked me to describe what I saw and experienced.

"What was your wife's name in that previous life?" Leo asked.

I thought for a second and then responded, "Diana."

"Your ex-wife's name is Diane, isn't it?"

"Yes," I said perplexed. "How is that related?"

"A person harboring repressed unhealed emotions will subconsciously attempt to recreate the situation that caused the emotional wound in an effort to heal it."

"What?" I struggled to understand the connection.

"For example," Leo explained, "a woman who was abused as a child by an alcoholic father will often marry an alcoholic. Subconsciously, she is attempting to recreate the past in an effort to now successfully resolve it.

"Now, in your case, what emotions did you experience when you were dying?"

"I felt like a failure because I was unable to defend myself. I felt responsible for causing my wife and child great pain as if I willfully abandoned them."

"Being strong is important to you," Leo commented. "That is why you lift weights and trained to be a black belt in Karate. That has been your compensation to feeling weak and defenseless in a previous life. You resolved in your dying moments to never be weak again. You also have a fear of being involved in a long term relationship with another woman because in part you are afraid of abandoning and hurting her."

My mind lit up as if I experienced a personal revelation. However, I remained skeptical.

"I am not sure I believe all this."

"Did you ever have a problem with your lower back?" Leo asked while pointing to it.

"Yes, I hurt it once lifting weights. I have pain in the lower back every once in a while."

"On what side does the pain originate from?"

"My left." The answer astonished me with the realization that it is the same side that the guard's sword penetrated. "Could it really be true? Or did my mind just make the whole thing up?"

"It does not really matter if the past life truly existed or not."

"How can you say it does not matter?"

"It does not matter in the sense that your personality and physical ailments match the consequences of those past events whether or not those events are real or perceived. In either case, such events need to be healed."

"How do we do that?" I asked.

Leo smiled. "You just have," he said. "You always had a lingering sense of sadness that you could not discern the source of. Haven't you?"

I considered his question and answered, "Yes, I have."

"Now you know why. You miss Diana."

*   *   *

Saturday night rolled around and I had, as usual at that time, no particular plans. Bored and not feeling like watching TV at home, I mulled over going to a place called the White Café. I had never been there before, but overheard fellows at the gym refer to the place as a "meat market". Further inquiries on my part revealed that the crowd there averaged over forty. Though this was an older average age than I generally socialized with, it had been my experience that mature unattached women are generally more promiscuous than their younger counterparts. Since I still did not feel ready for a serious relationship, the idea of a casual tryst with an older woman appealed to me. I threw on a shirt and tie, splashed some cologne on, and headed out.

True to its name, the décor of the café consisted of generous white marble styled in a classic Italian look. Situated in the center of the café was a dance floor with a large rectangle shaped bar to one side and a smaller bar and café area on the other side.

Patrons of the club were well dressed with most of the men wearing suits and the ladies in dresses. It was obvious from the atmosphere that the great majority of the patrons were seeking the potential company of an interested party.

I contented myself to just blend in and observe the movement and behavior of the crowd. A few particularly attractive women on the dance floor caught my attention. I leaned up against a rail and nursed a drink while enjoying the provocative show provided by some of the females while they danced. The sight of prancing females reminded me of an elaborate mating dance. As in nature, the goal of the female is to attract attention and then choose from a sequential selection of approaching males. The goal of the male is, well, obvious. From my perspective as an objective outsider, I found the intricate interaction of males and females attempting to couple fascinating.

After about half an hour, I turned my attention to the endless stream of people moving in a circle from one side of the dance floor to the other as if they were all searching for something. I inadvertently caught the eyes of one young lady and smiled more out of politeness than anything else. She returned the smile as she walked by me. I didn't think anything of it until she crossed my path again from travelling the circle. She came to stand very close to me, almost touching my shoulder with hers, looking out onto the dance floor. I had experienced this female tactic before. A woman will position herself so close to you that you cannot help but notice her. She stands quietly waiting for you to initiate verbal contact. If you do not respond in an appropriate period of time - about two minutes - she moves on.

Two things about her immediately caught my attention. First, unlike the majority of the crowd, she was very young. She did not even look twenty-one. Second, she appeared to be alone. That is very unusual, especially for young ladies who tend to go out in groups of two or more. An attractive young woman alone in a place like this was like throwing hamburger meat into a pool of piranha.

Deciding to be sociable, I turned to her. When our eyes met I greeted her with a warm smile and said, "Hi. How are you tonight?"

She responded with a typical "Hi, I'm fine. How are you?"

A light conversation ensued with the customary exchange of names, what we do for a living, little jokes, and so on. She wore a very nice short emerald green dress. She had the body of a high school cheerleader. Her face was young looking and very pretty. Despite her good lucks, her personality was somewhat reserved. During the conversation, I found out her name was Cathy and that she was nineteen years old. I wondered if she was being truthful. She might have been even younger.

We picked up a couple of drinks from the crowded bar and found a corner to sit down and talk. The light was somewhat better where we were sitting and I noticed that she appeared intoxicated. At this point in our interaction, I dismissed her as a potential conquest or a girlfriend. Yet, I did not want to leave her alone and at the mercy of some other man's advances while she was in an intoxicated state. She started to tell me about problems in her family and other personal matters.

"I don't know why I'm telling you all this," she said. "But for some reason I feel like I can trust you."

I listened intently offering only an occasional comment or asking a question. Two hours and a few more drinks went by. I then politely told her I was tired and going home. I kissed her on the cheek and said good-night. She wished me a goodnight but seemed confused. I assume this was because I did not ask for her telephone number. I picked up my jacket from the coatroom and headed out to the parking lot. I heard the clicking of high heels behind me. Cathy had followed me outside.

"Are you okay?" I asked. She was wobbly on her feet and obviously in no condition to drive home. "How did you get here?"

"I took my own car," she slurred slightly.

"Would you like a ride home?"

"Sure," she said with her eyes struggling to focus.

I opened the passenger door to my car and let her in. After I got into the driver's seat from the other side, she started to caress my shoulder with her hand. I looked over at her and she leaned over and gave me a sloppy wet kiss. Staring seductively into my eyes, both her hands went under her dress and she pulled down panties over her knees, ankles, and high heels. Leaning back in the seat, she continued to peer into my eyes invitingly waiting for me to make an entrance.

The temptation to take advantage of a situation most men only read about in adult nudie-magazines was strong but short lived. I couldn't help but wonder how a young woman could take such a risk by going out alone, getting drunk, leaving with a stranger, and be willing to participate in unprotected sex with him.

"Thanks for the invitation," I told her. "But I think I should just get you home."

In her alcoholic daze, she seemed confused and then disappointed.

"Where do you live?" I asked.

Cathy gave me directions to her parent's home where she lived. It was only fifteen minutes away. By the time we arrived at the house, her head bobbled freely against the back of the car seat. With her nearly passed out, I struggled to get her out of the car and to the front door. Searching through her small pocketbook, I found house keys and opened the door. I carried her inside by lifting her up and over my left shoulder. Her legs were hanging to one side in front of me while her body was draped over my back. The position of her body caused the skirt to hike up revealing the bottom half of her bare backside. I turned my head and found my nose just an inch away from the soft white flesh of her buttocks. I succumbed to the temptation to admire her rear assets at close range. A fleeting thought crossed my mind to explore more of the territory but I resisted.

Due to the late hour, it was very quiet in the house. Everyone must have been asleep. I gently laid her down on the bare wooden floor just inside the front door. She was out cold and not responding to my light taps on her cheek. I toyed with the idea of picking her up and carrying her to a sofa or bed. But I didn't see any such furniture nearby. It also occurred to me that if her parents should wake up and discover us, they would not take kindly to a stranger walking around the house carrying around their bottomless daughter. Considering my options, I decided to leave her on the floor assuming she would be found in the morning. I rolled her body onto her stomach in case she became ill and used her pocketbook as a makeshift pillow. After positioning her head to the side, I tiptoed to the front door and exited the house. Slowly, and quietly, I shut the door behind me and made my escape.

While driving home, I noticed Cathy's black satin panties on the floor of the car. I stored them in the glove compartment. They would come in handy at a later time.

*　　　　　*　　　　　*

Thanks to the communication skills Leo had taught me, I was doing quite well at my job in the software firm. I was able to deal with customers having problems effectively and smoothly. As my reputation grew for handling even the most irate customers, other technicians would occasionally ask me to take over a call from a particular unpleasant person.

The formula I used when managing a situation with an angry client was simple. First, I would psychologically pace the person by letting them vent their anger and at least to pretend to agree with whatever complaints they voiced. This tactic usually made the customer feel that they were speaking to a person who was listening and sympathetic. It also allowed them to blow off steam. Second, I would then take the lead in the conversation and then subtly guide the person toward a more desirable emotional state. Having achieved that, I would work toward a mutually satisfactory resolution. Using this formula, pace then lead, as a foundation to communicating with customers proved effective about ninety percent of the time. Leo was right. What he taught me had application in all facets of human interaction.

At the firm, the atmosphere of teamwork in the technical support department encouraged the development of personal friendships. I became a good friend with one fellow in particular by the name of Mark. Although he was seven years younger than I, we had much in common and got along very well.

During the time Mark and I spent together, he introduced me to a concept he coined "Joeness". Grammatically speaking, Joeness was a versatile word that could be used interchangeably to refer to a "Joe" or to describe the state of being a "Joe".

In its simplest form, Joeness is the act of being an excellent Joe. Slightly less prestigious, but still honorable, is being a "regular" Joe.

The state of being a Joe was not explicitly defined by it adherents - Mark and his friends. Rather, the term captured it's meaning from the observation of admirable behavior from fellow Joes. The best I could decipher from Mark and his friends is that Joeness is an intricate set of behavioral standards for young men who usually did not have a girlfriend but spent most of their free time looking for one. Interestingly, if a Joe found a girlfriend, he was almost automatically demoted from the Joeness title. This was especially so if he ceased former Joeness activities under pressure from the female. There were exceptions to this such as when the new girlfriend was a beauty pageant contestant, topless dancer, or willing to participate in threesomes.

Weekend Joeness activities often include three or four Joes in a car cruising down popular boulevards looking for "hot girls". Other popular activities include an adult video exchange and the use of electronic devices to ease drop on cordless telephone conversations of young females.

A portion of Joeness communication was coded for privacy. This code is a variation of police or military numbers, like 10-4. Using this convention, Joes could alert each other to the presence and location of hot girls without being too overt. Other Joeness communication methods included standard responses such as "cool" to indicate approval and "depression" to indicate disappointment.

On Mark's recommendation, I was honored with the title of fellow Joeness and inducted into the group after contributing to the common adult video library. To initially impress my new brotherhood, I used the panties Cathy left behind as a flag on my car's radio antenna when out with the fellows. It was a big hit.

I soon discovered that it was common for the Joes, all of who were in their early twenties at the time, to prefer girls in their late teens. This put me at somewhat of an awkward situation. While it was fun to watch the Joes pursue the filet mignon of the female gender, the age group they targeted was too young for me. Therefore, I usually limited my participation in the group outings to that of an observer rather than participant.

On one Friday evening, I had just spoken to Mark over the phone on the usual topics of girls, cars, and sports. There were no Joeness activities on the calendar for the evening. So, when I got off the phone, I decided to head out to the White Café again.

For some unknown reason I felt a bit depressed that evening. I decided to lighten my mood with a couple of vodka shots before leaving the house. I never did care to go out to clubs alone but I did not have any single male friends my age to accompany me. Most of the men my age I knew were married. I suppose in a way I was lucky to have divorced early to get a head start on the second time around.

The White Café was crowded again that night. It was a challenge to just walk from one end to another. I bumped into a woman I knew from work, exchanged pleasantries, and tried to squeeze myself into a spot at the bar to order a drink. The two bartenders were tall beautiful blond women wearing low cut tops and high top bottoms to show off ample cleavage at both the chest and buttocks. They provided pleasant scenery while I waited patiently to be served.

"Hi," A middle-aged woman next to me said.

"Hi, how are you?" I replied. She looked to be in her late forties and had short light brown hair and a few extraneous pounds on her frame. In the past, I would have avoided any interaction with a woman I had no romantic interest in. But I had a new policy of being politely friendly even if approached by a female I was not attracted to.

While I waited for the drink I ordered, we jokingly chatted about how packed and noisy the place was. She seemed overly interested in me considering the fact that I spotted a wedding ring on her hand.

"What is your name?" I asked.

"Olga."

Olga. That name always conjures images in my mind of a huge, fat, Nordic woman wearing a Viking helmet with horns protruding from it.

"My name is Tony."

"Hi," another fortyish woman on the other side said to me. She had a nice face and hair that was a unique combination of dyed blonde, silver, and brown. Though she was significantly older than me, I found her attractive. A quick scan of her hands revealed no wedding ring.

"Hello," I replied.

The three of us started to talk. I found out her name was Ann. Olga turned out to be her older cousin.

During the conversation, I discovered that Ann was in the middle of getting a divorce and that she had two young boys. Coincidentally, she lived in the same town as I did though on the opposite end from me.

Ann seemed good natured and pleasant. I began to think she had potential for a casual encounter. Since she was over ten years older than I and still technically married, I assumed she was not looking for a 'serious' relationship. I further assumed that, being practically divorced, she might be anxious for male companionship. My first experience some years ago with a recently divorced forty-year-old lady reinforced my stereotypical assumptions about divorced women. Two hours into a first date together we were, at her suggestion, intimately enjoying ourselves at a cheap motel. I thought that perhaps a similar opportunity was about to present itself.

Ann and I talked for a couple of hours and danced together a few times. She and Olga took turns playfully pinching my buttocks during the evening.

"Can I have your phone number?" I asked Ann toward the end of the night.

She hesitated and politely told me that she was not comfortable doing that.

"Why don't you give me yours," she suggested. "I have two boys at home and I would rather they not pick up the phone to have a man other than their father ask for me."

"Okay," I shrugged. I jotted my number down on a napkin not really convinced she would ever call. Given the late hour of the evening, I escorted Ann and Olga to the parking lot. Feeling a little giddy, they pinched my butt one more time and said goodnight.

*   *   *

The next day, Saturday, I went to Leo's office as scheduled. He seemed to be in a serious mood, which was unlike him. Instead of the typical fluff exchange at the start of a session such as "Hi. How have you been," Leo silently waited for me to get comfortable in the leather chair and then immediately proceeded with his instruction.

"The universe is a balance of opposing forces," Leo began. "Some people call these forces good and evil. I do not like those terms for they imply judgment. I prefer to call the forces light and dark for simplicity.

"The universe cannot exist without the interplay of both these forces. Perhaps you have seen the Chinese Yin Yang symbol. The dark side is female, mysterious, and passive. It represents the earth. The light side is male, direct, and aggressive. It represents the heavens.

"A warrior strives to mirror the balance of the universe. Therefore, he does not try to eliminate or diminish the light or the dark side. Instead, he strives to interact with each in harmony. If a person attempts to permanently align themselves with one side of the force, the counter force shall destroy them. A warrior attains mastery when he can willfully use either of the forces of the universe as it suits him."

"I'm having a difficult time understanding how I would apply this philosophy in my behavior," I said.

"Do not seek so much to understand as to be. Your personal power is not dependent on your intellect." Leo seemed somewhat impatient. He took a deep breath as if to calm himself.

"Do you recall anything unusual that happened to you in the last week?" he asked.

"No," I said trying to remember.

"Think hard! Did anything happen that frightened or startled you?"

I accessed my memory to review the events of the previous week. "There was one morning," I said starting to remember, "but I didn't think anything of it."

"What was it Tony?" he asked with a sense of urgency leaning forward in his chair.

"Well, one morning on my way to work, I accidentally stepped on a dead bird when getting into my car."

"What kind of bird was it?"

"It was a crow."

"How did you react?"

"I was startled at first before I looked down to see what it was. I have noticed a number of crows on the block I live on so I did not attach any significance to the incident."

Leo sat back into his chair. "It was a warning," he said grimly.

"A warning? A warning for what?" Leo always concerned me when he spoke like that. My immediate reaction to his mysterious warnings was to get annoyed at him.

"If you were a fully evolved warrior, you would have recognized the warning immediately. Because you are my apprentice, I have intervened in an attempt to save you pain and to increase your awareness. You did not notice let alone heed the warning. The next warning, if there is one, will be stronger to increase the chance you will stop and take notice. If you ignore the warnings and continue on your present path, you shall be destroyed."

I started to get a sick feeling in my stomach. "I don't even know what you are talking about," I said exasperated. "Come to think about it, how did you know to even ask me about the incident?"

Leo shook his head slightly from side to side to indicate disappointment.

"I was hoping you would understand on your own," he said in a resigned tone of voice. "But you do not and that is the problem."

"What is the problem?" I asked sincerely not knowing what he was talking about.

"The warning," he said slowly and deliberately, "is that the direction you are heading in shall lead to disaster. Under my tutelage, you have grown more powerful. However, your capacity to control and use that power responsibly has not increased proportionately. That is in part my fault. In order to convince you to learn the way of the warrior, I have taught you techniques to increase your power. You have immersed yourself in such instruction with an almost complete disregard for anything else. To use an analogy you can identify with, you are becoming muscle bound without any practical knowledge on how to use that muscle. When a man possesses power greater than he is, it ultimately destroys him."

Leo looked me intently in the eyes. "You always did have an abundance of power. That is another reason why I chose you. A troubled weak man will live a quiet life and seldom be a harm to anyone except himself. A troubled powerful man will cause great harm to both himself and others."

Leo leaned forward in his chair again as if to emphasize his words. "There have been a number of people in your life who either looked up to you or loved you dearly. You wound up carelessly hurting and disappointing them."

A deep feeling of remorse filled my heart. I sat there silently contemplating his words immersed in a profound sadness. Sensing my state of mind, Leo changed his tone of voice to a more kind one.

"The integrity of your behavior is determined by the extent your actions are in harmony with the universe. Ultimately, how you treat others is a reflection of how you regard yourself. Until recently, you denied your feelings of hurt and sadness and so you disregarded those same feelings in other people. You considered them weak and petty. The anger, frustration, and impatience you react to others with is really how you are reacting to yourself."

I did not utter a single word in response to Leo's observations. A heavy despair weighed down upon me.

"Let us call it a day Tony," Leo said standing up and putting one hand on my shoulder. "We have covered a lot of ground."

Downcast, I left the office without comment.

Shortly after I returned home, I lied down on the living room floor and meditated as Leo had taught me. Overwhelming feelings of sadness and regret surfaced and I wept for some time. The intensity of the release of emotions was so severe; I actually felt physical pain in my chest and stomach as the toxic repressed emotions dissipated. When the feelings subsided, I felt exhausted and empty but much lighter and peaceful.

*   *   *

The Wednesday night after we met, Ann called me. I was happy to hear from her. We made plans to have dinner together the next weekend. She expressed the preference to meet me at my apartment. Apparently, she did not want her two sons to know about her activities with another man.

"Va-Va-Voom! A hot divorcee," his Joeness Mark enthusiastically reacted when I told him about Ann.

"I don't get the impression she is like that," I said honestly.

"What do you mean? She is an older divorced woman! You'll score easily!"

Mark then changed the subject to give me a Joeness news report. From electronically ease dropping on a cordless phone conversation, he found out that the sixteen-year-old girl who lived across the street from him just lost her virginity. Mark enthusiastically described every detail of the conversation between her and a girlfriend discussing the occasion. Apparently, she had an enjoyable first experience though it was messier than she imagined.

"Well, I wish I could have heard it," I said.

"You can. I have it on tape."

"I think that's illegal."

"Well, don't tell anyone! Hey, and let me know how your date goes with that divorcee. Va-Va-Voom!"

My phone rang at 7:30 p.m., Saturday night, just at the time I expected Ann to meet me at my house.

"Hi, it's Ann," a very horse and squeaky voice said. She must be sick I thought, and calling to cancel the date.

"Are you alright?"

"Yes, I'm okay. I had a cold this week but I feel better than I sound," she said with a snuffled voice.

"Where are you?"

"I'm downstairs."

"Downstairs?"

"Yes. I'm on a cell phone."

I looked out the window and sure enough, she was there.

"I'll come down and get you," I said hanging up the telephone.

My memory of what she looked like was hazy but I was pleasantly surprised when I opened the door. She was more attractive than I recalled. "Thank you God," I said to myself.

"Would you like to see my apartment?" I asked. She smiled and nodded her head yes.

We walked up the flight of stairs and when we got to my door I requested, as I did with everyone, that she remove her shoes before entering. "Anything else is optional," I joked. She grinned with a look of feigned shock.

After I gave Ann the ten-second tour of my place, I took her to an Italian restaurant. The conversation at dinner was warm and friendly. Unlike many other first dates, I felt very at ease with her and I think she felt the same. When I looked into her eyes, I just knew that somehow she was very special. I didn't care whether or not we would wind up in bed in the near future; I just wanted to see her again. After all, the more a man genuinely likes a woman, the less anxious he will be to get into her pants. He will enjoy her company for other reasons. After that first wonderful night, Ann and I started to date regularly.

Early March arrived. The weather was unusually mild for that time of year. On one sunny and warm Sunday, Ann and I took a drive to an old Boy Scout camp adjacent to a state park on the eastern north shore of Long Island. I used to go to that camp when I was a young man in the Boy Scouts. The camp was, for the most part, empty until the warmer weather arrived in the summer.

I took Ann there with me because the area is very scenic. A long dirt road travels through thick woods, a pond that serves as a bird sanctuary, and ends at a sandy beach on the Long Island Sound. Since the trees were still bare of leaves, Ann and I enjoyed a clear view of the surrounding area for some distance.

We engaged in small talk as we enjoyed the natural scenery while walking on the dirt road. Then, for a while, we walked side by side in silence. I looked over at her and noticed that she seemed a little sad.

"Are you all right?" I asked wondering what was wrong.

"Yes," she answered quietly.

"You seem a little upset."

"It's just that," she paused, "It's just that I never did this with my husband."

"You mean you never took a nice walk with him in a park or on a beach?"

"No," she said with a sigh.

"Never?" I asked again surprised. "How long were you married to him?"

"Fifteen years."

"Fifteen years! And he never even took a walk with you! What was he doing?"

"He was always working long hours to build up his business," she started to explain. "When he was home all he wanted to do was watch sports. He didn't pay much attention to me."

A sad expression painted itself on Ann's face. I felt sorry for her. During the ensuing conversation, I found out that while Ann was married she knew her husband was having an affair with a female business associate. She never confronted her husband about it though and lived with the knowledge in silence for years. When I asked Ann why she did that, she replied it was an effort to hold on to her marriage and family. Upon returning home from an annual vacation in the Bahamas with her two boys, her husband announced that she should get a lawyer because he intended to divorce her.

"Am I wrong for being upset?" she asked.

"No," I answered. "You have a right to be upset. Why did you stay with him for so long?"

"I held on to hope and tried to keep the marriage together for my boys."

I stopped asking questions about her marriage because the subject obviously depressed Ann. She gave me a weak smile. I smiled back and took her hand in mine as we continued our walk together.

"It's a lovely day, isn't it?" I said to redirect her attention.

"Yes, it is," she replied. After a moment she said, "Thank you for listening."

"Your welcome." I kissed her on the cheek affectionately.

We walked along the side of the marsh serving as a bird sanctuary and watched the activities of a variety of waterfowl including cute little multi-colored ducks and big noisy geese. Following the path of the road we arrived at the beach and sat down atop a large sand dune that gave us a marvelous view of the blue ocean and sandy shoreline. The conversation was light and pleasant generally including comments on the scenery. We then walked along the beach and looked up at some houses built on high cliffs overlooking the Long Island Sound. The occupants of those houses must have a spectacular view.

"If we ever live together, we should get a house like that," Ann said lightly with a smile.

"Planning ahead already?" I joked.

After satiating ourselves with the natural beauty of the ocean and beach, Ann and I reversed our course and headed back to the dirt road that would eventually lead us out of the campgrounds to the parking lot about a mile away. The road stretched out straight in front of us for about fifty yards and then dipped down before a curve. Our pleasant stroll was abruptly interrupted by two loudly barking dogs that appeared over the crest in the road just after the curve. The dogs, running at full speed, were heading straight for us.

I became alarmed instantly. From past experience, I knew that there were some wild dogs in the area but they were mangy looking and usually avoided contact with humans. These two dogs appeared well groomed, big, muscular, and sleek. Yet, they had no dog tags or collars. No human being was in sight that I could assume was the owner.

The dogs continued to race menacingly in our direction quickly closing the distance between us. Had I been alone, I would have scurried up the nearest climbable tree out of harms way. Unfortunately, I was not alone. Ann was with me and she was not nearly athletic enough to jump up a tree with me.

"Move over there!" I shouted to a nervous Ann.

The ground on either side of the road was a foot and a half higher than the road itself. I directed Ann toward high ground about seven yards away interlaced with low, thick, thorny bushes. It was my hope that the thorns would discourage the dogs from pursuing us.

I followed Ann but walked backwards still facing the dogs that were barking wildly and still running at full trot. I pulled out a small pocketknife I had in my jeans and flipped opened the three-inch blade. With my other hand, I picked up off the ground a long but thin tree branch. It was the best thing that I could find to help defend myself in the few seconds I had before the two dogs were upon us.

"Keeping moving back," I yelled to Ann. She nervously made her way through the thick thorny bushes until her back was up against a large tree. The protruding thorns cut into her hands drawing thin lines of blood.

The dogs, which had been running side by side, split up. One continued directly toward me while the other moved off to our far left as if to flank us from behind. My nervousness increased. The dogs acted intelligent and organized.

The closest dog stopped about five feet in front of me. It barked menacingly and pulled its gums back to display sharp teeth. The dog appeared even larger close up than it first did when I saw it approaching. While I stared it down, I tried to keep the other dog in my peripheral vision. Ann grabbed me around the waist from behind obviously scared.

"Keep your hands off of me! I need to be able to move!" I shouted while forcibly pulling off one of her arms wrapped around my midsection.

She let go and started to cry.

As I prepared myself for an anticipated assault, it occurred to me that I had never before been in a situation where I had to fight for my very life. One dog would not have been too bad. I might be wounded, but I could easily kill it armed with a knife. However, two dogs were another story especially if they both went for the throat. I resolved to stand my ground and fight the dogs to the death if necessary. I did not concern myself with my fate, but summoned all my strength to protect Ann at any cost to my personal well being.

The well-groomed canine in front of me advanced two feet continuing to bark and snarl. Peering into its eyes with the most ferocious look I was capable of, I brandished my knife and growled back like a wild jungle cat in an effort to intimidate. I quickly planned that if the dog went for my leg, I would drive the knife into its eye socket. If it went for my upper body, I would pierce its throat and quickly spin around in case its partner tried to take me from behind or attack Ann.

Suddenly, both dogs hastily retreated by running back in the direction they had originally come from. Scanning the area they headed to, I noticed a middle aged woman walking along a small path away from us to our left. Relieved, I assumed she was the owner and quickly became angry. It was impossible for the woman to not have noticed Ann and I in the middle of the thorn bushes being hounded by her dogs. However, she did not so much as even look at us let alone offer an apology. The two beasts obediently followed her down the path and were soon out of sight.

"Lady, you don't know how close you came to losing your pets," I said to myself out loud. "Are you all right Ann?" I asked. She nodded her head in the affirmative though she appeared shaken by the experience.

When we finally got back to the parking lot, I pulled out a first aid kit I always keep in the trunk of my car. With Ann seated on the rear bumper, I took her hands one at a time and carefully cleaned the dirt and dried blood off with an antiseptic pad. Using a number of various sized adhesive bandages, I creatively covered the long scratches with crisscrossing patterns.

"There! As good as new," I announced with a grin.

"Thank you," she smiled softly looking into my eyes.

Something in her gaze touched my heart like a warm fire on a cold winter's day. I gently ran my fingers down the side of her face in admiration of her beauty. Staring deep into the well of her eyes, I sensed an incredible kindness and love I never experienced before. I leaned forward and lightly kissed her on the lips before we started our journey home.

*   *   *

"What did the dogs look like?" Leo asked when I told him about the incident.

"All I really remember is that they were huge," I answered.

"What color were the dogs?"

I thought about it for a moment and then answered, "Jet black. And they appeared well groomed."

"Ah," Leo said as if he were trying to figure something out. "The woman, what was the color of her hair?"

"Jet black," I said increasingly curious about what Leo was thinking. "You are starting to make me nervous again," I remarked. "Why are you so interested in these details?"

Leo looked at me as if he had formulated a conclusion. "You were scouted again."

"What? By who?"

"Undoubtedly by the same female who scouted you that time you were riding your bike."

"But why? Why would she try to scare me like that?"

"It was a test," Leo said nonchalantly as if the whole affair was very ordinary.

"I do not understand this whole so called scout business," I commented feeling annoyed. "What is the purpose? Why is this person bothering me?"

"As I have told you before, she probably crossed your path in an everyday setting. Perhaps you were grocery shopping for instance and she noticed you. She must have sensed you were different and decided to observe you."

"Different in what way?"

Leo sighed with a hint of trying to find patience. "Your energy field. You should know that by now."

"How would she be able to sense that?"

"The woman must be a sorceress to some degree. I believe you could use the word witch to describe her though that is not entirely accurate."

"A witch?" I said in disbelief.

"Something like that," Leo calmly replied.

"Are you kidding me? What does she want?"

"It is rather simple. The first time she encountered you, she must have sensed your rapidly expanding personal energy. She then started to scout you." Leo paused for a moment with a look of concern on his face. "I cautioned you in the past that your power was growing faster than your ability to manage it. She is stalking you looking for the right moment to make contact."

"Make contact for what?"

"I am not sure. She may have a personal interest. Or perhaps, she intends to tempt you to join her circle."

I sat there confused and disbelieving. The whole matter was beyond my immediate comprehension.

"I would not be too concerned," Leo said as if reading my mind. "She will think twice about ever getting close to you again!"

"Why is that?"

Leo started to smile. "At the risk of boosting your ego, you handled the situation masterfully!"

"Really," I said excitedly wanting to hear more. "How did I do that?"

"Your military background serves you well! Instinctively, you maintained your composure, occupied the most advantageous defensive position on thorny high ground with your back protected by a tree, and," Leo started to break out laughing, "you produced a weapon! And that was not even the best of all!"

"What! What was the best of all?" I asked like a young kid excited that he hit a home run during a little league game and wanted to hear from his father a recount of the event.

"You growled back at the dogs!" Leo slapped his thigh and roared with laughter. "I can imagine the face on the woman when she witnessed that!"

I laughed along with Leo. "That was a nice touch, huh?"

"Yes," Leo said, "She has now twice witnessed you are capable of great violence. She will be reluctant to approach you unless she feels you can be controlled."

"You are really crazy for believing all this nonsense," I said pointing to Leo, the two of us laughing at the top of our lungs.

After the session was over and I exited the office, I noticed the same young woman in the waiting area who witnessed me leaving a few months before when I was really angry with Leo. She looked at me wondering what all the laughing was about. I returned her inquisitive stare and said with a smile, "It's a guy thing."

CHAPTER 8

▼

SETBACKS

*"A true test of a man is not how many times he
gets knocked down, but how many times he gets back up."
from 'How I Got Lucky and Bumped Into God'—the author*

New baby buds sprouted from trees and flowers bloomed with bright colors as spring began to unfold. The weather turned from cold and gray to more sunny and mild. Thanks to Leo's help, my general state of mind reflected the change in seasons. Little day-to-day annoyances bothered me less. I tended to think of the bright side of things instead of the negative. I was kinder, more patient, and optimistic. This is not to say my mental disposition was entirely rosy, but it was far better than it had been in a long time.

It came as a surprise when Leo cautioned me about my new perspective.

"You will tend to view the world with rose colored glasses for a time. For a long while, you have focused your attention on the negative. Now that your eyes and heart have opened to the immense beauty of the universe, your mental scales have tipped the other way. You now tend to ignore the unpleasant and focus your attention on the positive. Though this state of mind is infinitely more enjoyable, it is not balanced. Remember that a warrior strives to reflect the balance of the universe. The universe is neither good nor evil. It is both, or more accurately, it is neutral.

"In time, your mental scales will shift back to balance and you will be aware of all aspects of the universe with a sense of detachment."

"I am not sure I understand," I said shaking my head to indicate lack of comprehension.

"Like much else I tutor you on, you will come to understanding after you experience it rather than just hearing it."

Leo paused then changed the subject abruptly by asking me about Ann.

"What is it you like about her? On the surface, it seems very unusual for a young handsome playboy like yourself to be interested in a mother of two."

His comment made me smile.

"She is very kind and warmhearted," I answered. "And I admire her sense of sacrifice of raising her children without a father in the household."

"Interesting," Leo said thoughtfully.

"What do you mean by that?"

"She possesses in abundance those very qualities you have so sorely lacked in the past. Historically, you have been selfish and impatient. You are attracted to Ann, at least to some degree, because subconsciously you hope to complete what you are lacking in personality with her."

"Do you mean we are like two pieces of a puzzle?"

"An excellent analogy! You both lack qualities the other has. Subconsciously, the two of you experience a sense of completion when you are together."

I did not fully understand the psychological factors concerning my relationship with Ann. Nor did I really care to. All I knew is that I felt more at peace with her than any other person I have ever known. She was like an oasis in the middle of the desert, a sanctuary in an otherwise cruel world.

Despite my feelings of affection toward Ann, I felt a growing anxiety with the realization that we had no future together. I wanted to have children; she did not want to have any more. Her sons were her priority in life and rightly so, but I wanted to feel I was first in a relationship.

Because there were many weekends I did not get to see Ann when she was busy with her children, I casually dated other women. However, no one else really interested me. What troubled me the most about the situation was the knowledge that if I seriously pursued a relationship with another woman, I would need to stop seeing Ann.

The conflicting feelings of love I had for her and the realization that we had no future caused me great distress. Still, every time I saw Ann or just heard her voice on the phone, my heart would melt.

*   *   *

Early one Saturday morning, I headed to the mall to do some spring clothes shopping. I casually made my way down the long corridors of smaller shops to one of the larger department stores. While fingering through some shirts on a rack, I became aware of a sensation. It almost felt like someone touched me lightly on the back of my head. For some reason, I thought it wise to turn around slowly.

In relative close proximity were three people. Two of them were an older couple shopping together. The third was a teenage girl. She looked about fourteen or fifteen years old and had short jet-black hair. Modestly dressed in bell-bottom jeans and a light colored button down shirt, she slowly browsed by some aisle displays. When I glanced at the old couple, I experienced no internal sensations. However, when I looked at the girl, I experienced a strange sensation of being both frightened and excited at the same time. Two thoughts spontaneously occurred to me. One, there is something different about this girl. And two, she is following me.

To test my intuitive feelings, I walked out of the department store into the main mall area and began to trace a slow random pattern through a number of shops. I could sense she was following me without even having to turn around to visually confirm. Occasionally, I glanced around to ascertain her position. There is no question about it I thought. She is trailing me.

Having attained that knowledge, the question became what to do now. I remembered how Leo taught me to 'disappear'. That is, he demonstrated a technique to allow me to go unnoticed by other people even if I was in close proximity to them. I thought briefly of trying it to lose her. However, I decided to turn the tables instead and become the hunter rather than the hunted.

At the other end of the mall was another large department store. I made my way in there and went down one floor using the elevator to a large women's clothes area populated by dozens of circular and rectangle clothes racks. It was still relatively early in the day so the floor was just about deserted. At a steady slow pace, I went over to one corner of the floor with no people around. I purposely stopped and milled around to give the girl time to close in. I could sense she was near by.

The clothes rack next to me stood about as high as my upper chest. Quickly, I ducked down below it out of sight and ran hunched over commando style in a clockwise wide circle toward the young girl's last position. I assumed she would head to the spot she last saw me. Using the technique to 'disappear', I hurriedly completed the circle to come up behind her. My calculation turned out to be correct. Unnoticed, I positioned myself directly behind the girl who was now standing in the area I vacated.

"Were you looking for me?" I asked.

Startled, she turned around quickly.

"Oh, you scared me," she said with her hand on her chest as if trying to catch her breath. "I didn't notice you! No, no, I wasn't looking for anyone." She flashed a nervous smile.

"You have been following me. What is it you want?" I asked in a serious tone of voice.

"No, no I wasn't following you. I wasn't following anybody," she replied defensively.

"You are lying," I said with a deadpan face.

"Look, I don't know who you are and I'm sorry but I wasn't following you." She acted annoyed and angry but I knew it was a pretense.

The teenage girl turned from me as if to walk away. With my left hand, I grasped the back of her shirt's collar. I hooked my right leg in front of her feet and forcibly pushed her forward so that she fell face down on the floor.

"What are you doing?" she protested.

Before she could say anything else, I pinned her down by placing my right knee in the middle of her back and pressing down with my full weight. I kept my lower body angled away from her center to prevent any counterattacks directed to the groin area.

"What are you doing!" she repeated with a more desperate tone.

Moving quickly with my right hand, I grabbed her right arm and twisted it behind her back. With my other hand, I ran my fingers through her short black hair to get a good grip and sharply yanked her head back.

"I don't like being followed and I don't like being lied to. Who are you and want do you want?"

"I don't know what you are talking about!"

In order to encourage a more honest answer, I twisted her arm further against its natural position to inflict a significant amount of pain.

"Ow! Please! I don't know what you want! Please leave me alone!"

I came to the curious realization that she purposely did not cry out loudly as if to avoid attracting attention.

Over her left shoulder, she carried a small black pocketbook. It looked like a tiny knapsack, barely big enough to hold my wallet. I picked it up, unclasped it, and emptied the contents on the floor.

"What are you doing?" she gasped.

Some cash, a little change, a small pink comb, one tube of black lip-stick, a hair clip, and cigarette lighter were the only things I found from the pocketbook.

"Who are you?" I asked her. "What's your name?"

"My name is Melissa! Now please let me go!"

I twisted her arm some more.

"Owwww! F—k! What are you doing to me?"

"You are lying," I said calmly.

I let go of her hair, reached around her neck, and undid the top two buttons of her shirt. I then pulled down the shirt's collar to expose the back of her neck and top of her shoulders to search for tattoos. Leo informed me that modern witches often sported tattoos symbolic of their craft. I didn't find any.

"Any place else I should look?" I asked.

She did not respond but continued to struggle vainly against being held down.

I pulled out her shirt at the lower back and tugged her jeans down to look for tattoos in the area just above her buttocks. There were no tattoos there either. I grabbed her hair again.

"Let me go!"

"What is your real name?" I asked.

She did not respond so I applied more pressure to the arm twisted behind her back. In pain, she slapped the floor with the palm of her free hand but she did not verbally protest. I noticed a neckband and reached around with my hand that had been holding her head by the hair to take a look. Hanging from the black neckband was a medallion with the figure of a five-pointed star.

"What is this?" I asked though I already knew the answer.

She did not reply.

I twisted the band about my hand to tighten it around her neck.

"Please stop!"

"We have ways of making you talk," I said in a German accent while tightening the band further around her neck.

Her face began to turn red.

"Please! Please don't hurt me." To my surprise, she started to cry. Her struggling body turned limp beneath me as if she had given up trying to free herself.

"Please don't hurt me," she repeated in a whisper with tears starting to fall from her eyes.

My feelings of anger and aggression quickly dissipated. I actually began to feel sorry for her. It occurred to me that she might be simply using another tactic against me. But I loosened my hold on both the neckband and her arm anyway. I lightened the weight of my knee on her back as well.

"Please don't hurt me," she repeated in a low voice.

I let go of her completely and then looked up to find three security guards staring at me. I had not even noticed them beforehand. They must have seen what was happening on surveillance cameras. Two of the guards were young men. The third was an older fellow with gray hair.

"Step away from her," the older guard commanded with a tentative tone to his voice. One of the younger guards looked nervous, the other had a tough guy look on his face.

I stood up. With the realization that I had just legally committed assault, I hastily reasoned that my best course of action was to run as fast as possible out of the department store to the parking lot and hope to lose them.

"Its okay. Its okay," the young girl said as she rose from the floor before I began my attempted escape. "Its okay. He's my boyfriend."

The three security guards and I looked at her as if she was crazy. She bent over and started to gather up the items I spilled out of the pocketbook.

"Really, its okay," she said to the three guards. "My name is Renee and this is my boyfriend Tony." Renee, or whatever her real name was, finished putting the stuff back in her bag and stood next to me facing the other men. "We got a little out of hand. I'm really sorry."

"Yes," I added getting into the act, "We're sorry if we caused you alarm."

The guards did not say anything but looked at us skeptically. In addition to the strange situation, I also looked twice as old as the girl. I gestured toward Renee and shrugged my shoulders to the guards.

"Sometimes she likes it rough," I explained. I then turned to Renee with a smile. "See? You didn't have the handcuffs in your bag after all."

The guards looked dumbfounded.

"Let's go Tony," she said. "I think we caused enough excitement for one day."

Renee took me by the arm and we turned around to walk away. We didn't look back but just made our way through the floor, up the escalator to the next level, then out to the parking lot. We walked at a moderate pace arm in arm. Curiously, I felt myself getting slightly aroused having her so close to me.

"Renee is your real name?" I asked.

"Yes it is," she said in a whisper.

We remained silent until out of sight from anyone that may be watching us from inside the store. I was about to ask her questions when she unhooked her arm from mine and ran off disappearing into the maze of the multi-level parking lot. The thought of chasing her down occurred to me. But I let both the thought and her go. I didn't need one of those sixty-year-old security officers patrolling the mall parking lot in a little scooter noticing me chasing a fourteen-year-old girl. It would be hard to explain.

"What do you think?" I asked Leo after telling him the story.

Leo sat pensively in his chair, chin in hand, considering his answer. "She will return to you some time in the future."

"I feel the same," I added.

"You do realize that the old woman you noticed while bike riding, the woman with the dogs in the camp grounds, and this young girl are all the same person?"

"That is impossible! Their ages differ widely."

"They are the same person," Leo repeated confidently.

"How can that be?" I asked with extreme skepticism.

"She simply disguised herself. After all, in two of the three encounters you only saw her from a distance."

"I find that difficult to accept. How could I mistake a young teenager for an old or middle aged woman?"

"She is not a teenager."

"How could you say that Leo? The last time I saw her close up. She has both the face and body of a young teenage girl."

"I'm sure she did," Leo said with a grin. "But she purposely altered her appearance to be that way."

I looked at Leo as if he had two heads and three eyes. "What are you talking about? How in the world could she so dramatically change her appearance?"

Leo sighed in a way that implied he knew the answer but did not want to share it.

"That does not matter. A warrior resists becoming obsessed with the attraction of his newfound awareness and abilities. For example, some people experience profound visions during intense meditation or discover that they can read minds. These are just flowery traps along the path of a warrior. Do not let them distract and pull you off your path."

"So what is the purpose?" I asked.

Leo looked as if he were trying to find patience.

"I have already told you. A warrior strives to live in harmony with the universe. Part of this is to take responsibility for your life. The meditation, Tai Chi, and breathing exercises are all designed to quiet your noisy consciousness and reconnect you through awareness to the spirit inside of you and outside of you. This reconnection leads to a discovery of innate abilities such as an advanced intuition.

"Some people succumb to the allure of these abilities. They become captivated by them and lose sight of the ultimate goal of being at peace with oneself and in harmony with the universe. The woman pursuing you is most likely one of those people who have lost sight."

"How should I deal with her?"

"I leave her to your own discretion," Leo said with a disarming smile. "Now, let us turn our attention to far more practical matters. You are troubled about something. Do you wish to talk about it?"

Leo's uncanny sense of my state of mind always amazed me.

"Its Ann," I replied with downcast eyes. "I have grown very fond of her. In fact, I am in love with her." Leo raised his eyebrows but did not interrupt. "I have never before felt so comfortable and at peace as when I am with her. I have never gotten along with any woman as well as I do with Ann. Yet, I feel torn because I can't envision a future together. I would like to have my own children. However, she is finished with child bearing. I would like to have a closer relationship with her. But most of her time is dedicated to her sons. And, well," I paused, "romantically speaking we are more friends than lovers if you know what I mean."

"You are not getting time in the sack with her," Leo stated with a nod and smile.

"Thank you for your sensitivity." I commented sarcastically.

"What is it you want in a relationship?"

"Well, I would like to eventually marry again and start my own family."

"Can you have that with Ann?"

"Well, not really," I sighed. "Legally, she is still married and she doesn't want to have any more children."

"So, you need to find someone else?"

"Therein lies the dilemma. I have strong feelings of affection for her and yet I am forced to end our relationship if I want to pursue my goals of marriage and a family."

Leo listened silently but did not offer any comment.

"Should I stop seeing her?" I asked Leo.

"That it is not for me to say. My appropriate role as a therapist and mentor is to advise you how to come to a decision, not to state what decision I think you should make."

"Okay. How should I make a decision?"

Leo rose from the chair he was sitting in, stepped over towards me, and lightly touched my heart with his index finger.

"Hey, that's what Tara told me," I said as Leo sat back down.

"Make your decision, Tony, not from fear or anger or selfishness, but from the heart. The heart will tell you." Leo pointed to his ear. "You just have to listen."

"Like I said to Tara, that all sounds good but it seems to me to be more of a cliché than have any real practical meaning."

"When you are fully evolved as a warrior, all your decisions will be from the heart. When you meditate, meditate from the heart. When you act, act from the heart. Let your heart be your guide and let Death be your advisor."

"Death be my advisor?"

"Yes, you will recall that you have already received instruction on that subject. When you get caught up in pettiness and self-pity, think of your death to put things back in perspective."

I left Leo's office reflecting on our conversation. On an intellectual level, I had some idea of what Leo was saying. However, on a deeper level, I was unclear on how to apply this philosophy.

At home, I sat quietly at my desk looking out the window wondering what I should do about Ann. Though I felt she was the most wonderful person I ever met, I was dissatisfied with the relationship and knew there was little hope for any improvement in the situation. To complicate matters, since our relationship was mostly platonic, I also found myself on the look out for other potential romantic partners.

After a long period of internal deliberation, I came to the decision to stop seeing her. The very thought made me feel sick to my stomach but I rationalized it was the best thing to do. That would give me the freedom of conscience to pursue other relationships with long term potential.

After making the mental decision to break up with Ann, a dark shroud fell upon my persona. I began feeling agitated and became short-tempered. The thought of telling Ann that it would be best if we stopped seeing each other made me ill as if someone had poisoned me.

I sought the counsel of his high Joeness, Mark. Despite the fact that he was younger than I, Mark was wise in the ways of male and female relationships.

"Yeah, she's too old for you anyway. You should be going out with younger girls and having some fun," his Joeness advised over the telephone.

"I suppose you are right," I said with a resigning sigh.

"Hey," Mark said changing the subject, "Rob is in the lead this month."

"Really? What's the running score?" I asked.

The running score was the equivalent of a Joeness fantasy baseball league. Each Joe would report the physical activities on his latest date. A score was then tabulated as follows:

> French kissing—First Base
> Feeling a private body part without overt permission—Stealing Second
> Feeling a private body part through clothes—Second Base
> Feeling a private body part under clothing—On the way to Third Base
> Oral gratification—Third Base
> Penetration of any kind—Home Run

The tabulation was cumulative and runs were scored for each pass at home plate. The winner of the most recent month was fellow Joe, Rob, who not only hit a home run with a promiscuous twenty-something female but also managed to cross the plate with her younger sister on the same night. Apparently, their parents were away from home last weekend. In addition to winning the month of April, this also put Rob in serious contention for Joeness of the Year. Such frivolous matters provided a temporary, but welcome, distraction from my personal problems.

*   *   *

"Hey Joeness," Mark shouted in a good-natured way to get my attention. I spun around my desk chair at work to face him.
"Hey Mark! What's up?"
"I got a good one!"
A 'good one' refers to a stock with a perceived high probability of significant appreciation. Mark and I often talked about money and stocks. He was fond of following different companies in the computer industry.

Mark began to tell me about one particular company he followed. It was doing well, the stock was going up, and they were going to announce earnings in two weeks. Mark was convinced that the earnings were going to come out better than expected and anticipated that the stock would jump up on the news. It was a Joeness Hot Tip for the stock market.

"I'm telling you," Mark said, "We can make a lot of money on this one!"

After being burned in the stock market so many times before, I was naturally cautious. However, over the next few days, I looked up all the news and financial information I could find on the company. The collective evidence supported Mark's view and the stock was still rising. I began to think to myself that maybe this would be an opportunity for me to make back all the money I had lost. I wound up investing thirty grand, most of my life savings. Mark invested five thousand dollars, which is about all he had at the time too.

The next day, the stock we purchased jumped up another half point. Doing the math, I made over six hundred dollars in one day. Mark and I felt like two financial geniuses and began to fondly look forward to the earnings announcement two weeks away.

"Joeness, what did I tell you? This stock is going to shoot way up," Mark enthusiastically proclaimed.

We followed the movement of the stock's price continuously during the week from our computers. The day before the earnings were announced, the stock had risen a full five points from the time we bought it. That meant I was ahead by almost seven thousand dollars in less than two weeks. Seven thousand dollars in two weeks! If I could make that much money consistently in the stock market, I would be able to quit my job!

"Hey Mark, you nailed this one right on the head," I said giving him a high five.

"Wait until tomorrow. It will probably go up another ten points!"

Hitting the buttons on my hand-held calculator, I figured out how much money that would come to. My plan was to let the stock spurt up and then bail out for a quick kill. Mark intended to hold on to it longer anticipating an extended trend up. Of course, all this was based on the assumption that their earnings would be good. If the earnings came out bad, I was going to sell as quickly as possible and get the heck out.

The earnings were announced after market trading hours on a Monday. Mark and I huddled in front of a computer screen watching for the posting of the financial information. We were both anxious and stared at the screen with a sense of Joeness solidarity.

"I hope you are right, Mark." My eyes began to feel the strain of staring at the screen.

"Joeness, you've got to be a believer."

A few moments longer and we discovered the earnings being posted to the electronic financial news. I felt an adrenaline rush as the news article headline appeared.

"Mark! Mark! You are a genius!" I excitedly shook him by the shoulders while he remained seated in the office chair. He seemed to be in a mild state of pleasant shock.

"Yes!" he shouted finally reacting.

The earnings were indeed significantly better than those forecasted.

Because the announcement came after market trading hours, Mark and I would have to wait to the next morning to find out just how much the stock would go up on the news. We were ecstatic and decided to celebrate our good fortune by going out to a steak house for dinner and a few beers.

"Dinner is on me," I offered.

"No, no. I got it," he insisted. We both laughed.

Our dinner conversation revolved around what we would do with our windfall. I was thinking of using the money towards the purchase of a new car. Mark considered buying a video camera so that he could secretly record sexual encounters in his bedroom. He mulled over where the best place would be to hide the camera.

The next morning I listened to the financial news on the radio before leaving for work. I heard the news report state that the stock we owned would be one of the hot stocks to watch during the day because of the positive earnings announcement. I smiled with glee and arrived at my job in a giddy mood.

"Mark! You ready for the big day?" I asked when I saw him at work.

"Hey, hey! We got it made," he replied with a big grin.

"Listen, you can watch the stock more often than I can with my work. If you see it go up by ten points or more, let me know because I'll probably sell it."

"No problem! I'm going to hold on because I think this company is going to keep doing well but I'll let you know what happens this morning."

As the early morning progressed, I went about my business with a sense of cocky confidence. The particular work Mark did enabled him to check the market prices more often than I could. I knew he would let me know in a hurry if anything big happened.

Shortly after the stock market opened, my desk phone rang. Mark frantically relayed the news.

"Joeness! Horrible news! The stock is down ten points!"

"What! How can that be?" I shouted so loud that people in surrounding cubicles looked over to see what the commotion was about. "Are you sure the stock is not up ten points?"

"Joeness! Joeness!" he replied with despair, "I checked three times!"

"That can't be! It must be a mistake!" Quickly, I pulled up stock quotes on my computer. It displayed that the stock was trading down eleven and a half points. "Mark, I am going to call my broker to confirm. I'll talk to you later!" I hung up and hurriedly called my brokerage firm. The representative confirmed that the stock was heading down and fast. "How can that be?" I asked not really expecting an answer.

"There is an old saying on Wall Street," the broker told me. "Buy the rumor and sell the news."

I have heard the same adage before but never personally experienced such a dramatic example to my financial detriment.

"Mark, Mark. We are doomed. It is true," I said over the office telephone.

"Depression!" he responded.

"I cannot believe this!"

"Joeness, just hold on. It is a good company. The stock will go back up eventually."

I was not encouraged by his latest prediction.

"Depression," I muttered in despair.

The stock ended the day down nine and a fraction, which was a thirty percent loss. The next day, it dropped another two points. I was now in the red over nine thousand dollars. My mood quickly turned to the extreme opposite of the enthusiasm I experienced when the price was rising.

Over the next few days the stock bounced up a little, then went back down. Feelings of disgust and frustration permeated my being. People at work sensed my rotten mood and avoided me when possible except for Mark who shared my grief.

Why was it that every time I tried to make money I wound up losing my shirt? I asked myself that question half-wondering if there was some kind of universal conspiracy plotting against me.

*   *   *

I involuntarily sighed as I mentally prepared myself for the unpleasant task of speaking to Ann about our future, or more accurately, our lack of a future together. Upon entering her home, I tried to hide feelings of anxiety and sadness. Ann's fat basset hound hurriedly wobbled over and greeted me with generous licks of affection on my face as I knelt down to pet him.

"He loves you more than he loves me," Ann joked.

"Yeah, but you kiss better," I replied with a smile.

Walking around the dog, Ann came over and kissed me. I hugged her tightly not wanting to let go. In the back of my mind, I wondered if it would be the last time that I would ever hold her.

After a little while, I asked Ann if I could talk to her about something that was bothering me. My tone of voice betrayed the fact that the subject matter was not a pleasant one.

"Sure," she said tentatively as we both sat down together on a couch. Her children were with their father that evening. So, Ann and I were able to speak without interruptions.

I took a silent deep breath and began to tell her how I felt.

In a slow apologetic tone of voice, I explained to her my desire to have my own children and to eventually remarry. I stated that, though I was very fond of her, I did not see a future together since her goals in life differed significantly from mine.

As the implications of my statements sunk in, Ann gradually pulled away from me. The expression on her face turned downcast. Her eyes became red and began to fill with tears. As if she had been afflicted by some black magic, she appeared to age twenty years right in front of my eyes. Witnessing the devastating affects that my words had on her made me feel like a knife had cut itself deeply in my heart.

"I'm sorry," I said.

How empty such words must be to her.

"How could you do this to me?" she asked in a low voice trying to hold back swelling tears. Her futile effort to repress her emotions failed and she started to cry.

"Please just leave," she asked no longer looking at me.

I gazed at her for a few seconds, my heart sinking further with each passing moment.

"Okay, I understand. I'll go."

I stood up to leave. The basset hound trotted into the room. The hound looked at Ann and then at me. Its head tilted quizzically to one side as if to ask what was going on.

"Bye, buddy," I said to the dog with a wave of my hand.

Usually, he would walk me to the door when I left the house. This time he stayed in the room with Ann. She remained seated on the couch with her head down and hands clutched tightly together by the fingers. Quietly, I let myself out and closed the door behind me.

It was a short drive home. Only five minutes. The dark night and clear sky provided a majestic view of the stars. However, the beauty above did not compensate for the ugliness within me. I parked in front of my house, disengaged the ignition, and sat in the car. I put my head down until it rested on the steering wheel and started to cry.

*   *   *

"Depression," Mark said when I told him about the conversation I had with Ann. "You need to meet a hot girl," he concluded.

My well meaning fellow Joeness suggested that meeting an attractive young woman who was, shall we say, eager to satisfy a man's primal needs would improve my disposition. However, I was not in any frame of mind to pursue an encounter for gratification sake alone.

Only a day had passed but I already missed Ann.

The combination of losing money in the stock market and breaking up with Ann left me depressed and with little energy. I called Leo and left a message on his voice mail canceling our upcoming session. I just didn't feel like talking to anybody.

Friday of that week came. I did not have or desire to make any plans for the weekend.

"Dude, why don't you come over to my house Friday night? We'll hang out," Mark suggested.

"Sure, why not?"

Taking advantage of Mark's invitation, I met him at his house that night. Using his computer, we first entertained ourselves playing a video hockey game. Mark instructed me in use of the controls for the game. He conveniently taught me only how to pass the puck between players, not to shoot the puck. I thought he taught me how to shoot. But every time I tried the puck passed to another player. He beat me 5-0.

"Joeness, are you going to teach me how to shoot the #$%@ puck?" I asked.

We ordered pizza and easily polished off an entire pie while playing a video karate game. It was one of those games where you can select from a number of cartoon-like characters. The animated opponents face off to do combat using a variety of martial art moves generated from operating the game controls.

Wham!

"Joeness, I knocked you out," Mark jubilantly announced.

"Do you have any other games I might actually have a chance at winning?"

"Hey! Why don't we go cruising for hot girls instead?"

I considered the suggestion with a shrug of my shoulders. "Sure. What the heck?"

It was around one o'clock in the morning on a sultry May night. We hopped into Mark's jeep and headed to a boulevard in Queens near where Mark lived. The boulevard was a popular place on weekends for young people in their late teens and early twenties to cruise.

Mark demonstrated an expertise at identifying females' cars. He was also adept at calculating just what lane and position to be in to wind up side by side with a desired car when stopping at a red light.

"Wahoo! Hot girls on the left!" Mark alerted.

Sure enough, there were five young females in the car to our left. They looked like high school girls.

"Hey there," Mark yelled smiling at them through the open window.

"Hiii," they giggled in unison.

"Where are you going?" Mark asked.

"Nowhere. Where are you going?"

"I'm going wherever you are going!"

The girls giggled again and sped off when the traffic light turned green. Mark followed their car for a while doing his best to get along side despite the other traffic.

"Joeness, did you see that? Those girls are cute!"

"Mark," I observed with a smile, "Those girls looked no older than sixteen!"

"Dude, that's the best age!"

I shook my head in amusement.

We approached a fast food franchise on the boulevard. Numerous cars and young people filled its small parking lot.

"Hot girl alert!" Mark announced.

He veered the jeep into the parking lot and into one of the few empty spots. We both combed our hair back and exited the jeep. To be sociable, we entered the franchise and purchased a couple of large sodas before mingling with the group of young people in the parking lot. Looking around me, I calculated that I was about ten years older than everyone else was. Thank heaven I look younger than my age.

"Hi Mark," a cute female voice said.

"Hey Tracey! How are you?"

Mark walked over to the girl with me in tow.

"I'm fine," Tracey smiled. She was a young good-looking brunette with a friendly smile.

"This is my friend Tony," Mark said gesturing toward me.

We exchanged greetings.

"This is my girlfriend Trish," Tracey introduced.

Mark elbowed me and winked slyly. Trish was a petite blonde graced with a pleasantly oversized chest for her stature.

"I remember you, Trish, from Rob's birthday party," Mark said.

"Yeah! Hi," she smiled widely.

A conversation ensued but my contribution was minimal. I gathered from certain contexts within the conversation that both girls were still in high school.

"So, what are you two up to tonight?" Mark inquired.

"Nothing much," the girls shrugged.

"Do you want to go for a ride in my jeep?"

"Yeah!" they enthusiastically answered in unison.

I began to wonder what I had gotten myself into.

"Tony! Sit in the back with Trish," Mark instructed as I stepped up to get into the jeep.

Though there was more than ample space in the back seat, Trish sat so close to me that our thighs touched. Apparently, she wasn't shy.

With heavy metal music vibrating loudly from the jeep's speakers, Mark drove us deep into a nearby wooded park and stopped in a dark, deserted place.

Mark turned around in the driver's seat to face me.

"Tony, Tracey and I are going to take a walk. You keep Trish company. Okay?"

"Okay," I answered with some hesitancy.

Mark and Tracey hopped out of the jeep and soon disappeared into the trees and darkness.

I glanced at Trish.

"Hi," she grinned with a little twinkle in her eye. I caught a whiff of alcohol on her breath.

"Hi," I replied awkwardly with a polite smile.

"So, how do you and Mark know each other?" she asked.

"We work together," I said not caring to expand the conversation.

"Do you have anything to drink in the jeep?"

"Unfortunately not," I smiled.

"Well, I guess we'll just have to entertain each other."

She leaned over and planted a wet kiss on my lips. Her tongue probed for an opening.

"Whoa! Just a second!"

"What's the matter?" Trish asked slightly puzzled.

I took a deep breath.

"You are very pretty," I said to her obvious pleasure. "But, I think you are a little too young for me."

"I'm seventeen. How old are you?"

"Let's just say I graduated from high school some time ago."

She laughed. "You're cute!"

Obviously, I was not getting through to her.

She stared seductively into my eyes. Without breaking eye contact, she reached down and tugged on my belt to undo it.

"Hey!"

"Yes?" she giggled.

"Don't do that!"

"Why not?"

"Well, you never know what might pop up!"

"You're funny," she laughed unzipping my pants.

"No, really, I don't think this is a good idea."

"What can I do to convince you?" she asked and started to probe my ear with her tongue. Her hand went on a fishing expedition in my pants. She found what she was looking for.

"You wouldn't happen to have ID with your birth date on it?"

She did not answer but simply engulfed my manhood deep in her mouth.

"Whoa!" I involuntarily blurted out.

Trish, obviously experienced at playing the bagpipes, began to perform a masterful symphony with hand, tongue, and lips. My private part gave her a standing ovation.

With her free hand, she opened up her shirt and undid her bra to expose her wonderfully round, ripe cantaloupes. I am unsure if she did this for my visual enjoyment or if she just wanted to keep her clothes free of any potential stains.

"Look, really, you don't have to do this," I said weakly sinking into the seat.

The statement seemed only to inspire her to bring me to greater heights.

At first, I squirmed around feeling tense and uncomfortable. After a few minutes of exquisite pleasure, I resigned to my fortunate fate and relaxed to enjoy the fruits of her talent. The end of her impressive performance was marked by the biological equivalent of fireworks.

"How was that?" Trish smiled.

"You score a perfect ten," I said attempting to compose myself.

She kindly tucked the bagpipe back in and zipped up my pants. However, she left her shirt open. I couldn't help but admire the exposed anatomy.

"Would you like to touch them?" she asked while taking my hand and placing it on one of her melons.

I started to inspect the merchandise by checking for firmness and texture. I was tempted to taste test, but we then heard Mark and Tracey returning from their walk. Trish quickly put the melons back in the rack and buttoned up her shirt.

"Hey, you guys get to know each other better?" Tracey asked with a grin as she settled into the front seat of the jeep.

"Yeah," Trish answered loudly.

"Well, at least in certain respects," I added.

The girls laughed. Mark looked over at me to silently ask what happened. I gave him a facial response that I would tell him later.

Mark and I drove them home and then headed back to his house.

"Joeness! What happened?" Mark asked.

I proceeded to tell him about the festivities in the back of the jeep after he left for his walk with Tracey.

"Man!" Mark pounded the steering wheel. "I knew that girl was a slut!" He seemed amusingly angry he missed an opportunity to be with Trish himself. "The seat didn't get messed up did it?"

"No, she was quite good at cleaning up after herself."

"Man!" Mark repeated to himself. He then reached over and put his hand on my shoulder. "Joeness, do you feel a little better now?"

"Yes, I do. Thanks."

Despite my answer and my happy bagpipes, I did not really feeling any better emotionally speaking. While the evening activities did help distract me for a time, a flood of depression soon returned as reality set back in. My life felt empty without Ann.

*　　　　　　*　　　　　　*

"What time are the classes?" I asked Steve, an Aikido master.

"We have classes on four weekday nights, Monday, Wednesday, Thursday, and Friday at 7:00 p.m. and 8:30 p.m. We also have a Saturday class at 10:00 a.m."

Because my Tai Chi lessons with Tara had ended, I thought about continuing my martial arts education in Aikido. Aikido is considered a soft martial art. Unlike karate, which includes many offensive movements, a soft martial art is entirely defensive. An opponent is neutralized by redirecting the force generated by an aggressive attack. Usually, this is accomplished when the aggressor is thrown off balance in some fashion.

After observing a few classes in Steve's school, I was favorably impressed and decided to join. Unfortunately, that decision would turn out to be detrimental to my well being.

During my third class at the Aikido school, Steve demonstrated a defensive technique designed to disarm an attacker who approached from behind and planted a knife in the middle of the lower back of an intended victim. The technique involved the defender simultaneously turning and sweeping one arm across to direct the attacker's knife wielding arm away. The defender then grabs and twists the assailant's wrist to disarm him.

As I watched Steve demonstrate using a wooden knife, I observed that if the attacker seized the defender around the neck with the other arm the defensive move would be useless. After the class, I approached Steve and relayed my observation.

"That's interesting," he said. "Let's try it."

Steve turned around so his back faced me. I placed my left arm around his neck and my right hand pressed the wooden knife into the small of his lower back. He looked for an opening to strike my groin. But I strategically placed my lower body at an angle to keep my private parts safe.

"Hmm, a smart attacker," Steve commented.

He then executed a movement to take me successfully down to the mat. But I was able to slash him with the wooden knife before hitting the ground.

"Okay, let's try that again," Steve said.

A small group of students gathered to watch us.

Again, Steve used a technique to bring me down, but I was able to make contact with the knife before being neutralized.

"How about you give it a try," Steve suggested to a black belt, John, who was standing nearby. John was new to the school and to my misfortune decided to try to make an impression.

John and I assumed the positions of attacker and defender just as I had done with Steve. I foolishly assumed that since John was a black belt, he knew what he was doing.

Without warning me in advance so that I could yield to his movement, John grasped my left arm which was around his neck with both hands and yanked down as hard as he could in an attempt to flip me over his back. Not being very talented, John failed to flip me over. He did, however, pull violently on my arm. In the split second his action took, I felt and heard a snap in my left biceps. I slid off John's back and doubled over on the mat. I pinned my straightened left arm to my body in response to the violent contractions in the biceps muscle as it hung from one tendon instead of the usual two. The pain was excruciating.

"Are you alright?" Steve asked alarmed.

"No! He pulled my biceps!"

I had to keep the arm straight and pinned tightly to my body with the other arm to minimize the convulsions in the muscle.

"I'm really sorry," John said apologetically.

"We need to get him to a hospital," a student by the name of Mike suggested.

After about ten minutes, I was able to at least stand. With great difficulty, I got out of the martial arts uniform and into my street clothes. Mike drove me to a nearby hospital using my car. Steve and John followed in another car. Fortunately for me, there were few people in the emergency room. I was attended to in a timely fashion. An x-ray revealed no insight to the injury. The first indication was that the biceps suffered a partial tear. The attending doctor simply recommended that I see an orthopedic surgeon as soon as possible.

In physical pain and emotional despair, I went out into the waiting area of the emergency room and sank into a hard plastic seat. I continued to pin my left arm to my body. Any other position resulted in extremely painful contractions as my biceps tried in vain to stabilize in one place.

Steve, Mike, and John looked at me sympathetically.

"I'm really sorry," John repeated.

"What were you thinking?" I verbally lashed at him with anger in my voice.

"Tony, is there anyone you could call to take you home?" Mike asked.

I couldn't think of anyone immediately. Mark lived all the way in Queens. My father lived 50 miles away. I didn't even know my mother's phone number since I had not spoken to her in years. Leo resided in the city. Besides, I usually ended up getting his voice mail when I called anyway.

Despondent, I sat there with my head down feeling sorry for myself.

Who, I asked myself, could I depend on to help me?

CHAPTER 9

▼

HEALING

"Is it true everything that happens has
a purpose?" I asked the white haired man.
"No," he answered. "But it is true that
everything has a lesson."
From "How I got Lucky and Bumped into God"—the author

A nurse in the emergency room was kind enough to allow me to use a telephone in her office.

"Hello, Ann? I'm sorry to bother you but I've had an accident."

I had not spoken to Ann in a couple of months and felt awkward asking her for a favor. Yet, I somehow felt I could still trust and depend on her.

"Are you alright?" she asked.

"My arm is injured but otherwise I'm okay. I can't drive though."

"I'll come pick you up! Where are you?"

With the assistance of the nurse, I gave Ann directions to the hospital.

After I spoke to Ann, I told Steve, John, and Mike that someone was coming to pick me up. They decided to keep me company while I waited. I surmised that their motivations for waiting with me differed. I think Steve, the owner of the school, was worried about being sued. John felt guilty for hurting me. Mike, I think, was just being a nice guy.

While we waited, the fellows made small talk amongst themselves. I sat alone quietly for the most part wishing the biceps muscle would stop convulsing. About half an hour later, Ann arrived with her cousin Olga.

"What have you done?" Ann asked as if I was a little boy who hurt himself in the playground.

"I didn't do anything. He did." I pointed to John who was outwardly embarrassed. "Hi Olga. How are you doing?"

"Better than you at the moment," she joked.

For etiquette's sake, I made introductions.

"This is Steve. He is the instructor at the Aikido school. This is Mike, a student of the school. Mike drove me here. This is John. John is the one who decided to dismember my arm from the rest of my body."

"I'm really sorry," John said again.

I flashed a sharp look that communicated to him he was better off keeping quiet.

We left the hospital. Olga drove me back home in my car while Ann followed in her SUV. Conveniently, Ann lived only two miles away from me.

"Thank you," I said to Olga and Ann when we arrived at my apartment.

"You're welcome," they replied.

"I'll help you up," Ann offered.

Ann walked me upstairs carrying my gym bag and opening doors for me.

"You know," I said to Ann, "When I was sitting in the hospital wondering who I could call, I thought of you. Thank you for helping me."

"I'm happy I was the one you thought of," she said with soft eyes and a warm smile. "I'll give you a call tomorrow and see how you are doing."

"Thanks," I said giving her a kiss on the cheek.

After Ann left, it took me over fifteen minutes to just get my shirt off. Sharp pains kept shooting through my arm forcing me to move very slowly. The hospital had given me painkillers, but I refrained from taking them. I crawled into bed and put an ice bag on my biceps and shoulder.

"Why did this happen to me?" I silently bemoaned.

I thought it would be difficult to fall asleep. However, in less than half an hour I drifted off. The next morning I called my supervisor, Rick, who was also a friend. I told him about the injury and that I would be out for at least the next two days. I reasoned that once the involuntary contractions subsided, I would be able to drive with at least one hand. Mark found out from Rick that I was hurt. He called me.

"Joeness! Dude! What happened?"

I told Mark of my misadventures at the Aikido school.

"Depression!" he responded. "Do you want me to kick that guy's ass who did this to you?"

"No," I grinned, "He was not malicious, just stupid."

"Listen, Tony, I have got to get back to work but I'll call you later."

"Later," I said in confirmation.

I got out of bed, filled a plastic bag with ice, grabbed a doctor's directory, and went back to bed with the ice covering my arm. A black and blue mark the size of an orange appeared overnight on the site of the injury.

Leafing through the directory, I called an orthopedic surgeon to make an appointment. The earliest one I could make was for Saturday. Today was Thursday. I made the appointment, put the directory down, and went back to sleep. I remained in bed for another four hours.

That afternoon, I called Leo. It was a rare occasion to reach him in person instead of his voice mail but this time he picked up the phone. I told Leo about the accident and resulting injury. He listened quietly not offering any expression of sympathy such as, "I'm sorry to hear that" or "Gee, what a bad break".

"All warriors are tested," Leo philosophized. "In addition to the arena of daily life, there are sometimes traumatic events that test the mettle of a warrior. With the correct response, a warrior can often turn a setback to his advantage."

"I fail to understand how getting injured could be to my ultimate advantage."

"I am not telling you that the injury is in any way beneficial by itself. What can be beneficial is what you learn and what you do in response to it."

"Well, what I learned is to not let anyone touch me in martial arts practice and my response is to be angry and even more depressed than what I was before," I said in a sarcastic tone of voice.

"That is your conditioned response, Tony. You get angry and depressed when things do not go your way. As you evolve into a warrior you will learn to use your anger for motivation and your depression will give way to determination in those matters in which you can affect the outcome."

"What about those things I have no control over?"

"There may be times when you are helpless to change a situation but those times will be few. And, you always have control over how you emotionally respond to a situation whatever it may be."

"I think right now I am in the helpless stage."

Leo laughed. "I assure you. You are far from helpless. I would like to give you some homework since you have some time on your hands."

"What would that be?"

"First, I am going to send you via electronic mail a list of three books. Purchase and read the books in the order of the list."

"Is this your equivalent of a home study course?"

"Yes, you could say that."

"What else?"

"Second, I want you to practice the following at least three times a day. Place yourself in the most comfortable position possible with your injured arm. Relax and use the breathing techniques to bring yourself into a light trance state. You are already adept at this from your daily meditation.

"Before your arm can begin healing, the damage must be cleared. It is like a building damaged in an earthquake. There is debris and rubble. This must be cleared away before reconstruction can take place. In your arm, the debris is in the form of internal bleeding. This blood produced by the injury needs to be cleaned out.

"While you are in a relaxed state, imagine your arm as a damaged structure. Picture in your mind construction crews and trucks cleaning up the rubble and carting it away. Continue to imagine this in the most vivid way possible for at least fifteen minutes."

"This is supposed to really help?"

"Yes. What you consistently imagine in your mind will eventually manifest itself in reality. This technique is a form of visualization, a technique I introduced to you already."

"Okay, Leo. I'll do it. I suppose it can't hurt."

"When the black and blue area on your biceps disappears, give me a call and we will progress to the next stage."

"Will do. Thank you for the advice," I said before hanging up the telephone.

Four days later, I drove myself to work using only one hand. Luckily, my job was only a few miles away.

I still could not move my left arm on its own power. So, I placed the computer keyboard on my lap and positioned my left forearm on the chair's armrest so the hand could dangle down and reach the keyboard. Though it was a bit awkward, I could at least type and perform my job duties within reason.

In the aftermath of the accident, Ann showered me with love and attention. Each day after work, she picked me up at my apartment and took me to her home for dinner. We'd eat together and then relax on the couch watching TV. I sat with an ice pack on one arm and Ann affectionately wrapped around the other. Occasionally, she dozed off with her head resting on my shoulder. As she lightly snored, I would gaze at her face and marvel at just how wonderful and caring she was. As the days went by, she did my laundry and helped me with grocery shopping. Because of her unselfish love and caring, my feelings of anger and depression began to fade. Thank heaven for Ann. She made me start to feel at peace again.

At the end of the first week, the visible bruise on the biceps disappeared. As instructed, I called Leo and left a message on his voice mail. Two hours later he called me back.

"You are now ready for the next step in your recovery," Leo stated. "Change your visualization exercise to imagine that the construction crews have cleared away all the damage and are now beginning reconstruction. Picture the construction workers laying down strong steel beams and pouring deep cement to repair the structure. The construction workers symbolically represent the healing powers of your body. The structure represents the torn biceps. Do this for about fifteen minutes.

"Following this, imagine yourself weightlifting and performing all the sport activities you like with a totally healed arm. Do this for fifteen minutes as well."

"Okay. Got it," I responded.

"Did you acquire the books I recommended?"

"Yes, I received them by mail the other day. I'll start reading the first book on the list today."

"Good. Keep your spirits up, Tony. Some day soon, a very pleasant surprise may come to you."

Leo sparked my interest with his comment.

"What kind of surprise?"

"The kind that puts a smile on your face."

"What? What is it?"

"Patience, Tony. It shall come soon enough. I'll check up on you next week to see how you are doing." With that, he hung up.

The next week I saw an orthopedic surgeon who recommended an MRI. Ann drove me to the MRI center. They used one of the older machines that looks like a torpedo tube and sounds like a washing machine on its last legs. Being inserted into the tube created feelings of near claustrophobic panic in me. I closed my eyes tight and imagined being in a big open field to keep me calm for the thirty minutes it took the clanking machine to take the images of my arm and shoulder.

"There is some damage to the shoulder, but that should heal," the doctor said during my next appointment to get the results of the MRI. "The real problem is a partial tear to the biceps tendon in the upper part of the arm where it attaches to the chest. It cannot be repaired by an operation and there is a chance of a complete rupture if the tendon is stressed too greatly."

"Depression," I whispered.

"What was that?" he asked.

"Nothing."

Basically, the doctor was telling me the injury was inoperable and that the partial tear would never heal completely. Translation - it was a permanent injury.

I thought of getting a second opinion. However, after making numerous informal inquiries with people I knew in my gym, I discovered two different bodybuilders with the same type of injury. I found out that the prognosis they were given was identical to mine.

Depression.

As angry and as down as I felt, I was determined with full resolve to rehabilitate the injury completely. During my meditative visualization exercises, I pictured huge steal beams being placed to reinforce the tendon. I imagined the partially torn tendon getting thicker and stronger with exercise. I pictured myself working out in the gym with heavy weights. I used my feelings of anger to motivate me toward a full recovery.

The next Saturday, my doorbell rang late in the morning. It was very unusual for me to have an unannounced visit. I assumed whomever it was rang the wrong bell or it was a young person selling newspaper deliveries. I opened one of the windows of my second floor apartment and looked down.

"Tara!" I shouted with surprise.

"Tony! Hello!"

"Wait a second! I'll come down to let you in!" In my rush, I accidentally attempted to open the door with my injured left arm. A sharp shooting pain reminded me not to do that. I opened my apartment door with the right arm, ran down the flight of stairs holding on to my hurt arm, and opened the door to let Tara in.

"What a pleasant surprise!" I smiled suddenly remembering what Leo said about me getting a surprise soon. "What brings you here?" I asked as I escorted her up the stairs to my apartment.

"You bring me here," she grinned. "I heard about what happened from Leo."

"It's very nice of you to pay me a visit."

"I'm here for more than just a visit," Tara said with a smile.

"Really? Are we going to get naked and take a shower together?"

She laughed loudly, put her hands on her hips, and said, "It's apparent that you still have your unique sense of humor. The answer to your question is no." In an exaggerated fashion, I slumped my shoulders to indicate disappointment. "I'm here to help you rehabilitate the injury."

"Does that mean at least you are going to walk on my back naked?"

Tara rolled her eyes up in her head but could not help but grin.

"How about you get naked while I work on you," she joked.

"Okay."

"I should have known better to kid around like that," Tara said shaking her head.

"Can I offer you anything to drink?"

"No thank you. Let's get started. Shall we?"

"Okay. What are we going to do?"

Tara had me lie on my back across my futon bed. Standing on the side of the bed my head was at; she carefully took my injured arm with both her hands and started to move it very slowly.

"Tell me if you have any pain," she instructed. She moved my straightened arm across my body, away from the body, then over my head.

"That hurts," I winced.

Tara stopped moving the arm in that direction and headed in another direction in a circular motion.

"Your range of motion is very limited now. This will help restore it," she explained.

She continued the circular back and forth movements with the arm for about ten minutes.

"How does that feel?" Tara asked.

"It hurts. But I guess that is to be expected."

I slowly rose off the bed. Tara and I went into the living room where she asked me to assume the preparatory Tai Chi position.

"We are resuming our lessons?" I asked with a grin.

"Yes, we are."

She had me start the opening movement of the form. The first movement is basically just raising the arms slowly straight out to shoulder level. The pain in my shoulder and biceps made me clench my teeth as I attempted it.

"Go very slow," Tara advised. "If you feel a very sharp stabbing pain, stop. Just do the best you can."

I struggled and became disheartened that my once strong muscular arm could now hardly move. "Be patient. It will take time," Tara said.

Tai Chi, by its very nature, is comprised of slow movements. However, I was moving at less than half the speed one normally would.

Tara had me go through the entire Tai Chi short form consisting of twenty-four movements. After a brief break, she had me do it again. But this time she joined me matching my exact tempo and speed. Our synchronized movements made me feel very centered and calm. A thought flashed through my mind wondering how well we would move together in more intimate ways.

"Practice at least twice a day. It will help bring healing and balance to your body."

Tara asked me to lie down on the floor on my back with both arms relaxed at my side with the palms of my hands facing up. She leaned over me on the injured side crisscrossing her two hands, one over the other, about six inches above the torn biceps.

"What are you doing?" I asked.

"Shhhh. Just relax and be quiet."

She closed her eyes and maintained the position of her hands and body over me. At first, I stared at her for a while, but then I started to feel sleepy and closed my eyes. In about five minutes, I felt a warm sensation envelope the area of the injury. I opened my eyes and Tara was still in the same position. She remained there, motionless, for another fifteen minutes.

"Okay, that's enough for now," she said as if she were talking to herself.

"What were you doing?" I asked again.

"The universe is comprised of infinite energy. I used myself as a conduit for that energy to direct some of it toward healing your arm."

"You're getting mystical on me again."

She laughed at my comment. "There is really nothing mystical as you put it. The universe is the source of infinite power. However, you are just beginning to learn how to open to it and use it."

"Can you teach me how to open to it completely?"

"That would not be wise," she counseled. "Without adequate preparation, such a tremendous revelation could destroy you."

"Destroy me? But how?"

"A person could go mentally insane unless they have the foundation of a warrior. It is better to open the window of awareness slowly."

"You are scary sometimes."

"So are you," she jokingly replied.

"Would you like to have lunch?"

"Sorry, but I should get back."

"Are you sure I can't interest you in getting a bite to eat together, or perhaps taking a shower?"

Tara put her hands on her hips and smirked at me.

"No thank you," she said.

"How did you get out here?"

"I took the subway, then the bus."

"That must have taken a long time!"

"Hmm, about two hours."

"I feel honored that you went so out of your way to visit me," I said lightheartedly. "Let me at least drive you to the railroad station. You can take that back to the city instead of the bus. It's much quicker."

Using my one good arm, I drove Tara to the village railroad station a mile away from my apartment. I escorted her to the platform and kept her company while she waited for the train.

"Here, take this," I said to Tara handing her a ten-dollar bill.

"What's this for?"

"That's to pay for your ticket." She was about to protest but I didn't give her a chance. "You are being very kind to me. I still wonder why you are even helping me so much. Sometimes, I don't think I deserve it. Moreover, I feel helpless in the sense that I don't know how to repay you. Okay, you did get to see me naked once but I won't count that. Anyway, paying for your ticket is the only way I have now of thanking you."

In the distance, I heard the sound of the train approaching. I turned around to look at it.

"That's going to take you away from me," I said solemnly watching the train draw near.

"I'll visit you twice a week to help with your healing," she said reassuringly.

"What about after that?" I took her by the hand and gazed deeply into her eyes. "Perhaps I am not as evolved as you but even I can sense a connection between us. It's like a beam of energy from me," I pointed to my heart, "to you." I made a straight line to her heart.

"I think you are trying your tricks of seduction," she reacted suspiciously. "I question Leo's judgment for teaching you those skills."

"It's not your body I want. Rather," I paused for affect, "it's your heart I desire. Perhaps you are already hopelessly in love with me, but can't accept it yet."

For a brief moment, her face softened with eyes peering longingly into my soul. However, Tara quickly regained her composure and said to me with a grin, "You are hopelessly egotistical."

The train had stopped at the platform. The doors opened.

"Thank you for your help," I said as she walked in.

Tara disappeared into the train. The train faded from view down the tracks. I stood alone on the platform feeling empty in her absence.

*   *   *

With an ice pack on my arm and the basset hound licking my hand, I sat on the couch that night watching the wide screen TV in what Ann referred to as the 'little room' in her house. I stared blankly at the TV, my mind preoccupied with thoughts of Tara.

"Are you okay?" Ann asked a little concerned.

"Yes, I'm just tired and a little agitated from the pain."

The basset hound hopped on the couch and started to lick my face. Though the dog had a conventional name, I was in the habit of calling it the Fat Basset or Fatso for short. Ann did not appreciate the nicknames I gave the dog.

"He's not fat!" she objected.

"You have got to be kidding me." We both started to laugh.

"Well, why don't you take him for a walk?"

Walk! All Fatso had to hear was that one word. He excitedly jumped on the couch, then leaped off on to the floor and charged down the hall to the front door. When I didn't follow, the Fat Basset charged back and hopped on the couch vigorously licking my face while whining.

"Someone wants to go for a walk," Ann chimed.

"Don't your sons walk him?"

"No, they don't."

"Well, that would account for why he is so fat. Okay, okay. I'll take him for a walk. Do you want to go for a WALK fatso?"

The dog momentarily froze at the word WALK then ran full speed to the front door again jumping up and pawing at it while wildly wagging his tail. It took Ann and I a minute or two to just get the leash on the Fat Basset's collar. I opened the front door and he charged out running as fast as he could pull me along with him.

"Whoa! Slow down!"

I held the leash with my good arm and put my hand of the other arm in my pant's pocket to avoid using it out of habit.

That Fat Basset was so happy to get out that he peed on every lamppost and tree he came across. By the eighth tree, the dog had exhausted his supply of urine. He raised his leg and scrunched his doggy face as he forced out two or three drops. Suddenly, dog poop shot out of his behind.

"You Fat Basset! Stop that!"

He put his tail between his legs, sat down, and looked at me with sad eyes. The walk resumed with a gentle tug on his leash.

By the second block, he was already slowing down, obviously in no shape for the kind of effort required to keep pulling me at a fast pace. His tongue began to hang low and he occasionally wheezed for air. Despite his fatigue, the basset hound indulged in earnest with exploring the outside world. He sniffed, listened, and watched everything within his sense of awareness.

Gradually, we walked at a more normal pace. Fatso's initial gallop turned into a waddled walk. While stopping to allow the dog time to sniff around, I looked up at the sparkling stars admiring their silent beauty. The night sky and air were clear. Suddenly, a strong gust of wind hit me. Dust and dirt stung my eyes forcing me to shut them tightly. The wind then stopped as abruptly as it started. I suspiciously noticed no movement in the trees to indicate a breeze. Fatso stopped walking and sat down. He quizzically darted his head back and forth wondering what went by. I looked down at Fatso, and he looked up at me. We then both turned our heads to the direction the rush of wind came from.

"What was that Fatso?"

He gave me the dumb dog 'I don't know' look.

Down the block, barely illuminated by the street lamps, I saw a small slow moving whirlwind of leaves and dust headed in our direction. The rest of the air around us was very still. I glanced at the dog. He was captivated by the same phenomena. His tail went down between his legs.

"What is it Fatso?"

He began to tug anxiously on the leash, away from the approaching whirlwind.

"What is it?" I asked again.

A sudden feeling of belligerence came over me. I decided to stand my ground. However, Fatso tugged harder to get away.

The whirlwind headed toward us. As it approached, it became larger and faster. I stared at its center. The dog began to whine and pace anxiously in circles. He was obviously distressed. I felt sorry for him, so I decided to concede.

"Okay, Fatso. Let's move out of the way."

Fat Basset pulled me to perceived safety across the street where we watched the wind pass by and dissipate down the block.

I peered in the direction of the whirlwind's origin. In the dark shadows of trees and bushes, I thought I saw the figure of a woman. Without taking my eyes off the image, I rushed toward it.

"Come on Fatso! Let's go!"

The dog, sensing some kind of urgency, ran excitedly with me. We reached the spot where I thought I saw the image, but there was nothing there. Bewildered, I concluded the shadows created an illusion and my imagination did the rest.

Fatso and I finished our walk a few blocks later and returned home.

"How was the walk?" Ann asked.

Fat Basset headed straight to the water dish to replenish his supply.

"He marked his territory on every standing object on the block. When he emptied the tank, he resorted to other waste material."

"No! Bad dog!"

Fatso looked up at her with the dumb 'I don't know what you are talking about' look.

Ann's two boys came home shortly after the dog and I came in. They exchanged polite greetings with me.

"Mom, why does the dog look so tired?" her younger son John asked.

Fat Basset was lying under the kitchen table, head on its paws with its tongue hanging out.

"Tony took him for a walk," she answered.

"Good," Ann's older son Mike said. "That dog is fat."

I gave Ann the 'I told you so' look. She couldn't help but smile.

Ann and I went into the 'little room', and began to watch a movie on cable TV. When Fat Basset finally decided to move, it joined us and plopped itself down on top of my feet.

"Aww, he loves you. Isn't he cute?" Ann said.

"Yeah, I guess so." He scrunched his face in delight while I scratched him behind the ears.

About an hour into the movie, Ann dozed off with her head on my thigh. The dog fell asleep too. They both snored lightly. I shut off the TV using the remote and sat in silence alternately gazing at Ann and the basset. They both made me feel very loved. For the first time in my memory, I actually started to feel like part of a family.

I gently nudged Ann and wiggled my toes to tickle the under belly of Fatso to wake him.

"Time for me to go home," I said to a sleepy eyed Ann. She rubbed her eyes, smiled at me, and gave me a kiss. The dog and Ann walked me to the front door and then stood out on the porch together as I walked to my car.

"Oh, look a star," Ann said looking up at the sky. "Star bright, star light, first star I see tonight. I wish I may, I wish I might, I wish my wish comes true tonight. I wish...Do you know what I wished for?"

"No, what is it?"

"I'm not telling you," she smiled, "because then it won't come true."

I laughed and drove off while Ann waved goodbye.

              *   *   *

"Leo, something a little strange happened to me last Saturday night."

"What is it?"

I told Leo over the telephone about the whirlwind incident. The end of the line went silent.

"Leo, are you there?"

"Yes, I am here." The line got quiet again.

"Well, what do you think about it?"

Leo sighed and then said with a tone of resignation, "You blundered. The female who stalks you finally discovered a weakness."

His assessment alarmed me.

"Leo, you are getting spooky again. What do you mean I blundered? What did I do wrong?"

"Thus far, every time you have been probed, you have acted fearlessly. This time, however, you avoided confrontation. She has found a way to manipulate you."

"I'm not sure what you mean. What should I have done?"

"Ideally, you should have stayed put and let the wind harmlessly pass you by. You could have stood in front of the dog to shield it. Instead, you became attached to the dog's distress and moved away."

"So, what is wrong with that?"

"She succeeded in moving you. She found a weak link. If you were alone, you would have stood firm in the face of the wind. However, you felt fear for the animal. The dog's fear hooked you just as if you feared for yourself."

I sighed and found myself getting annoyed. "What does this all mean?"

"It means you are vulnerable. She has found a way to influence your behavior."

"What should I do?"

After a few seconds of silence, Leo spoke.

"The more evolved you become as a warrior, the less likely you will be open to manipulation of any kind. Simply continue your training and be ready."

"Ready for what?"

"Just be ready," Leo said with an air of mystery.

"You are not making all this up just to frighten me into behaving a certain way? You know like some parents do with children by telling them they had better be good or the boogeyman will get them? Are you?"

"You have an active imagination."

"Maybe, but my imagination is not nearly as bizarre as your reality."

Leo laughed but I did not share the humor.

"How is your arm feeling?" he asked changing the subject.

"It improves every day though it is far from one hundred percent."

"Tara stopped by to assist you. Correct?"

"Yes. She did. Hey, would you mind if Tara and I…well if Tara and I got to know each other better?"

"I would not advise it. Tara has informed me of your advances." He started to chuckle. "It amazes me that you so easily found her weak spot."

"I didn't do anything on purpose," I said defensively.

"That amazes me too! You did it intuitively! You are even more powerful than you realize. You are just too dumb to know it."

"I think I resent that comment."

Leo chuckled again. "Tara is a fine warrior. She is far more advanced than you are at the moment. But somehow you quickly pierced her defenses. Do you love her?"

Leo's question took me by surprise.

"I don't know. I am fond of her though."

"Do you care for her?"

"Yes."

"I will do you the favor of telling you a secret. You are not to repeat this to anyone or even discuss it with me further. Understood?"

"Understood."

"Tara has a troubled past. She has done well to heal and follow the path of a warrior. However, she is not ready to fall in love yet. Not with you or anyone else. Be kind to her and cease your advances. If you do not, she will become troubled and may flee from you."

"Why would she flee?"

"If she finds herself falling in love with you, she will go very far away." I fell silent with the weight of his words. "Do you understand?" he asked with great seriousness. "Do you understand that in a sense she is taking a risk to help you?"

"I understand."

With that, Leo concluded the conversation.

Four weeks went by as the warm summer weather engulfed the Long Island area. Tara visited me twice a week on Tuesday and Thursday night. At my suggestion, she took the railroad to the village and I picked her up at the station. At my insistence, I reimbursed her transportation costs. As Leo suggested, I ceased any romantic advances. We were friendly and polite with each other. But, it seemed strained as if we were both trying to hold back more intimate feelings.

Tara had a clearly defined routine during each visit. She would skillfully manipulate my arm to stretch it, practice Tai Chi with me, and then do the 'healing hands' thing over my biceps.

At the end of four weeks, my arm had complete range of motion. That was a marked improvement although the pain and weakness remained.

"You now have full range of motion," Tara announced.

"You would make a good physical therapist."

"Thanks for the compliment. It will now be a matter of strengthening the arm. That is the next phase of your recovery. Contact Leo. He shall assist you with the rest of your healing."

"What about you? You're not going to visit me any longer?"

"No. You no longer need me," she said with a forced smile.

"Well, please forgive me for saying this, but what if I told you I would like to see you anyway?" I gulped hard waiting for her response.

"That would not be a good idea."

Her disappointing answer angered me. I tried to hide my feelings without much success.

"I'll take you to the station," I said dryly.

We drove to the train station in silence. As was my habit, I escorted her to the elevated platform.

"You don't have to stay with me," she said.

"That's okay. I'll wait with you."

We stood together on the platform. She was close to the edge of the platform with her body turned so that her back faced me. I nervously glanced down the tracks dreading the inevitable arrival of the train. I tried to think of something to say.

"Tara…"

She quickly interrupted.

"Tony, you have to let me go." She didn't turn around to face me. "Please, just let me go."

Her somber words saddened me.

"But we Tai Chi so well together."

She started to laugh softly while still facing away from me. I detected distress in her laughter.

"Always with that sense of humor," she said shaking her head.

I caught first sight of the train in the distance. I walked over to her and tugged at the bottom of her shirt like a little boy trying to get the attention of an adult.

"Please don't go."

She turned around and looked into my eyes briefly before looking down and placing the fingertips of her left hand over the center of my heart.

"It's not time for you and I yet. It's not time." She then affectionately wrapped her arms around me. Almost with a sense of caution, I returned her delicate embrace. "What did you do to me?" she whispered.

"Not nearly as much as I would like."

She started to laugh again but tears soon appeared. I gently touched the corner of one of her twinkling brown eyes. A warm teardrop slowly ran down my finger.

It seemed that no sooner had we lost ourselves in each other's arms that the train pulled into the station.

"I have to go," she told me while reluctantly untangling arms.

The doors of the train opened and Tara walked in taking a piece of my heart with her. I stared at the tracks for a long time even after the train moved out of sight.

When I got back to my apartment, I called Ann and told her I wouldn't be coming by for dinner that night.

"Are you okay?" she asked.

"I'm okay. I just need some time to myself."

"I hate hearing you sound so depressed! Would you like me to come over by your house?"

"No, really I'm okay. I just need some time alone."

"Alright," Ann said with a concerned tone. "I'll talk to you tomorrow."

I took a walk to the village park. I sat on a bench buried with my thoughts until the sun went down and darkness engulfed me.

*   *   *

"Hi Leo. Tara said I should get in touch with you. My arm now has full range of motion."

"Excellent. She has done well to aid your rehabilitation. I will meet you at your gym tomorrow night at six o'clock."

"You are going to meet me at my gym?"

"Yes."

"Uh, okay. Do you need the address?"

"No, I already have it."

"How?"

"You have mentioned to me in the past the name of the health club. I simply looked up the address in a telephone directory."

"Alright. I'll see you tomorrow night."

I was perplexed as to why Leo wanted to meet me. My assumption was that he was going to demonstrate some exercises for my arm. However, I was already very experienced with lifting weights and he knew that. I doubted that he could really teach me anything I didn't already know.

At the appointed time the next evening, I went to the gym and found Leo waiting just outside the entrance.

"They are going to ask you for a ten dollar visitor fee," I informed Leo while pulling out the money for him.

"Do not concern yourself with that. Go in first and I shall follow behind you."

"Hey, you are going to do that trick where you just go right by people without them noticing, aren't you?"

"Being a wizard does have its advantages," he smiled.

We entered the building. As required by the establishment, I stopped by the reception desk to show my health club ID card and sign in. I then headed to the locker room but turned around to watch Leo. Sure enough, he casually strolled by the reception desk to the complete obliviousness of the usually alert staff.

"Can you teach me that trick so I can lurk around in the women's locker room unnoticed?" I asked.

Leo laughed. "You already know how to do it. You just are just not completely convinced it works."

After I put my belongings into a locker, Leo and I went to the section of the gym where the resistance equipment was located. On the way, we passed the aerobics area that was liberally populated with very fit women attired in workout outfits that accentuated their hard bodies.

"I am beginning to understand the source of your dedication to working out," Leo joked. "Now, let's get down to business. I would like to observe you doing a set of dumbbell curls with your good arm. Select a moderate weight to use."

"With my good arm?" I asked for verification.

"Yes."

I picked up a forty-pound dumbbell off the rack and curled it ten times with my good right arm.

"Ah, just as I suspected," Leo commented.

"What? What did I do wrong?" I asked a little defensively.

"The way you lift weights is a mirror of how you live life. You struggle against the weight. Your attitude is that the weight is your opponent and you have to defeat it. You approach your whole exercise routine as an adversary."

"Well of course it's a struggle! How else should I work out?"

Leo looked around the gym for a moment.

"Come here with me," he said walking a few feet to our left. "Do you see that woman there?"

Leo motioned to a very attractive blonde young woman. She was in the middle of performing seated dumbbell presses in front of a long mirror on the wall. "Do you notice her form?" he asked.

"You bet I do."

Leo poked me in the head.

"You know what I mean! Do not be distracted by her beauty. Observe her form on the exercise."

She lifted the weights overhead in a controlled and steady motion. This was in contrast to most of the men working out who forcibly jerked the dumbbells up.

"Yeah, but she is a girl."

Leo poked me in the head again.

"Yes, and you could learn something from her if you stop staring at her chest."

"Oh, Leo," I said shaking my head in admiration, "Do you see those? They are perfect!"

Leo rolled up his eyes giving me the 'what am I going to do with you' look.

"Tony," Leo sharply snapped his fingers in my face, "Use a twenty pound dumbbell and do another set of curls with your good arm."

"Okay," I said walking back to the rack. I picked up a dumbbell and started to curl.

"Stop!" Leo shouted.

"What? What did I do?"

"Slow down! Raise the weight for a count of two, and lower it for a count of four. Concentrate on the muscle, not the weight. If you concentrate on the weight that means it is too heavy. Become one with the weight. Pretend that it is an extension of your physical self. Work with it, not against it."

"Alright coach."

I lifted the dumbbell in the manner Leo prescribed. It was much more difficult to perform the curls in that fashion even when using half the weight as the first set.

"That's a big difference," I said a little surprised. "Wow, I can really feel it."

"Good. That is the proper way to exercise. Do not punish your body with undue strain. Listen to your body and it will guide you flawlessly. Now that you know the proper form to use, let us begin."

We started with some exercises for the chest. Because of the severe damage in the area that attaches the biceps to my chest, I could only manage using a two and a half-pound dumbbell.

"Should I lift heavier weights with my good arm?"

"No. Though the weight you are using will be too light for your uninjured side, it is important to build the body in balance."

I felt embarrassed using such a puny weight. My injured arm struggled to lift the dumbbell. The pain was significant, but it did not worsen during the exercise. I lifted as if I was moving in slow speed.

"How did that feel?" Leo asked after I finished the set.

"It still hurts a lot."

"Does the pain get better as you exercise, or worse?"

"Well, it's about the same."

"As long as the pain does not get worse, that is okay. If, when doing the exercise, the pain increases or there is a sharp pain, stop immediately."

For the next hour, Leo observed my form and provided encouragement. From experience, I knew what exercises to do to build the injured biceps and shoulder. Therefore, I did not need Leo's assistance in that regard. However, through his keen powers of observation, he showed me slight adjustments to my form that made the exercises feel much more effective.

When we were finished, I sat on an exercise bench feeling discouraged that I was so weak.

"Tony, it will take time," Leo said as if reading my thoughts.

"Yes, I know. I know," I replied unhappy with the situation.

Leo and I strolled over to a row of stationary bikes. I got on one bike and he hopped on the bike next to me. We both started to pedal enjoying an advantageous view of the aerobics area and the females working out there.

"You look a little heavier. Have you adjusted your calorie intake to account for less activity?"

"No," I answered. "In fact, I have been eating more. Ann has been very generous by letting me come over to her house for dinner."

"I see," he said. "And how are you two getting along?"

"We get along perfectly. She is a wonderful woman."

"I detect distress in your voice."

"Well, yeah. The old problem of her not wanting to have a family and putting me a distant second to her children still exists. What can I do? If I stay with her, I have to give up the idea of having children and accept that until her children get older; I take a back seat in her priorities. If I leave her, I wind up feeling miserable and missing her." I sighed deeply.

"That is a dilemma," Leo said.

I was disappointed with his answer as I hoped he would offer more concrete advice. I looked over at him.

"Follow the heart. That is what you and Tara have told me. But what if the heart is torn?"

Leo silently considered his answer for a few moments.

"In meditation, go to the heart and politely ask for the best possible resolution to the situation. Then sit silent for a time. Do this every day. An answer will present itself eventually."

"You have to be kidding me."

"No, I am serious. Give it a try."

We cycled in silence enjoying the occasional pass by of a well-toned female. After half an hour, we left the gym.

"How did you get here? Do you need a ride anywhere?" I asked Leo.

"I have my own transportation thank you."

Leo walked in the opposite direction from where my car was located. I assumed he had his car parked on the other side of the block. Out of curiosity, after getting into my own vehicle, I drove around the corner but there was no sign of him or his black sports car.

CHAPTER 10

▼

SEARCHING

"Before you begin searching, be certain
of what you are looking for"
From *"The Dark Side of a Warrior"*—*the author*

"How are you feeling?" Ann asked referring to my arm.

"It's getting better. But, I still have a long way to go."

It was a pleasantly warm and sunny summer Sunday. Ann's two boys were with their father.

"Do you feel like doing anything?"

"What do you have in mind?" I asked.

Ann suggested a game of miniature golf at a recently opened course in our neighborhood.

"Are you able to play with your arm?" she asked.

"I think I can handle that."

The Fat Basset jumped up on my leg vigorously pawing my thigh.

"Guess what he wants?" Ann smiled.

The dog jumped off my leg and began to nudge his leash hanging from the doorknob.

"Not now you Fat Basset!" I scolded.

He began to whine and lick the back of my hand.

"I'll take you for a walk later!"

He bolted to the couch in the living room, did a U-turn, and then ran back jumping up on my leg again. Wagging his tail furiously, he gave me the sad doggy face look.

"Let's get going," I said to Ann trying my best to ignore the hound.

When the Fat Basset realized that not only was I not taking him for a walk but I was also taking his mommy with me, he began to whine and cry.

I let Ann out the front door first while I admonished the dog, who was trying to push his way out with us, to stay put. After both Ann and I were outside, the dog jumped up on the living room window that looks out to the driveway. He began to howl loudly like a lonely wolf atop a mountain.

"Aww, I feel so bad leaving him like that," Ann said.

"That's what he is counting on; your sympathy. He'll be all right. When we get back, I'll take him out for a while."

Ann and I drove to the mini golf course five minutes away. After a short wait in line, I paid the fee and we headed to the first hole. Ann gripped her golf club backward with her lead hand lower than the other hand. I attempted to correct her.

"But I like it this way," she responded stomping her foot down for emphasis.

"If that's what you want," I said shrugging my shoulders.

Being a gentleman, I allowed Ann to putt first. She hit the ball with that cockamamie grip. We watched as it rolled over little hills and curves until it plopped into the hole.

Son of a gun. She scored a hole in one.

"Yes!" Ann yelled.

"I don't believe it," I muttered under my breath. "Must be beginners luck."

A sudden pick up in the wind around us caught my attention. I looked up to see the recently clear sky darken with thunderstorm clouds.

"It looks like rain. Just our luck," said a disappointed Ann.

The wind picked up dust and blew in circles. A part of me felt intuitively suspicious. I scanned the area. Sure enough, I noticed the figure of a dark haired woman by the fence that separated the course from the parking lot. A few hard raindrops hit my face. Some of the people on the course headed for cover.

"Should we go back to the car?" Ann asked.

"No, let's keep playing."

I continued to stare at the dark female figure. It seemed to have an eerie hue about it.

"What if it starts to pour?"

"We'll get wet, go home, and dry off."

Ignoring the weather, I teed off and finished the hole four shots later. A full down pour never materialized and few minutes later the sky cleared. The next time I looked around, the dark haired woman was nowhere to be found.

Ann and I continued to play. To her delight and my bemusement, she scored a hole in one again on the fifth and eighth holes. I remained hole-in-one-less though I did manage to lose a ball in one of the course's water fountains. Ann took playful pleasure at handedly beating me at the game.

"Pretty good, huh," Ann gleamed.

"Yes, you're pretty amazing," I smiled.

Upon returning home, the Fat Basset jumped up and slobbered all over me. I took him for a walk and he repeated his new ritual of urinating on every standing object possible. He may have been a little dog with a little hose, but he had a big tank.

Ann and I barbecued a few steaks and sat out on her backyard deck enjoying the comfortable late afternoon weather. A soft wistful breeze rustled the leaves of a large tree in Ann's yard. Despite such a serene atmosphere, I was not at peace. The uneasy feeling that Ann and I would go our separate ways sometime in the near future gnawed at me. I also thought about Tara. Should I try to see Tara or just let it go? I needed to consult an expert on such weighty matters.

"Dude! Go after her," his high Joeness Mark counseled when I asked his advice on the situation with Tara. "She's into you. She's just scared."

"You think so? All I have is a phone number to leave her a message. I would feel stupid leaving a message. What would I say?"

"Do you know where she lives?"

"No. I don't even know her last name. All I know is where we used to meet for the Tai Chi lessons."

"Joeness, why don't you look for her there?"

"I have no idea if she'll even be there."

"Hey, what do you have to lose? If you want, I'll go with you to look for her."

"That might be an idea," I mused.

"Sure. If we don't find her we'll just hang out in the city for a while. Maybe we'll be able to pick up some Manhattan girls."

Mark convinced me to go looking for Tara with his assistance. So, the next Saturday morning, he and I drove into downtown NYC to the big old building I used to meet Tara at for our lessons. It was relatively early in the morning for the weekend, so we were able to find parking close to the building.

"This is it," I said to Mark.

We walked up a few flights of stairs to the floor where the ballet room is located.

"Okay, if she is anywhere here, it would be on this floor. The ballet room is down one end. The woman's locker room is on the opposite side. There are other rooms for aerobics, basketball, and stuff, but I have never been in them. It's probably better for us to split up. You take that end, and I'll take the side with the ballet room."

"It's a plan," Mark nodded. "You said she is a short Asian babe with a great body. Right?"

"Right."

"If I find her, I'll come back to look for you and let you know where she is."

"Good. If we lose sight of each other, we'll meet back at your jeep in half an hour."

"Got it," Mark replied. Off we went on our search.

I walked down the long hall and headed to the ballet room. I did not really expect to find Tara there. However, that part of the building was the only one I was familiar with so I decided to start my search there. When I reached the room, the large door was open giving me a clear view inside. There, sitting on the floor with her back leaning against a wall, knees up by her chest, and arms wrapped around her legs, was Tara. She seemed deeply pensive. Her solemn appearance diminished my initial excitement of finding her.

I leaned forward to poke my head into the room. "Hello," I said in a low voice to get her attention without startling her.

"Hello," she answered without any hint of surprise.

She turned her eyes briefly towards me then resumed looking straight ahead as if staring at something in the distance. I entered the room slowly and quietly, walked over, and sat down beside her. I assumed the same position she was in. We sat silently for a few moments until I decided to break the ice.

"I thought I would stop by to visit you. You don't seem surprised to see me."

"I knew you were coming."

"You knew? How could you possibly know?"

"I just knew," she said turning her head toward me and grinning slightly.

"Sometimes you are spooky just like Leo," I commented. "Look, I just wanted to see you to let you know that well, um, I think that maybe you and I have potential for a possible relationship."

Tara shook her head from side to side indicating disagreement.

"I can't be with you," she said.

"Why not? What's wrong with me?"

"I am not ready for a romantic relationship with you or anyone else."

"May I ask why?"

She sighed deeply.

"My father died when I was a young girl. My mother remarried a year later. Her new husband, my stepfather, soon began to abuse me."

"Abuse you? How?"

"He raped me from the time I was ten years old until I left home when I was fourteen."

The revelation shocked me. Tara always seemed so composed, so emotionally centered that I never suspected such a traumatic past.

"Wow. I am sorry to hear that! Have you ever had a boyfriend?"

"Oh, yes. I have, but I was very troubled and the men I picked were always abusive. I ran away from home and came to New York City. I lied about my age to find work and moved in with three other girls in a small apartment. I thought that, by running away to the East Coast, I could leave the pain of the past behind. However, the demons remained inside of me. Geographic distance cannot heal a troubled soul.

"I was very depressed and angry. One day, the emotional pain overwhelmed me. I attempted suicide by overdosing on sleeping pills. Luckily, my roommates discovered me unconscious and called an ambulance before it was too late.

"After the suicide attempt, I was required to undergo counseling. That helped, but I was still very troubled. I met Leo after one of the counselors asked him to help me."

"Judging by the way you are now, I would say Leo did a great job."

"Yes. He has. The other counselors were sympathetic and kind but that did not ultimately heal me. Leo used a different approach. He didn't express any sympathy or feel sorry for me. He told me that that would only reinforce the image I had of myself as a victim. Leo taught me how to be a warrior instead of a victim.

"I have achieved much over the years with Leo's guidance. However, I still have more to accomplish." She paused for a few seconds. "You have provided the catalyst for me to transcend to the next level."

"How did I do that?"

Tara laughed.

"That Leo is a crafty one! He knew exactly what he was doing when he asked me to teach you Tai Chi!"

"I'm not sure I understand what you mean," I said perplexed.

For the first time in the conversation, Tara turned her body to face me as if to emphasize her words.

"I never thought…" Tara said her voice getting a little choked up, "After what happened to me, I never thought I could feel love again. That is, until you came along."

"Me?" I asked trying to hide my delight.

"Yes, you. You, you egotistical male chauvinist. Leo is clever. He used me to help you find your center and power with Tai Chi and he used you to unlock feelings buried deep inside of me."

"I still don't quite understand what you mean when you say you are moving to the next level."

"The next level in my evolution as a warrior. That is what I mean. I am going to California."

"California? What for?"

"To slay my demons," Tara said seriously. "I am going to confront my father-in-law for the crimes he committed."

I scratched my head. "What do you hope to accomplish? Are you looking for revenge?"

"No, I do not seek revenge or wish him any harm."

Her answer just confused me more.

"If that is the case, why not just let it go? Forget him and move on. I've heard that the best thing to do in a case like this is to just forgive the person that wronged you and move on."

"When I first met Leo, he asked me if I forgave my father-in-law. I said to him, 'Yes, I do.' Leo laughed at me and said I did not really forgive him. Leo said that I just used the facade of forgiveness as an excuse to not confront him. Leo then asked me if I forgave myself. At first, I did not know what he meant, but I soon realized that I was angry toward myself for letting me be abused. Leo told me that to heal, the most important person I needed to forgive was ultimately myself.

"Leo and I worked together in therapy towards that goal. However, in order for me to earn my own forgiveness, I have to show I can stand up and defend myself in front of my father-in-law. I have forgiven myself for being abused as a helpless child but now I am an adult and a warrior. A warrior stands up for and defends herself. That is why I must confront him."

"So," I said trying to make sense of her explanation, "You are going to confront your father-in-law to prove to yourself you can stand up to him. By doing that, you earn your own sense of forgiveness. Do I have that right?'

"That is basically it," Tara smiled.

"How about I just go to California and beat him up for you?"

She just laughed without answering the question. "By the way, Tara is not my given name."

"I thought that name was a little strange for someone of Asian ethnicity. What is your real name?"

"I would rather not say. Tara is the name I have given myself and the name I wish to be addressed as. I only tell you the fact to be honest with you." Her head tilted and her eyes shifted up and to her left. "Your friend is looking for you," she said.

"How do you know that? How do you even know a friend came with me?"

"I just know," Tara said with a wink.

"You are getting mysterious on me again!"

"Come. Let's go find him."

We got up and left the room together. Tara looked over to her left and told me my friend was in that direction.

"By the way," she added, "Does your offer for lunch still stand?"

"You bet! Whenever you would like."

"How about today?" she asked with a grin.

"That would be wonderful," I replied touching her eyes with mine.

We found Mark wandering about the large building with a lost look on his face. I shouted to get his attention.

"Hey Mark! I found her. This is Tara."

"Hey, hello Tara. It's nice to meet you," Mark said while conspicuously checking her out.

"Is he picturing what I would look like naked?" Tara asked with feigned anger.

Mark and I exchanged quick glances.

"Uh, no. Mark is a nice guy. He is just naturally curious about you."

"Oh, okay," she said with a sly smile. "Hey Mark, if you are single, I have a friend you may like to meet."

"Really?" Mark asked with his face lighting up. "What is she like?"

"She is a very attractive Asian woman. But, there are two important things you should know about her. First, she wants to meet a nice handsome guy but she is not looking for a serious relationship."

"Okay, what is the other thing?"

"Well, she has a twin sister. They share everything, including the men in their lives, if you know what I mean."

Mark's eyes popped open. His jaw dropped at the implication.

"No! You are kidding!"

"You could meet her now if you would like."

Mark and I exchanged glances indicating why not.

Led by Tara, we walked downstairs to a part of the building that had a large room filled with aerobics equipment. About two dozen people were working out there. She walked in by herself to find her friend and then came back to introduce us.

"This is my friend Tony and his friend Mark." We nodded our heads in a gesture of hello. "This is Kathleen," Tara said to us.

Kathleen stood about five foot two with a perfect body adorned with surgically enhanced breasts. Her tee shirt was completely soaked with perspiration from exercising providing Mark and I an opportunity to appreciate the fine details of her upper body protrusions. A wide smile added to her attractiveness.

"Hi," we all said exchanging greetings. Mark and I glanced at each other and then involuntarily stared at her breasts. Kathleen noticed our fixated eyes.

"Do you like them?" she asked looking down at her own chest.

Her bluntness took Mark and I by surprise.

"Nice job," I answered pointing at her chest and nodding my head in approval. "Nice, right?" I nudged Mark with my elbow.

"Oh, yeah! Very nice!"

"I just got them done a few months ago," Kathleen smiled widely.

"If you two are good boys, maybe she'll show them to you," Tara joked or so I thought.

Turning to Kathleen, Tara said, "We were all about to go out to lunch. Would you like to join us?"

"I'd love to! Just give me a few minutes to shower and change."

"Can we join you?" I asked.

"I don't know you that well - yet!" Kathleen said with a mischievous smile. "See you soon," she waved as she went to the women's locker room. Tara excused herself and joined Kathleen. She said they would meet us outside. Mark and I waited outside in front of the building while the girls got ready.

"She's hot!" Mark commented about Kathleen. "Is that true about her sister?"

"I have no idea."

"Man, am I glad I came with you!"

In the fifteen minutes it took for the girls to get ready, Mark amused me by pondering out loud the potential fulfillment of various fantasies involving two females.

The girls eventually came, and we all headed on foot led by Tara to a nearby café. After we were seated, the conversation at the table turned animated and silly.

"So tell me," I began in true Joeness fashion, "the men's shower area in that building is just one large room with a couple of dozen of nozzles. Is the women's shower the same?"

Tara and Kathleen nodded yes.

"So, does that mean you girls shower together and get to see each other in the nude?"

Mark and I both tried hard not to break out laughing.

"Oh, yes. All the time," Tara teasingly answered. "Kathleen and I shower together often. Don't we Kathleen?"

"Oh, yeah!"

"Sometimes, if we are bored, we soap each other up," Tara added.

Now it was the girls' turn to try not to break out laughing. Mark clenched his hands in a fist in an attempt to maintain his composure. He must have been creating vivid pictures in his mind of the two girls soaping each other in the shower.

"So, why did you decide to get your breasts done?" I asked Kathleen.

"I like to be noticed."

"Well, you certainly accomplished that," Mark chimed in.

"Thank you. I work out hard to keep my body in shape so I just wanted that extra touch."

"Are you planning on getting yours done?" I jokingly asked Tara who is less than gifted in that area.

"No. When I want to know what it is like to have big boobs, I reach around Kathleen from behind and play with hers."

The girls broke out laughing loudly. Mark and I looked at each other wondering if there was any truth to the statement.

"They are just teasing us," I reassured Mark.

Food was served and the conversation became lighter though just as equally irrelevant. When the bill arrived, Mark and I offered to pay but the girls insisted on contributing their share. As we left the café, Tara and Kathleen walked side by side a few feet ahead of us. Both were wearing shorts on this hot summer day. Though Kathleen's rear assets were a little larger than Tara's, it was impressive in shape and form. Our eyes were glued to the wonderful twin view.

"What do you think Mark?"

"I think I'm about to explode."

The girls were talking to each other, but I could not overhear the conversation. They stopped walking to allow us to catch up to them. Tara took me aside.

"Would you like to take a walk together alone?"

"Sure," I replied welcoming the idea.

Tara and I rejoined Mark and Kathleen. Tara announced that she and I were going to spend a little time together and suggested that Kathleen show Mark their apartment.

"Oh, you two live together?" I asked.

"Yes, the two of us and Kathleen's sister," Tara answered. She then told Kathleen that we would meet them back at the apartment in about half an hour. Mark and I exchanged glances. He gave me a look that it was okay with him.

Tara and I strolled off in one direction while Mark and Kathleen headed the other way. We first walked in silence and then engaged in small talk much like two people on a first date. I had an impulsive urge to hold her hand but refrained from doing so.

The city streets were busy this hot summer Saturday and the steady movement of people around us distracted my attention from Tara somewhat. After ten minutes, we reached a small park and settled down on one of the benches overlooking children playing in a water fountain. Some of the children were very young and watching them made me start to wonder if I would ever be a father.

"Hello," Tara said to get my attention. "Where are you?"

"I'm here," I said breaking out of my daydreaming.

Tara turned to the direction I was staring.

"You are wondering if you will ever have children of your own."

"How do you know that?"

"I just know," she said with a coy smile. I shook my head in acceptance of the futility of asking her the source of her cognition.

We sat quietly for a while. I somehow became aware that Tara was observing me closely although she did not outwardly appear so. I asked her when she planned on going to California and she told me she would be leaving in two weeks. I then asked her when she planned on returning.

"I don't plan to come back," she responded.

Her answer hit me like a thunderbolt. I had assumed that she was returning to New York. Before I could question her, she started to explain.

"I have family in California and there is nothing keeping me here. I ran away to New York and now it is time for me to go back home.

"When I came to the East Coast, I was depressed, angry, and defeated. Thanks to Leo, I have reclaimed my life. I shall return a warrior with the rest of my life in front of me."

She turned to me with a look on her face that indicated she hoped I understood.

"I'll miss you," I said taking her hand in mine.

She gently placed her other hand on top of mine.

"I'll miss you too."

We gazed into each other's eyes for a time until I broke away and fixed my attention again on the children playing. Sadness steadily began to envelop me like a dark veil dropping from the sky. Tara patted me on the arm and shook me lightly. She suggested we head to her apartment. Mark and Kathleen were waiting for us she reminded me. We got up and started walking back.

"Was that true what you said about Kathleen and her sister sharing boyfriends?" I asked trying to distract myself from the fact that Tara was leaving New York for good.

Tara smiled and said, "No. But the two of them are pretty wild girls. If Mark is looking for a little action…" she winked, "he may find it."

After a few minutes, we arrived at the apartment house Tara lived in with her roommates. It was an old four-story building with narrow halls. The apartment itself was rather small despite the fact there were four rooms. It looked well kept.

"Boy, it is hot in here!" I commented pulling the collar of my tee shirt out to let some air in.

"It's expensive to use the air conditioners all day so we try to keep them on only when we sleep," Kathleen explained.

"Gee, how do you stand the heat in here during the summer?" I asked.

"We usually walk around in the nude," Kathleen answered with a big smile.

"No!" Mark responded opened mouthed.

"I walk around naked all the time when it is hot. So does my sister. Just ask Tara."

Tara nodded in the affirmative.

"Uh, what about you," I asked Tara with the same opened mouthed expression Mark had, "Do you walk around in the nude too?"

"I tend to be more modest but sometimes I do."

The girls started giggling. Kathleen offered me something cold to drink but I politely declined. My imagination went wild picturing them both prancing around the apartment in the buff.

I asked if Kathleen's sister was home but it turned out that she was working. After some utterly meaningless yet colorful conversation interlaced with sexual innuendoes, Mark and I got ready to leave. It is an unwritten Joeness rule to not overextend a visit. I gave Tara a kiss on the cheek, the most physical contact I ever had with her up to that time, and said goodbye as well as wishing her luck in California. She promised to call me once she got settled. Mark told Kathleen how much he enjoyed meeting her.

"Why don't you and Tony hang out with me and my sister some time," Kathleen suggested. "That is, if Tara doesn't mind," she added. Tara smiled and shook her head to indicate she had no objection.

"Cool!" Mark reacted. He then asked for and received Kathleen's telephone number.

Mark and I started to head out the door. I stopped suddenly and turned around toward the girls while shaking my finger as if trying to remember something.

"You know, I have to ask...if it's okay with you..." the girls waited on edge for me to finish the sentence, "Can we see them?"

I directed my eyes at Kathleen's chest.

"Should I?" she turned and asked Tara with a grin.

"Oh for heaven's sake! Whatever makes you happy!"

"Okay," Kathleen said.

She reached around her back and undid the bra underneath her light blue tee shirt. She then slipped the bra off by pulling it down under the tee shirt and playfully tossed it on the floor.

Mark gripped my arm tightly in anticipation of the curtains going up.

I suspected she was just bluffing, but she then placed her two hands at the bottom of her tee shirt and lifted it up fully exposing her enhanced breasts.

Tara started to laugh loudly no doubt amused by the look of delightful shock on Mark's face and mine. Regaining our composure, Mark and I began whistling and making catcalls with requests to take it all off. Kathleen responded by twirling around, hiking up her shorts to show off the bottom curves of her buttocks and wiggling them around.

"Okay, that's enough guys!" Tara shouted to end the show.

We thanked Kathleen profusely and headed out.

On the ride back home, Mark and I joyfully recounted Kathleen's unveiling numerous times.

*   *   *

As the summer weeks passed, I dedicated myself almost entirely to rebuilding my arm. Progress was slow but steady. Leo provided helpful assistance in the gym until he was satisfied that my exercise form was consistently correct.

I had finished reading the books Leo recommended to me. During our sessions, I asked him questions on the subject matter of the material. He was patient with me and answered my questions but always encouraged me to practice what I was learning rather than just developing book knowledge.

Meanwhile, Mark and I were both doing well at the software company. He received an Employee of the Quarter award and I was given an outstanding review accompanied by a substantial raise. Unfortunately, our stock picking skills did not match our career accomplishments. The stock we bought together continued to decline though at a slower rate. Mark was content to just hold on to the stock and wait for an anticipated turn in the price while I internally berated myself for not being smart enough to do better.

During that summer, Ann and I continued to see each other. My feelings of attachment for her grew along with my anxiety that the relationship was a dead end. This intensifying conflict caused escalating feelings of irritability and depression.

"Is there anything wrong?" Ann asked me.

"No," I said both lying and faking a smile.

It was a pleasant Sunday evening near the end of the summer. Daylight slowly faded as the darkness crept into both the sky and my heart. Feelings of sadness grew within me. The sun setting was a sign that I would soon be going home.

Sunday nights had become a special ritual for Ann and I. We would often sit on the deck of her backyard chatting or just relaxing. She always had the radio set to one of those stations that predominantly play love songs. I used to tease her by referring to the station as Mush FM.

If he wasn't asleep, the Fat Basset would join us outside occasionally nudging one of us to be petted. If he didn't get the attention he sought, he would lay his little head down on top of one of our feet. The dog was a mush too.

"Isn't he cute," Ann would say to me more of a statement than a question.

"You took a perfectly good dog bred to be a hunter and turned him into a mush ball," I teased her. She slapped her thigh and gave me a 'how can you say that' look while trying to repress a smile.

Her children were home that evening having returned from a weekend with their father. It always impressed me just how close Ann and they were. Being a witness to their relationship made me long for the same type of family of my own.

"Children are not everything," Ann said to me often. The hypocrisy of the statement amused me. Ann's life completely revolved around her children. Sensing my unhappiness, she asked, "What is it you want?"

"Someday, I would like children of my own," I answered.

Her face turned sad.

"Does that mean I have to let you go so that you can find someone else who can give that to you?"

I leaned over in the deck chair I was sitting in and took her hand in both of mine.

"I would rather not even think about it."

That said, the subject was dropped for the moment.

Every Sunday night with Ann eventually came to an end. Ann and the Fat Basset would escort me outside and see me off as I drove away. Most of the time, I felt sad driving home after seeing Ann. I suppose it was because

I anticipated the end of the relationship and wondered how long we would still see each other. On one occasion returning home from her house, a police officer pulled me over for speeding. Sensing my deep melancholy, the officer must have felt sorry for me. He refrained from writing a ticket and just politely asked me to drive slower.

"Joeness! Cheer up!" Mark encouraged me one day at work. "You look like someone died!"

I laughed. Mark has the curious reaction of trying to cheer me up whenever I was depressed even if he felt depressed too.

"Let's go out tonight," he suggested.

"For what? It's a workday tomorrow."

"Who cares for what? We'll go out to celebrate we are alive and have two functioning arms and legs!"

He made me laugh.

"How about we plan to go out Friday instead? That way we can stay out late if we wish and not have to be concerned with getting up early for work the next day."

"That's good with me. It's a plan."

That evening, after I returned home from work, I decided to ride my bike to the village park. The weather was mild and comfortable. I slung a small gym bag over my shoulder that contained a paddle and a couple of balls. I figured I would play a little paddleball with my good arm and get some exercise. Riding the bike was a little difficult, as I had to do it with essentially one arm. The left arm could not bear the normal stress of supporting its portion of my upper body weight on the handlebars of the bike.

Like me, many people were at the park taking advantage of the nice weather. Fortunately, one of the handball courts was empty. I pulled out the paddle and started to hit the ball off the wall in an easy fashion. I was careful to not move abruptly and risk aggravating the injuries to my left arm and shoulder. Being out of practice, I soon sent the ball over the wall on one of the shots. Some teenagers on the other side graciously tossed it over.

"Thank you," I yelled over the wall. I knelt down to scoop up the rolling ball.

"Could you tie my shoe?" a little voice asked.

A young boy, maybe four years old, had wandered over to my side of the court. One of his shoelaces was untied.

"Could you tie my shoe?" he asked again.

"Sure," I said walking over to him. "What is your name?"

"Michael."

"Hi Michael. My name is Tony. Let me show you how to tie your shoelace." I positioned myself to be on the same side as him as I tied the lace.

"First, make a loop like this. See? Then pretend this is a tree and the other string is a rabbit. The rabbit goes around the tree making this little hole and then goes into the hole. Like that. There, now the shoe is tied."

Being more concerned with the details of the instruction than actually tying the knot, I made a mistake and the lace became undone as soon as I tried tightening it.

Michael gave me a funny look.

"Uh, let's try that again." I repeated the knot-tying lesson, this time successfully.

"Can I play with you?"

The question caught me off guard. I looked around for a potential parent but there were only young teenage boys and girls in the nearby area.

"Sure. Have you played before?"

"With my father."

"Okay then."

I handed him the paddle and the ball. He swung at the ball missing it.

"Try bouncing it first."

He bounced the ball, swung as hard as he could, and sent it careening off the fence and on to the other side. The teenagers threw the ball back.

"Here," I said, "Watch me."

I demonstrated to him in slow motion how to hit the ball.

"Now you try it."

He swung the paddle again as hard as he could missing the ball but whacking my knee hard. I should have known better than to stand so close. He didn't offer an apology but just silently looked up at me. I handed him another ball and stepped back.

"Try it again."

He swung, making enough contact for the ball to bounce weakly to the wall. I found myself getting impatient and a little annoyed. Catching myself, I became aware of my inappropriate reaction and experienced a mental flashback.

I remembered the time I was a young boy when my father was teaching me how to play baseball. He was very impatient with me and quick to berate me for mistakes. It was common when I was a boy for my father to stop talking to me for days if I had a bad outing in a little league game. Whether he realized it or not, he taught me that my self worth depended on my performance in sports.

Leo told me during our sessions that I emotionally internalized the stern father figure within me. This is one of the reasons I was impatient with other people and myself he explained. That internalized figure was one of the demons Leo said I must defeat to become a warrior.

I looked at the little boy and realized that it is not really important if he learned to correctly handle a paddle or hit a ball. What is important is that he feels loved.

"Okay. I'll bounce the ball to you and you hit the ball back to the wall."

Though I made every attempt to softly toss the ball right to him, he did not succeed once at getting it back to the wall though he did hit the fence on either side of the court a couple of times.

"I'm not so good at this," he concluded. His shoelace became undone again. "Could you tie my shoelace?"

I knelt down to tie the shoelace.

"Always remember Michael, that anytime you try something new, it takes time to get good at it. That is true for everyone. All you need to do is practice and be patient."

He gave me a funny look as if something about me confused him. I started to toss the ball to him again and after five or six attempts he was able to actually get the ball to hit the wall once.

"There you go! See? You are getting better already!" Michael smiled though it seemed a bit subdued.

Looking up after I congratulated my little friend, I noticed a young woman on the other side of the fence. It appeared she had been watching us for a while. She had strawberry blond hair, a nice face, and pleasant features. I ascertained that she was about my age.

"Is he yours?" I asked.

"Yes," she said nodding her head with a smile, "I have been looking for him. I hope he wasn't bothering you."

She started to make her way around the fence to the court.

"Oh, not at all. I needed someone to play with anyway."

"It's very nice of you. He can be a handful at times."

I introduced myself. She reciprocated and told me her name was Elise. I glanced down at her hands; no wedding ring.

"He's learning rather well but his backhand needs work."

She laughed and knelt down in front of Michael.

"I told you to not wander off. You just think you can go anywhere, don't you?" she said patiently to a silent Michael.

"They have difficulty understanding negatives and sarcasm," I offered.

Elise looked at me puzzled.

I attempted to clarify myself.

"At that age, a young child has difficulty understanding negatives such as 'Don't do this'. They also do not really understand sarcasm. They interpret everything literally, which means it is better to structure sentences in a positive way. For example, instead of saying, 'Don't wander off,' it would be better to say, 'Make sure you always stay where Mommy can see you.'"

"How do you know this? Do you work with children?"

"No. I just learned it from a fellow by the name of Leo who is well educated in these matters."

"Do you have children?"

"No. I'm still waiting to grow up myself."

She smiled widely and laughed. "Well, from the little I have seen and from what you seem to know, I would say you are better at being a parent than some actual parents are."

I thanked her for the compliment, but pointed out that it is easy for me to be patient with a child for a short period of time as compared to a parent who is around a child constantly.

"Will you be here tomorrow?" Michael asked me.

"No, sorry, I won't be."

He did not show any outward sign of disappointment. In fact, his entire demeanor was very unexpressive.

"You'll have to forgive him," Elise said apologetically, "He gets lonely sometimes."

"Lonely?"

She looked down and her face tightened.

"His father passed away six months ago. Motorcycle accident..." Her voice trailed off.

I expressed polite condolences. She nodded her head in a gesture of thanks.

"What about you Elise? Do you get lonely sometimes too?"

The question caught her by surprise. Her eyes sank down and her face tightened. Inadvertently, I think the question made her feel uncomfortable.

"We have to get going," she said taking Michael's hand, "It getting close to dinner time." She paused for a moment and then looked up at me. "It has been nice meeting you."

"Its nice to meet you too." I turned to Michael, "Bye Michael! I'll see you soon." I handed him the paddle. "Practice, but only use it outside the house." His eyes locked on me as if we were unsure to take it, but he did not utter a word.

"You don't have to do that," Elise said.

Her mannerisms indicated she wished to leave quickly.

"Its okay. I have a collection of paddles at home."

She thanked me and then left the park with Michael.

CHAPTER 11

▼

DIRECTIONS

"This fire does not consume,"
she said staring into the flames,
"It transforms."
The Dark Side of a Warrior—the author

During one of our sessions, Leo recommended that when I needed to regain a rational perspective in life, I should remind myself that anyone or anything I hold dear will one day cease to exist. This reminder included the realization that someday I too shall cease to exist.

"Look around you when you are with friends or loved ones, and remind yourself that someday they will all be gone. Look into a mirror, and remind yourself that one day you shall be gone as well."

I objected to the suggestion telling Leo the idea depressed me.

"A warrior uses the knowledge of impending death to eliminate pettiness and become acutely aware of how precious time is. Time is our most valuable resource.

"Ordinary men waste time as if it were limitless. They are caught up in petty matters as if death did not exist.

"If the knowledge of imminent death depresses you, it is a sign that you have not yet transcended to the mindset of a warrior."

When I found myself getting annoyed or angry at trivial things, I would remember Leo's advice. I'd look around me and realize that some day it will all be gone. That thought helped center and calm me when I was caught up in the craziness of the world.

Much of what Leo taught initially impressed me as being idealistic and impractical. However, I have to admit that when I followed his advice, it was usually to my great benefit.

Still, despite all the wisdom Leo imparted to me, my heart was not at peace.

How could it be?

I treasured every moment spent with Ann like a precious gift. A gift that someday I knew I would lose. How could I be at peace with that knowledge? Inside, I realized our days together were numbered and that eventually we would go our separate ways. For me, the path would be to follow the desire for a wife and family. For her, the path would be to have a companion without the legal approval of a marriage license or the procreation of any additional children.

"Tony, something is wrong with that woman," Ann alerted me as I was leaving her house one Saturday night.

An older, but not elderly, woman was walking down the sidewalk looking confused. Her eyes squinted tightly trying to discern the address number on houses.

"Can I help you?" I asked.

Perplexed, the lady said she was looking for a certain house and told me the address. I did not know the location of the street. I asked her if she wished to use a phone to call the people at the house and ask for directions.

"Oh, no," the lady said, "It's my home."

While driving back home from wherever she had been, she apparently became confused and disoriented. I politely asked to see her license to check the address. I asked her if she was taking any medication but she ignored the question.

"I don't know what happened. I'm just trying to find my house."

I could see in Ann's eyes a genuine concern for the poor woman.

"We will help you," I assured her. "Is that your car up the block?"

She nodded her head. The vehicle blocked a driveway and protruded half way in the middle of the road. I asked her for the keys.

"This is so embarrassing," she said with increasing distress.

A small crowd of curious neighbors began to gather. Someone called the police.

"Please help me," the woman began to cry.

Ann took her by the hand in an effort to calm her.

"Please God, please help me. I don't know where I am."

She looked around her confused by the unfamiliar surroundings and nervous with the increasing number of onlookers.

I noticed a dog tag on the woman's ring of keys.

"You were in the army?" I asked to purposely interrupt her growing panic.

"Yes", she answered with tears rolling down her cheeks. "It was one of the worst mistakes I ever made!"

Her comment made me laugh and she seemed to calm down a bit.

"Is there anyone home you can call?" Ann asked.

"No, my husband is away."

Ann and I looked at each other. We silently wondered if the lady even remembered her husband. For all we knew, he could have been deceased.

Two police cars arrived. A bit overkill I thought.

The number of inquisitive neighbors increased at the sign of police vehicles.

I briefly described the situation to one of the officers. He called an ambulance out of a concern that the woman may have possibly suffered a minor stroke or some other medical condition.

"This is so sad," Ann commented.

I knew, without any awareness of how such knowledge came to me, that the woman did not suffer from any acute attacks like a stroke. Rather, her condition was the result of a slow but steady deterioration in her mental capabilities. Her energy field was weak around the head area. Somehow, I could sense it.

As the officer continued to question the lady, I became aware of a shift in my perception. My eyes scanned the people on the street and I visually discerned a silver white hue around their bodies. I assumed that I was seeing their energy fields.

I walked up the street to move the woman's car so it would not be blocking the driveway it was in front of. Before I could enter the vehicle, I noticed the figure of a female under the' dark shadows of a tree just a few feet away. The figure lacked the silver white hue I observed around the other people. I stepped closer to investigate.

The image of the female seemed surreal as if it moved and adjusted its appearance according to the surroundings. I thought for a moment that my imagination created the vision from the combination of nighttime, the glow from the street lamps, and the shadows cast by tree branches swaying in the breeze. However, as I drew nearer, details of the figure clearly emerged. As I peered at its face, I recognized it as being the same as the teenage girl who followed me through the mall.

My stomach tightened with anxiety. My faced clenched with anger at her imposition into my personal life.

I did not say a word or move. I simply stared into her eyes; eyes that somehow appeared red in the darkness though I know that it is impossible.

She began to speak. Her words sounded as if they originated inside my head.

"Nature eliminates the old, the sick, and the weak without mercy. That is the way. Yet you feel compassion for the sick woman. That is your weakness," the dark female figure hissed.

I turned away ignoring her and opened the door to enter the vehicle.

"Your feelings of attachment are your undoing. You are about to lose everything to learn that lesson!"

"I already know that," I impulsively answered without looking back at her.

"When you are empty inside with no one to turn to, come to me." I stopped and looked at her. She opened her arms invitingly. "Come into my bosom and find safety and power."

As if a magical spell had been cast upon me, my anger dissipated and my heart began to race with the temptation of moving toward her. It felt as if something attached to my midsection pulled me.

She opened her arms wider. In the backdrop of the night, her surreal figure sparkled with silver and black.

"Join me. Together we can find everything we have searched for.

"Become one with me and complete yourself. With me, you can forever leave the ordinary affairs of men."

She extended one hand, opening it to take mine.

My heart pounded excitedly and I felt strangely aroused.

"Take my hand. Touch me and you can leave this place and all of your worries."

As if in a trance, I walked around the car stepping closer to the figure. Her face glowed with an indescribable dark beauty. The arousal in my heart and below my waist intensified.

My arm rose toward her hand as if under its own power. Spellbound, I stared into the red diamonds of her eyes.

Abruptly, a hoarse but loud bark broke me out of the trance.

The Fat Basset wasn't as dumb as he looked. Apparently, he sensed the urgency of my situation and ran down the block to rescue me.

"Woof! Woof!"

This dog was the only one I knew that sounded like he had asthma when he barked.

He jumped up on my leg and frantically scratched with both paws.

"Alright! Alright you Fat Basset!" I yelled.

The Basset leapt off my leg, scampered over to the tree immediately next to the black and silver female figure, lifted his short leg, and let loose a healthy stream of urine. The dog scrunched its face to squeeze out every drop.

The seductively beautiful vision faded into the night as if it had never been there.

I guess the Fat Basset showed her who was boss.

Picking up the dog's leash, I went back to the driver's side of the sick woman's car. The Basset, taking advantage of the open door, jumped into the car onto the front passenger seat.

I got into the car and the dopey dog tried to sit in my lap and lick my face while I parked it.

When I returned to the front of Ann's house, an ambulance had arrived and the paramedics attended to the woman and shortly took her to a hospital for observation. The small crowd of neighbors lingered about talking about what happened. Some of them made small jokes to make light of the situation. I sensed that those who reacted to the situation with humor were actually afraid inside. Afraid that they too someday may lose their mind.

Ann was visibly saddened by the experience of witnessing someone so helpless that she could not even find her own way home.

"Where were you? Bad boy!" Ann scolded the dog.

One of the neighbors outside also had their dog with them. The Basset promptly ran over and tried to hump the other dog. I took the leash from Ann and smartly whacked the Fat Basset on the rump. He immediately sat down with his tail between his legs and gave me the sad puppy dog look.

"Bad boy!" Ann scolded again.

A little girl, who thought the Fat Basset was cute, walked over.

"You can pet him if you like," I told the girl.

With that, the little girl grabbed the Basset's nose and squeezed it. The dog quickly withdrew and hid behind my legs.

"I think that was enough excitement for one night," I said to Ann. "I'll get going now." I handed her the dog's leash. With a hint of sadness, she looked into my eyes.

"I love you," she whispered.

"I love you too."

We hugged each other tightly. The Fat Basset looked on feeling left out. As it pressed its face into my thigh, I petted it on the head and said good-bye. He started to whimper.

"Aww. He loves you," Ann cooed.

"I love him too. Even if he is stupid," I said with a grin.

Ann stomped her foot in mock anger and smiled too. I got in my car, waved goodbye, and drove home.

When I returned to my apartment, there was a message on the answering machine. It was Leo. It had been some time since I had visited him for a session.

He asked how my arm and I were doing. He left the suggestion that we see each other soon. However, I had no desire to do so. What would I say to him—that even after all his instruction I still felt confused? That my life lacked any kind of coherent direction? That I was still filled with guilt and anger?

I pondered, with great seriousness, if I should be thankful to Leo for exposing me to a way of life that gave me hope for happiness, or if I should accuse him of plunging me into a strange world I didn't quite understand.

It was late, and I was tired. I set aside the internal debate about Leo and decided for the time being to not return his calls.

*　　　　　*　　　　　*

After work on the Tuesday of the next week, I took a walk to the village park. Strolling around, I looked for my little friend Michael and his mother Elise but did not find them. I decided to go over to a relatively secluded area at the far end of the soccer and baseball fields and practice Tai Chi.

My Tai Chi movements were purposely very slow. The shadows my body cast on the ground provided guidance for both form and speed. The ruptured biceps and injured shoulder still hurt but not as badly.

With each circle of the form and each breath taken, I felt increasingly centered. After ten minutes, my mind cleared. The body moved without effort and flowed in harmony with the universe. I performed the long form, which I just recently learned before Tara departed. I then came to the form's closing breathing deep into my stomach and feeling completely relaxed.

"That was very pretty," a female voice said.

I turned around to find Elise watching me. I felt happy to see her.

"I'm not interrupting you, am I?" she asked.

"No, not at all. I was just finishing."

We exchanged greetings and I told Elise that I had looked for her earlier. She said that she and her son just recently arrived at the park.

"Where is Michael?" I asked.

"He's in the kiddy playground."

I offered to walk back to the playground, which was on the other side of the field, with her. We engaged in some small talk and settled down on one of the picnic benches just outside of the playground.

"There is something different about you," Elise observed.

"In what way?"

She squished her face as if trying to figure it out.

"I don't know. You strike me as being very kind."

I could not resist an outburst of ironic laughter. If anything, up to that moment in my life, I was guilty of being unkind and thoughtless much of the time.

"I can assure you that your opinion is in the minority."

"I don't know," she looked at me quizzically. "There is something about you."

Her statement reminded me of a time Leo said that people would be attracted to me if they sensed strength and kindness that was devoid of any emotional attachment.

Leo stated, "If your kind actions are not motivated by selfish desires, people will be irresistibly attracted to you. If, however, a person senses that you simply wish to gain favor with them or manipulate them in some way, they will resist you."

"Are you married?" Elise inquired. "I ask because I get the impression you're not."

"I used to be. I am divorced now."

"What happened?"

"I was not happy and I made my ex-wife miserable." I flashed a smile. "See? I'm not as kind as you thought." Elise looked puzzled at my answer. "Sorry if I altered your first good impression of me," I said.

"But I saw you with Michael the other day. You were very kind to him." I shrugged my shoulders in response to her observation. "Maybe you are more kind than you give yourself credit for," Elise said.

I did not comment on her statement. The conversation then turned less serious and more typical of two people getting to know each other. The subject matter included common topics such as where we work, live, what our hobbies are, and so forth.

"You mentioned that you lost your husband in a motorcycle accident."

"Yes," she said with a frown. "He was only thirty two years old."

"That's a shame."

"Have you ever lost someone you really love?" Elise asked.

"Yes, I have. However, they are still alive."

Elise hesitated to say anything else for fear she inadvertently brought up a topic I was uncomfortable with.

Michael came over from the playground. He did not seem nearly as animated or energetic as the other children did. I assumed this was an emotional consequence to the loss of his father.

"Michael, you remember Tony. Right?"

He nodded his head affirmatively.

"Are your shoe laces all tied?" I asked jokingly.

He looked down and answered yes.

"Are you having fun?" his mom asked.

He nodded his head and then ran back to the playground area.

"He's a good kid," Elise said. "He just misses his father."

I nodded my head to indicate understanding.

"I'm going to leave now. I have some things I need to get done at home."

"Oh, okay," she replied with a hint of disappointment in her voice.

I stood up from the picnic table and then asked, "Would you like to have dinner together sometime?" Her smile betrayed the answer.

"But I hardly know you," she said retaining her smile.

"Well, this is your opportunity to change that."

We exchanged telephone numbers and arranged, by her preference, to meet me at my place one night during the week.

The next day at work, I told Mark about Elise.

"Is she hot?" was the first thing Mark asked.

"She's attractive."

"Joeness, do you really want to get involved with someone who has a kid?"

"Its possible," I answered with some hesitation.

"Dude, you should be sticking with the young girls."

I laughed and shook my head. That statement seemed to be his standard advice to me.

"How are our stocks doing?" I asked changing the subject. Mark and I continued to dabble, quite to our collective financial detriment, in the stock market.

Mark pulled up a quote screen on his computer. His grim face expressed disappointment. He closed down the screen and suggested that I not worry. He believed the stocks we had purchased would rebound someday. In a strange way, I admired his naïve enthusiasm.

"When are you taking Elise out?"

"Thursday night."

"Do you think you'll get any action?"

"My intentions are honorable."

Mark looked at me puzzled. "Honorable? Joeness, is that you?"

"It's like this," I started to explain. "Casual sex may be a fun Joeness kind of thing to do. But it does not lead to lasting happiness. I believe, like the ancient Greeks did, that a male and female are born incomplete. By coming together, they form a harmonious union of love and become one."

"Joeness, that's a beautiful thing! No wonder why you get the girls!" We both started to laugh.

"So, you're looking for a nice girl you can be happy with?"

"Yes, I guess you can say that."

My thoughts turned to Ann for a moment. She made me happy and even when we weren't together, I experienced a sense of stability in my life because of her. Now, I came closer to having to make a decision whether or not to pursue a relationship with someone else. In this case, that someone was Elise.

That night, I had a dream. Ann was in her bedroom crying. I was watching her from the outside through the window. I banged on the window but she did not hear or chose to ignore me. I pounded my fist on the front door but no one answered. Looking back into her bedroom, she was still crying.

I tasted something foul. Using my hands, I began to pull out a sticky black sludge from my mouth. No matter how much of the substance I pulled out of my mouth, there seemed to be more.

I awoke feeling horrible guilt and depression.

*　　　　　*　　　　　*

The telephone rang the next morning at seven o'clock. I was just out of the shower getting ready to dress for work. It was very unusual for anyone to call me that early.

I picked up the phone. It was Leo.

"You have not returned my calls," he said with no hint of offense taken. "It is important that we speak in person."

"Why is that?"

My question was greeted with momentary silence.

"Your training is incomplete and you are entering a dangerous time," he finally answered.

"Look, Leo," I said with extreme politeness, "I believe you are very sincere about helping me. However, this mysterious stuff about danger and all the other strange things…well, I'm just losing patience with it. I mean, what kind of therapist are you? Are you even certified by any organization?"

I took a deep breath and continued.

"Your world is sometimes very bizarre. Your philosophy seems at times equally bizarre. I don't feel any better off for it sometimes."

"Tony, it is time I did you the favor of a small secret."

"What is that?" I asked beginning to lose patience.

"With the correct instruction, you can not only learn to be a warrior you also have the potential to become a wizard like me."

His statement bewildered me. I then became agitated.

"A wizard? Are you joking? Look, I came to you because I was unhappy and depressed and I did not like being that way. That's all. You know, I often thought you were a bit crazy but this proves it."

"Tony, the way to happiness is the warrior's way. That is why I have been training you to follow that path. It is also your destiny to go beyond that. Your fear and anger have aligned you with the shadow side, your kindness and compassion have aligned you with the other side as well. With the proper training, you can use both forces interchangeably at will. If you rush to exercise that power without the temperament of a warrior, it will destroy you."

His words had no meaning to me.

"I just want to live a normal happy life," I said with a feeling of growing mental fatigue.

"To be a warrior is to have control over ones life. The more control you have, the happier you will tend to be. Everything I have taught you are tools to realize that control."

Conflicting thoughts raced through my mind and I had no inclination or energy to sort them.

"I'm sorry Leo, but I don't really feel like thinking about all this now."

"Contact me when you are ready. Your time is short! Do not wait long!"

I hated it when he spoke with such urgency. In a way, I wished that I would never hear from him again.

Thursday evening came and Elise met me at my apartment right on schedule. It always impresses me when a woman is on time. She was dressed far nicer than when I saw her at the park. Her face was pleasantly touched up with makeup. I could tell from her promptness, mannerism, and body language that she liked me.

"Wow, you are even prettier than I first thought," I said.

She smiled broadly and replied, "You are either very nice, or very smooth."

"Well, I might be both."

"A woman could only dream of a man like that," she grinned.

I avoided giving Elise a short tour of my apartment. Ann had given me a number of stuffed animals over the months and I didn't want to upset them with the presence of another woman. You may think me strange for this but trust me. They have feelings too.

Elise and I got into my car and I took us to a popular Italian restaurant. It was crowded for a weekday night but we were seated in a short time. The ensuing conversation and meal were both pleasant. At one point, without any connection to the context of the most recent conversation topics, Elise asked me an unusually blunt question.

"Do you get around?"

"Get around? You mean like sleeping with a lot of women?"

"Yes."

The directness of the question caught me off guard.

"Why, may I inquire, do you ask that?"

"You are just too good," she said with a serious grin and look of concentration as if studying me. "You are just too smooth, like a Casanova."

"What gives you that impression?"

"You know just the right things to say to a girl."

"Maybe I'm just a nice guy."

"I thought of that, but then again, you are divorced. That leads me to suspect you may be something of a ladies man."

I could not resist smiling a little.

"I'll take your suspicion as a compliment and leave it to your intuition to discern whether or not that is true." She leaned back in her chair as if trying to decide. "I didn't take you out to dinner to try to get into your pants," I said.

She was mildly shocked and amused by the comment.

"Why have you taken me out then?"

"I think you are worth getting to know better. If sometime in the near future you get an irresistible urge to tear your clothes off and throw yourself at me, that's okay too."

My wide grin indicated to her I was joking and she took it as such.

During Leo's lessons he said that if you want a woman to become attracted to you, get her to laugh and mentally link her states of pleasure to yourself. Simply stated - if a woman enjoys herself with you and feels comfortable, she will want to see you again.

After dinner, we drove to a nearby park with a small pond. There was still a half-hour or so of sunlight left in the late summer day. Elise and I strolled through the park around the pond. I consciously avoided holding her hand for the time being.

We stopped at the pond's edge and settled on a small wooden bench. We sat quietly with me staring over the water and her staring at my face. She gently placed one hand on my thigh.

I turned, looked into her eyes, and placed a hand on top of hers. Elise leaned over to kiss me. Our lips met and gently touched. I ran my hand slowly through her hair and our lips pressed tighter and then opened invitingly. Our tongues passionately encircled and explored. Our arms pulled each other closer together. Honking geese on the pond serenaded us.

After an exquisite thirty seconds or so, we disentangled tongues and limbs and gazed at each other affectionately.

"Wow! You can kiss! You must be a ladies man."

"Perhaps you just inspire me."

She laughed and then we just sat quietly together for a while enjoying the pleasant surroundings. The day then began to turn to night, so we left and headed back to my apartment.

While in the car, Elise asked if she could turn the radio on. She depressed the power button and tuned the radio to the 'Nothing but Love Songs' station that Ann likes - Mush FM as I referred to it.

My thoughts turned to Ann and to the moral complications that I had started to date another woman while I was still seeing her.

My head hurt as it tried to find a satisfactory reconciliation to the situation. The thought of breaking up with Ann gave me a sick feeling in the pit of my stomach. I liked Elise, but I was just getting to know her and there was a part of me holding back—the part of me that loved Ann.

Dusk turned to darkness. My car made its way down side streets heading toward home. A streak from the outside circle of the illumination of the car's headlights on my right side caught my attention but it was too late. A loud thump resounded from the front end. The vehicle screeched to a stop as I stepped down hard on the brakes.

Elise did not see what happened. The sound of impact with another object and the sudden stop alarmed her. I flung open my door and quickly vacated the car. A few feet from the front of the vehicle was a small dog lying in the road. Its stomach raced in and out from rapid breathing. Its face looked up at me in shock.

"I didn't see him in time," I said to Elise who was now out of the car. She looked at me without saying a word and then turned her eyes to the pooch.

I knelt down beside the dog, placed one hand on its head and ran my other hand over the exposed underside of its belly without actually touching him. He had extensive internal damage and bleeding. I do not know exactly how, but I could feel it. The dog's energy field was mortally disrupted. He had only an hour or so of life left.

"Snooky!!" a young boy hollered running toward the scene. "Snooky!!"

The boy looked down and reached toward the dog.

"Don't touch him," I cautioned. "Is this your dog?"

He nodded yes. Tears started to roll down his face.

"Get your parents. I'll watch him."

He ran off quickly yelling for his mom and dad.

I asked Elise to engage the emergency blinkers of the car. Fortunately, there was very little traffic at the time.

"How bad is it?" Elise asked.

"Bad," I replied grimly. "He is not going to survive."

"Maybe its not that bad. It may just be hurt."

"Trust me on this. I can tell."

She looked at me a little puzzled no doubt wondering why I seemed so certain.

I kept one hand placed on the dog's head and looked into its eyes. It seemed to have a calming affect on him and his breathing slowed. The boy and his parents soon arrived at the scene.

"Oh my God!" the mother said with her hands on her face.

"What happened?" the father asked.

"He ran in front of my car," I explained. "I wasn't able to stop in time."

"He just ran out of the yard when I opened the gate. I tried to catch him but couldn't," the boy cried. I could tell that he blamed himself for the accident.

The father kneeled down as if to pick up the dog.

"Don't move him," I warned. "He is critically injured. Get a flat board or something similar to slide him on. You will then want to get him to a vet as soon as possible."

The father looked at me skeptically as if he debated taking my advice.

"He doesn't have much time," I whispered. "At least do all you can so that you and your family can feel everything possible was tried to save him."

The boy's father backed away from me and then told his wife he would be right back. He ran off while she knelt down and softly petted the dog's head telling it that it would be all right. The dog's tail wagged weakly in response.

"I didn't mean to let him out," the boy cried. "Please Snooky don't die! Don't die!"

"He's going to be all right," the mother attempted to reassure her son. I could tell though, they both knew deep inside the dog was not going to make it.

The first emotional response to facing eminent death of the self or loved one is denial.

I stepped back and away from them and scanned the area. A few people from nearby homes stepped outside to find out what was happening. My eyes scanned quickly from left to right. I then expanded my awareness to alert me to any unseen presence. I sensed nothing unusual. I half expected my personal stalker to make an appearance. However, she did not.

The father soon returned in his sport utility vehicle. There was a little girl in there with him. I assumed it was the younger sister of the boy. He brought a wide piece of cardboard. It looked like a hastily cut out side of an appliance box.

I helped him carefully slide the cardboard under the dog. He then picked up the dog, handed it to his wife and ordered the family into the SUV. They quickly sped off without saying a word to me.

I motioned to Elise to get into the car.

"Let's go," I said.

It took only a few minutes to get back to my apartment. We drove in silence. My emotional response to the whole incident was to feel angry.

"I'm sorry the evening did not end on a happier note," I told Elise after we returned.

"It wasn't your fault."

"I know. But, I still feel bad about it."

We said good night to each other accompanied by a polite kiss. I waited for Elise to get into her car and drive off before going into my apartment.

There were three messages on my answering machine. For me, that was an usually high number for the few hours I was out. I hit the play button on the machine. All three messages were hang-ups.

*   *   *

Mark asked how the date went when I saw him at work the next day. He was disappointed that my description of the evening events did not include any sexual exploits. I distinctly got the impression he thought that I was slipping with my Joeness prowess. I mentioned to Mark how I hit the dog on the way home from the date.

"Depression," he responded. "Are you going to go out with her again?"

"Probably."

"Probably? You don't know for sure?"

"I like her, but my heart is still with Ann."

"Yeah, but you know that's not going anywhere," Mark said referring to my relationship with Ann.

"Yes, I know but I still have strong feelings for Ann. Its difficult for me to pursue another relationship while I still feel that way."

His High Joeness Mark carefully considered his response to my dilemma and then simply said, "Depression."

Work responsibilities soon interrupted our private conversation and we returned to our cubicle cages to continue the manipulation of electronic devices called computers.

I went to the health club directly from the job at the end of the work-day and then returned home. A few minutes after entering my apartment, the telephone rang. It was Ann. For her to call that early in the evening was unusual. It was more typical of Ann to try to reach me later at night.

"I tried calling you last night. You weren't home," Ann said with a bel-ligerent tone in her voice.

I immediately sensed impending relationship disaster.

"Yeah, I was out," I replied nervously knowing the conversation was about to head quickly downhill.

"Where were you?"

"I went out to dinner with a friend."

I cringed inside with the anticipated inquiry from Ann.

"Who were you with?"

"Just a friend. Nobody you know."

"What was her name?"

Adrenaline pumped into my veins and my heart raced with the full realization that I had been found out somehow.

"I plead the fifth," was the only answer I could come up with.

Ann then directed an angry verbal assault at me. A friend of hers noticed me at the restaurant and carefully observed the interaction between Elise and I. This friend, whose identity was never revealed to me, made it clear to Ann that I appeared to be out on a date. This information was conveyed to Ann the very same night. It was she that left the hang-up messages on my answering machine. In an effort to confirm if the story was true and be sure it was not a case of mistaken identity, she tried calling me several times.

"Do you know how embarrassed I am to have someone tell me that they saw you out with another woman? I feel like a fool! Do you know how hurt I feel?"

Her voiced crackled as her emotional state shifted violently and repeat-edly from anger to sadness.

I got that sick feeling again. If I could have crawled under a rock and stayed there for the rest of my life, I would have.

"What do you have to say?" she yelled.

Simply telling her I was sorry was not going to be sufficient, but I said it anyway.

"I'm sorry."

"Is that it?"

"No. I suppose its time we spoke. I have been avoiding it until now but given the current circumstances I suppose its time."

I took a deep breath.

For the next five minutes I told Ann, in as kind a way as possible, that I didn't see a future with her. It was an old conversation between us and it was painful to repeat. I could not have children with Ann because she did not want any more. I could not live with Ann because her soon to be ex-husband could cut off the support she depended on if I did. I wanted more out of a relationship. That is why, I told her, I elected to explore other possibilities.

Ann countered with her usual arguments that having children wasn't everything in life and that I needed to be realistic about how much money it took to support the standard of living she and her children enjoyed. In other words, she could not jeopardize her husband's financial support. She pointed out correctly, though it hurt to hear it, that I did not have the means to support them myself.

"I won't see you if you are going to date other women," was Ann's final statement.

I could not argue with her position. After all, she was right. How could I reasonably expect her to see me if she knew I might be dating others?

"I'm sorry," I said in a low voice. "I can't promise you that."

My own words made me cringe inside knowing the consequences of saying that to Ann.

"Then its over between us! Don't ever call me again!" She slammed the phone down the sound of which felt like a sledgehammer hitting my heart.

I put down the phone and sat on the futon couch in the living room slumped forward with my head in my hands. Tears soon followed.

An hour later, Ann called back. It was apparent from her voice that she had been crying too.

"I know you want your own family," she started to say, "but you can be a part of my life. My children would be your children. When the divorce is over, you can move in if you want to. My husband will never find out. It is none of his business.

"Even the stupid dog loves you." Her voice trailed off as she tried to repress her tears. "Having children together is not the most important thing in the world. Please, I don't want to sound like I'm begging."

I closed my eyes and tears flowed down my face. I realized that Ann just offered me everything she had in the world despite her feeling betrayed just a short while ago.

"I'm sorry," I said filled with grief. "I just don't know if I can be satisfied with that."

"Do you love me?"

"Yes."

"Then why are two people who love each other breaking up?" She started to cry again. "Just tell me its over between us then."

My stomach tightened into a hard knot. I could not bring myself to say it was over.

"Just say it," Ann cried. A moment passed and she caught her breath enough to collect herself. "I'll say it then. It's over! There is no more you and me! Don't ever call me again!"

She slammed the phone down again. A knife might as well have thrust itself in my heart.

I sat down at the kitchen table and stayed there for a long time without moving or even thinking. My mind and heart went numb. Later, I crawled into bed and drifted off to an uneasy sleep.

For the next few days, I felt empty inside and mechanically went through the motions of life's daily activities. Not much of anything mattered to me. I avoided socializing with anyone beyond being polite with the exception of Mark who accurately described the entire situation as 'depression'.

Elise, who was probably wondering why I had not called her, phoned me but I was in no mood to speak to her.

"What's wrong?" she asked feeling confused by my behavior.

"I'm sorry. I'm just in a bad mood."

"You sound angry. Are you angry with me for some reason? Did something happen?"

"I'm angry. Yes. But not at you."

I silently contemplated if my feelings of anger were indeed directed at least in part toward Elise. Perhaps a subconscious part of me blamed Elise for the breakup with Ann. The irony of my attempt at self-psychological analysis amused me.

"Can I help somehow?" she asked.

"No. I just need time to myself."

Elise honored my request by expressing her concern, offering support if I wanted it, and getting off the phone.

*   *   *

Time heals all wounds they say. The tremendous stupidity of that statement amazes me. Time does not heal all wounds. In fact, Leo taught me that the subconscious has no concept of time. Time is only experienced at the conscious level. Since unhealed hurtful emotions are stored subconsciously, the passing of time from an emotionally damaging event is irrelevant.

My state of depression only deepened with the passage of time. I missed Ann terribly.

A week passed. I stopped bothering to answer my telephone and shut off the ringers on both my phones.

Leo called and left messages on my answering machine. I did not return the calls.

Elise called to find out how I was. She left a message too. I did not return her call either.

The only voice I wanted to hear was Ann's. But Ann never called me again. And who could blame her?

*   *   *

"Two thousand four hundred and thirty three seconds."

This is what Brian, the security guard at work, said to me when I left for the day. Poor fellow. He was so bored that he periodically calculated the number of seconds left on his shift and recorded the number into the margin of the newspaper he read daily. Each time I passed him during the day he would tell me the latest count.

"Good night Brian," I said with a sympathetic smile.

"Good night Tony."

I walked to my car in the parking lot noticing just how beautiful the early autumn weather was. It was dry and mild with a bright sun overhead. Such a sharp contrast to my dark frame of mind I thought to myself.

Instead of returning home, I decided to take a short ride to a nearby park adjacent to a harbor on Long Island's North Shore. It is a large park with a long beachfront, playground, basketball courts, and picnic area. When I arrived there, the parking lot was just about empty, just my car and a few others. The relative absence of people in the park pleased me. I wanted solitude in the midst of my gloom.

I settled down on one of the wooden benches along the concrete walk that stretched the entire distance of the beach overlooking the harbor. A cool breeze caressed my face and filled my lungs with sea air. I breathed deeply and started to relax. My eyes focused at the long shadows cast by the late afternoon sun. For a moment, however temporary it might have been, I felt peaceful.

My attention became distracted by the presence of a person who chose to sit on the same bench as I. This struck me as peculiar since the park is large and only a few people were scattered around in it. I glanced to my left to look at the person.

"Leo!" I shouted with immense surprise. "What are you doing here? How did you know where I was?"

Leo broke out into a jovial laugh. "You seem fit to ignore my messages on your answering machine. I therefore determined that a personal visit is in order. After all, it has been some time since we last saw each other."

I was dumbfounded.

"But, how did you even find me?"

"I first went to your apartment. When it became clear to me you were not there, I speculated that perhaps you were here."

"Still, how did you even know to look for me here?"

"You mentioned one time that you come to this park on occasion to meditate when you are troubled."

I honestly had no recall of ever telling Leo that. I looked at him suspiciously.

"This is quite a surprise to me."

"You are troubled," Leo said preventing me from commenting further on his unannounced visit.

"Yes. I am," I responded while looking out over the water beyond the beach.

"Perhaps, if you told me what is bothering you, I can be of some assistance."

"What would you like to hear about first? How I hurt and broke up with Ann; the most wonderful woman I ever met? How I have lost most of my savings playing the stock market? How I still can't lift more than ten pounds with my left arm? How I wish I could just run away from everything and everyone?

"I know…I know you sincerely wish to help me. You have in some ways. I also think you are a kook but that's beside the point.

"Leo, I just find it hard to go on. I don't see any hope. Everything I try seems to fail."

I expected that Leo would begin chastising me for feeling sorry for myself. However, he actually seemed sympathetic - something unusual for him.

"You have two choices," Leo said. "You can give up and live angry and bitter to die a miserable death or you can continue on the warrior's path and have at least a chance to live a full and happy life."

"Sometimes, I don't feel I can go on," I responded in a low voice. "Is that an acceptable option?"

"Surrender is only acceptable when there is no hope. You learned that a long time ago in the military but have yet to apply that philosophy to your personal life."

"But I don't feel like there is any hope. That's the point."

"Tell me," Leo said, "If a soldier is still capable of fighting and there is at least a chance of victory, even a remote chance, is it his duty to continue on?"

"Yes," I answered.

"Were you a good soldier when you served in the armed forces?"

"Yes."

"If need be, were you willing to fight to your last breath in combat?"

"Yes."

"Don't you believe that you should have that same conviction and courage in your daily life? In the army, they taught you to be a soldier. In life, I teach you to be a warrior. As you have found, the arena of ordinary daily life is ultimately our greatest challenge as human beings.

"Some people may be defined by a brief moment of achievement in their life. However, for the great majority of mankind, how we define ourselves is by our day to day actions and behavior. What you are is determined by how you live every day. The measure of a man or woman is determined each day by every action great or small.

"I use the term Warrior because it is a struggle to live life with consistent proper action. Neither you nor I will ever achieve perfection. To be a warrior is always to strive toward an ideal while having the sobriety to realize that ideal will never be permanently obtained. There will always be setbacks and there will be times when even the most enlightened of us makes mistakes."

I sat silently while my eyes gazed upon a descending sun that lit the horizon with red and gold. Leo turned his head toward the same scenic view. I began to laugh softly.

"You are very good at what you do Leo. You skillfully used the core values I learned in the military and created an analogy for every day life. You then structured your questions to get me to answer yes at least three times before making your persuasive appeal."

I turned my head to look at Leo and thought I detected, for the first time since I have known him, a hint of sadness.

"Sometimes you are too smart for your own good," he sighed. "By learning the art of manipulation, you have also mastered your defense against manipulation.

"Let me ask you," Leo continued, "Would you agree that manipulation can be a good thing? For example, if someone has convinced themselves to be miserable and destructive and I use a benevolent form of manipulation to lead them toward more constructive beliefs and appropriate behavior so that they can lead a productive and happy life, is that morally acceptable?"

"Yes, but only if that person wishes it so."

"Okay," Leo said, "then it is morally correct for me to use my skills to help someone assuming, by your criteria, they want to be helped."

"Correct."

Ten seconds of silence passed. Leo studied me intently and then asked slowly, "Do you want to be helped?" I looked at Leo sharply as if his words touched a hidden nerve. His eyes were strikingly clear and kind.

I did not answer and turned away from him. Tears began to well in my eyes like a dam no longer able to hold back the water that pressed against it.

Leo asked with a soft voice, "Tony, you don't feel that you deserve to be helped. Don't you?"

I shook my head no while tears rolled freely down my face despite my best effort to restrain them.

"What is stopping you from feeling that you are deserving of help?" he asked.

"I don't deserve it," I said shaking my head while wiping the tears on my face with my shirtsleeve. "When I was a little boy, I never felt loved. They hurt me, Leo." My body tightened and doubled over as I began to sob openly. "What did I do to be beaten like that? What did I do to be told by my own mother I was worthless?" My stomach muscles contracted violently from the anguish as I cried. My face cringed as if caught in a vise. I could barely speak beyond a raspy whisper. "Now that I am older, I hurt other people. I became like my parents. I became one of them."

Teardrops fell from my eyes dotting the cement beneath me like raindrops from the sky.

Leo sat quietly and waited for me to regain some degree of composure.

"It is because you felt unloved by your parents that makes it difficult for you to accept love as an adult," Leo began to explain in a kind-hearted way. "You subconsciously believe that if your own mother and father did not love you, how could you be deserving of love from anyone else? Your experience as a youth made you fearful of being hurt and rejected. That is why you became involved with women who are tremendously loyal and loving. However, you were unable to accept that love, so ultimately you hurt and rejected them."

"Gee, that's it in a nutshell. I'm a mess."

"Tony, though you understand the problem intellectually, you have not internalized the resolution."

"What resolution?"

"You need to forgive yourself and sincerely believe you are deserving of love and happiness."

"That is easy for you to say."

Leo sat pensively for a moment and then asked me, "Has anyone who ever wronged you asked for forgiveness?"

"Yes."

"How did you decide whether or not to accept their apology?"

"Well, if I thought they were sincere and that they would not repeat the offense I would forgive them."

"It is the same with the universe," Leo said gesturing toward the sky, "and with the conscience."

"How do you mean?"

"Do you wish to be forgiven?"

"Yes, of course."

"Then you must sincerely ask the universe and your conscience for forgiveness. However, that is not all. You must demonstrate your sincerity and earn trust by ceasing to repeat the offense and living in harmony with the universe through right action and correct behavior."

I nodded my head in agreement.

"What about those people I hurt? Should I ask them for their forgiveness as well?

Leo paused before giving an answer as if he were considering his words carefully.

"It is appropriate in most cases to ask a person for forgiveness when you are sincerely sorry. However, I caution you. Sometimes a person will not be willing to forgive. So, you must ask sincerely but keep in mind the other person may or may not accept the apology.

"Keep in mind as well, that at times it is better to leave a person be especially a person who you have not seen in a long time. You will have to listen to your heart to make that decision."

"I am not sure what you mean Leo."

"When you are inclined to ask an apology from someone you have wronged, ask yourself if the apology is beneficial in some way to them. If not, or if you are asking forgiveness to just gain a feeling of absolution, then it may not be appropriate.

"In most cases, the mere act of admitting you are wrong and apologizing does wonders to heal the infraction. In some cases however, the wronged party is not forgiving or is not available to ask forgiveness. In any case, you must always forgive yourself first and be willing to change your behavior and make amends if appropriate to earn that forgiveness."

Leo waited a little while before saying anything else as if to allow me time to consider his words.

"It is up to you, Tony. Choose your path and choose well. The wrong path leads to destruction. The right path, the way of the warrior, leads to healing and redemption. No matter how you have suffered, no matter what you have ever done, you have the opportunity to create the life you desire from this time forward."

"Your words give me comfort and hope Leo. But, when I leave here, I will be going back to the same world I find so troubling. I then slip back into old habits and behavior. It's very discouraging."

"That," said Leo pausing for emphasis, "is the struggle of a warrior. You either accept the challenge of the struggle or surrender to it. Your question is to be or not to be a warrior."

I looked down at the ground without saying anything.

"You learned how to be a good soldier in the army. You can also learn how to be a warrior. Though you may not realize it, in many ways you have progressed. Your perspective, however, is to look at how far you have yet to go without giving yourself due credit for the distance already traveled.

"May I tell you a true story?"

I nodded my downcast head yes.

"In the eighteen-hundreds, when the British were excavating the pyramids in Egypt, an archeologist came upon a seed stored in an ancient urn. The seed laid dormant in that urn for thousands of years.

"The archeologist took the seed back to England with him. Curious, he planted it. To his astonishment, it sprouted and grew into a healthy plant.

"Like that seed in the urn, there is seed inside of you. Perhaps it has been dormant for a long while. When the ancient seed's time arrived, it grew and flourished even after thousands of years. Perhaps now it is time for the seed within you to blossom as well."

Peering into my eyes, Leo reached out and touched me softly on the back of my neck with his hand. It did not feel like a physical touch. Rather, it felt like a minute vibration of energy upon my skin.

The sun began to dip under the horizon and stars at the far-east end of the sky began to shine through the approaching night.

Leo stood up.

"Twilight is upon us. It is time I go."

The announcement that he was leaving saddened me.

"Will I see you again Leo? Or are you going to disappear from my life the way Tara did?"

He smiled in a reassuring way.

"You know enough and are powerful enough to not require my guidance any further. However, if you should ever feel a need you may call upon me."

I stood up and faced Leo.

"I realize that words alone are woefully inadequate but I wish to say thank you anyway. Thank you Leo."

"You are welcome Tony.

"Live your life always like a warrior; each day, each hour, each minute. Listen to your intuition and follow your heart. Accept that life will test you, sometimes severely. Accept that you will make mistakes. Resolve to learn from them. Let experience temper your character and increase your knowledge.

Open your spirit to the light and accept the darkness. One cannot exist without the other. Bring the two to harmony." Leo paused, bowed as if ending a curtain act, and then finished by bidding me goodnight.

I succumbed to an overwhelming urge to embrace him. I stepped toward Leo and gave him a big hug. Unexpectedly, I became frightened after experiencing a strange sensation of a lack of a physical contact when I hugged him. It was as if I felt a vibration instead. His kind eyes and warm smile disarmed my fears when I stepped back.

Leo walked off in the direction of the parking lot about a hundred yards away. I sat back down and looked out over the harbor for a few seconds. Suddenly, I became curious. I got up and walked along the concrete path. Within a few yards, I had a clear view of the rest of the park and the parking lot.

Leo was nowhere to be found nor did I see his black sports car.

It was impossible for him to have walked or even ran a distance of a hundred yards in the ten or so seconds I sat back down on the bench when he left.

"Hey, fellow, park's closing," a county employee on a little tractor told me.

"Yes, I know, thank you. Say, did you see a man just leave a few seconds ago?"

"No," he said shaking his head.

I scanned the park and the clearly visible road just outside of it. No cars or people were there save for the fellow I was just talking to.

Leo did it to me again.

I took a deep breath and one last look out into the water. The sky was now brightly decorated throughout with stars and a half moon. In the west, a light blue hue marked the sun's last glimmer.

Detouring off the concrete path, I walked on to the sand of the beach and looked up to the heavens. I folded my hands together by my waist as if in prayer.

"Please forgive me," I asked the universe.

I gazed fixedly upward. The stars twinkled silently in the sky. I listened intently for an answer. There was only a quiet soft breeze.

"I suppose I can't blame you for not wanting to speak to me either," I said.

I turned around to head back. A sudden gust of wind rushed by me as if to get my attention. I stopped and looked up again at the sky. The stars seemed much kinder somehow.

"Thank you," I said impulsively.

I began to slowly walk back to my car.

"What will the future bring?" I wondered silently.

As I pondered the unanswerable question, I thought back to one of my early sessions with Leo.

"You worry too much," he observed.

"Of course I worry. I worry about the future and how everything will turn out."

Leo laughed and said, "A warrior acts with confidence in all his or her endeavors. By confidence, I do not mean cockiness. Rather, I mean that a warrior makes a personal conviction to do the very best he or she can each and every day.

"When you are committed to always doing the best you can, the outcome of anything is irrelevant."

I was about to open my car door but hesitated. As the night surrounded me in the deserted parking lot, I contemplated his words of wisdom.

"Do your best. That's all anyone can ask of you."

I suppose that's a step in the right direction.

The End

About the Author

C.J. Regan is a hypnotherapist and personal coach in the Long Island New York area. He may be contacted at *MindCoach33@Yahoo.com.*

Printed in the United States
3056

9 780595 192113